Acknowledgements

So many good-willed souls have helped to get me this far. Former literary agent Kate Jones first gave me the confidence to continue, but alas she is no longer with us. Agents Peter Straus and Broo Doherty have also been very supportive. I'd also like to thank friends and family, who have encouraged me over the years.

Most of all I'd like to thank the nitty-gritty brigade, those that have got down and dirty in helping, by sharing their skills and giving up their time. These are headed by my supportive partner Kate, and also include Tina Orr Munro, Tim Kevan and Gina Skinner. Thanks to anyone else who has helped, you know who you are!

Professional help has come from the likes of Naomi Chapman with her social media insight, and Rebecca Keys, whose proof and editing skills were much appreciated.

And finally a word for my book cover designer Jamie Keenan. He might be used to designing covers for the likes of Irvine Welsh and Stephen King, but not only did he offer his services most reasonably, but supported my promotion as an author.

Defending Elton

By TJ Cooke

First Edition, March 2013

www.tjcooke.com

CHAPTER 1

At precisely two o'clock, Judge Llewelyn-Davies nodded to the clerk who was sitting below him, and the spindly man in the yellowing wig got to his feet.

'Elton Spears, please stand up. Elton Spears, you are charged on an indictment containing one count of murder – that between Saturday 14th and Monday 16th January 2012 you murdered Sarena Gunasekera, contrary to common law. How do you plead? Guilty or not guilty?'

Defence counsel, Mr Harry Douglas QC, was concerned that Elton's unpredictable mind might not deal with a straight question like 'are you guilty or not guilty?'. Consequently, he had the judge's permission for me to stand right next to Elton in front of the dock, while the indictment was read out.

After an awkward pause, and a surreptitious poke from me, Elton blurted out 'not guilty' as loud as the Old Bailey had ever heard it. I couldn't help but notice that a few of the jurors were taken aback, both by his volume and demeanour.

I returned to the defence solicitor's bench and sat directly behind Harry, who was as immaculate as ever. Statuesque, with a pale complexion and distinctively arched eyebrows, he was always extremely well turned out. He was a barrister who I knew better than any, and it was no accident that I'd instructed him in this particular case.

Sitting on the far side of counsel's bench was Raymond Lefevre, or 'counsel for the Crown', as he insisted on being addressed. He was very much an old-school brief, the old school in question probably being Harrow. With a confident air and perma-tanned self-reverence, he checked his notes, wetted his lips, and stood up in preparation to deliver the prosecution opening.

The jury – seven male, five female – had the look of a dozen pupils about to sit a chemistry exam, but their faces were soon captured by intrigue as the indictment was read out. The very word 'murder' seemed to mix a potent cocktail of dread and prurient anticipation. They appeared a pretty conservative bunch, though the pretty young woman in the white cotton smock, wearing African beads, looked anomalous.

The theatre of it all, though matinee fodder to the likes of Lefevre and Harry, seemed an exciting place to these twelve random souls, most of whom had never set foot in a court before. Normally I would have been sharing counsel's confidence, not least because this was my seventh murder trial. However, I was, as my dear Aunt Marj used to say, fidgeting like a frightened ferret.

A varnished air drifted from the recently polished oak benches, as Lefevre began to address the jury. I was determined to hang on to his every word. So much depended on it.

'Good afternoon, members of the jury. My name is Raymond Lefevre and I represent the Crown in this case, the prosecution. My learned friend Mr Harry Douglas QC represents the accused, Elton Spears.'

As Harry nodded in acknowledgement to the jury, Lefevre did the first of many pulls on the lapels of his robe, before refocusing his attention.

'So, members of the jury, it was during the morning of

Monday 16th January, some months ago now, that a Mrs Brandon was walking her dog at the foot of Beachy Head cliffs... and I'm afraid Mrs Brandon came upon a rather gruesome sight. What she came across was a sack... one that appeared to contain a dead body.'

Lefevre paused, allowing the jury to brew up their own mental image. A middle-aged woman on the far right of the jury briefly looked over at Elton, before quickly looking away again, as if she'd seen something rotten. Lefevre took the opportunity of inhaling a chestful of breath, before interpolating further, with dexterous precision.

'The young woman, who, the prosecution say, was murdered by this defendant, was twenty-seven-year-old Sarena Gunasekera. She was a law student, originally from Sri Lanka, who had in fact undertaken the bulk of her studies in Perth, Australia. She had taken various exams abroad and was here to gain experience of our legal system... still thought of, members of the jury, as the best in the world...'

Lefevre unfolded a sycophantic smile for the jury. Judge Llewelyn-Davies acknowledged with a brief look over his half-moon glasses. Harry, however, was already busy scribbling some notes, not being one to join in with such sanctimonious mumbo-jumbo. Lefevre tugged away at his robe again.

'Now, we'll return to the victim later. I'll just deal briefly with the defendant's arrest. You will hear that on that same Monday morning, the defendant, Elton Spears, was found wandering along a hotel corridor in Eastbourne, which is just a few miles along the coast from Beachy Head. You will hear that Mr Spears was unkempt and soiled, and that he had beach tar on his shoes and clothing, but that wasn't all he had on his clothing: the defendant had smears of blood, and when that blood was sent for analysis, it was found to be that of the victim, Miss Gunasekera. You may well come to ask, how did it get there?'

I looked over to the dock where Elton was rocking forwards and backwards in his chair. He was flanked by two burly prison guards, but they still looked like midgets in comparison. At first glance Elton could have passed for a heavyweight boxing champion. There was a touch of the George Foreman about him, though he was far too uncoordinated to have stood a chance in the ring. For some reason he had a huge cheesy smile, which was quite incongruous to the moment.

My mind briefly recalled all the times I'd made Elton his coffee with six sugars, and let him spout lyrical nonsense in my office. There were also many times when I'd rescued him from homelessness, battled in vain to get him housing, and fought in court to get him off a trumped-up charge when a junior street constable had used him for fun and statistics.

I also thought of all the offences he'd probably committed, and not been caught for, and knew that none of this tumultuous trumpery would have been taking place if they'd diagnosed his condition earlier.

CHAPTER 2

I was thinking all sorts while on the hands-free phone to Loren, driving back from Eastbourne to my little London flat. She eventually answered my question, with tautological ease.

'She'll be found dead at the bottom of the cliff.'

I couldn't help a spontaneous huff.

'I know. What I was asking you to think about, Loren, is what was she doing there?'

Nothing in reply for a good few seconds. The silent beat briefly raised my pulse. I checked the mobile to see if we'd been disconnected, but three bars were clearly visible. Then Loren's broken voice vibrated my earpiece.

'So...? So what?'

'Loren, are you being thick?'

She huffed back, before adding:

'Oh, don't be in that mood, please... not now.'

'What mood?'

I silently chastised myself. I knew I couldn't afford such lapses, and needed to keep Loren onside.

'Jim... You've got to keep yourself together... Are you watching the road?'

I didn't answer. Of course I was watching the road. In fact I was focused on the lorry in front, a huge Norbert Dentressangle juggernaut. The snow had turned to wet sleet. It was melting on impact with the windscreen, and I was envious of the thaw.

'What I meant, Lol, was what the hell was Sarena actually doing on Beachy Head? I mean why was she there? That's what they'll ask!'

'I don't know... rambling?'

'What? She'd been out rambling? In a black velvet party dress?'

Loren didn't come back at me with a response. I didn't know whether it was because she didn't have one or if the mobile signal had been lost. It took me a few seconds to realise that she was no longer connected, but it wasn't the signal. My battery had failed to charge, and finally given up the ghost.

My hands tightened around the steering wheel. As I stared ahead at the Norbert Dentressangle juggernaut, appalling visions of death began to appear on the car windscreen. They were blurry – wavy even, like the first few seconds of a film seen through the cinema house curtains.

The first was of Sarena, in her flat, with her dead head resting on top of an old Hello! magazine, partially obscuring Angelina Jolie's cover pose. The rhythmic brushes of the wipers swept the image away, but then another appeared, and another...

-The steel-handled knife sticking rigidly through one of the bright green dragons of her shiny silk kimono.

-Her moribund body floating face-down in the bath.

-Me, towelling her dry.

I recalled the grotesque feeling of forcing her lifeless body to squeeze into her black velvet dress, pulling her deadweight arms through the armholes, first one and then the other. I had to fight not to be physically sick.

Who is Norbert Dentressangle? I forced myself to ponder, as if somehow this would release me from these awful scenes. Was he born in Paris? How old was the little haulier before he could spell his name? I searched for more distractions, but then the letters 's.a.n.g' in the middle of his surname leapt out at me from the back of the truck, as if in some 3D animation. 'In sang,' I muttered to myself. 'In crimson red sang.' It was no use. Nothing could stop the bloody images.

I had seen many albums of murder in the stuffy atmosphere of court, 'scenes of crime' locked in time and place. Yet these particular frames flashed before me, more briskly than before, and with rhythm, as if an old carousel projector was casting them onto my windscreen.

The last one I remember showed Loren in my arms, with me trying to convince her that it was no time for 'the truth and nothing but the truth'. It was time for lies, I had told her... to be constructed with care, and delivered with skill.

It would have been crazy to go to the police and plead accident. Yes, that was the truth: I had never meant to harm Sarena. Her demise had happened in a flash of misfortune, but truth plays little part in an adversarial trial. I'd seen far too many criminal trials to risk that, and either Loren or I – or more likely both – would have been convicted.

The scenario would have been presented to the jury as a classic 'boy kills girl to get girl/girl kills girl to get boy/love triangle/'crime passionnel.' Call it what you will, but the Old Bailey had certainly heard it all before, and either way we were shafted.

I had imagined police officers arriving, blue and white tape being pegged on the street outside, forensic scientists gathering, pathologists, detectives, interview rooms. I could see Jim Harwood and Loren Granger in the devil's dock... and it was then that my thoughts turned to Elton – imaginings I would almost immediately regret and despise myself for, but once the stage had been set and the script written, the players would surely follow their lines.

CHAPTER 3

I could ill afford to miss a word. If there were to be any last-minute surprises, then Lefevre's opening speech might reveal a clue. He raised his voice a tiller touch, just enough to guide the jury to follow his course.

'Further, when Mr Spears's football top was analysed, a considerable number of black fibres were found. These fibres were, the prosecution say, from the victim's clothing, specifically from her black velvet dress. Due to their rare nature, the prosecution will suggest to you that it is tantamount to an impossibility that these fibres came from any other source.'

I was still sitting behind Harry, happy to hide myself from the judge's view. Every now and again I'd poke my neck around from behind Harry's back to note the looks on the jurors' faces, before snapping it back like a terrified tortoise. My ears remained poised throughout, like radar dishes, primed to detect every conceivable signal.

I'd regained so much focus that I hadn't noticed Loren coming in from the back of the court. I just felt her shuffling up close to me on the defence solicitor's bench.

'Is everything okay?' Her mousey voice trembled.

I gently squeezed her hand under the desk that ran along the bench. I could feel three ice-cold digits in my palm.

'Nothing bad's happened?' she added in a whisper, almost nibbling my ear with her lips. I slowly shook my head, whilst wanting to shout out loud 'Nothing *bad*? Are you crazy?'

Lefevre was now telling the jury about Sarena. He was painting the usual 'victim' canvas, totally unaware of her duplicitous past.

'You will hear that the victim, Miss Gunasekera, was not only a studious and ambitious young woman, but a loving daughter who respected her family and kept in daily contact with her father in Sri Lanka...'

It was then that my attention was drawn to the public gallery. I'm sure that I did a distinct double-take. Another of my clients was up there, Sammy Todd. I briefly guessed that a mate of his was on trial next door and they'd adjourned, or that Sammy himself was due in the dock and was 'sussing out the judge', as he might put it. Whatever, I couldn't afford to get side-tracked, and forced myself to concentrate on Lefevre once again. He briefly studied a forensic statement before continuing to address the jury.

'Now, you will also hear that the victim, Miss Gunasekera, was possibly raped before she died. The Crown cannot prove rape, but there was evidence of recent sexual intercourse. Due to her exposure to the elements, we cannot be certain whether it was this man Spears, or another, who had sexual intercourse with her.'

I felt myself shrinking next to Loren. Of course she knew that we must have made love that fateful night, but bringing home my affair with Sarena in such a brutal way made her bristle with loathing, I'm sure. I knew then that Regina versus Spears would encourage the flow of magma from within. This was to be a battle of damaged minds, with my own sanity being as much on trial as Elton's.

Then, as Lefevre turned to speak to the jury again, I noticed that his lips weren't moving in time with the emanating sounds. For a brief moment I thought I might have been going into shock, as if imagining some out-ofsync black-and-white movie.

'The Crown will, however, invite you to consider the fibre evidence, and even if the offence of rape itself can't be proved, it goes some way towards showing the defendant's contact with the victim. You may have little difficulty in concluding that those fibres were found on the defendant's football top. Yet again, members of the jury, the question we will invite you to ask is, how did they get there…?'

Lefevre's words were almost too much for me to take in, very nearly forcing my childhood Tourettes to resurface and rant, '*Fuck off, wankers! It was me!*'

Lefevre had paused for a good few seconds after the 'how did they get there?' line, leaving it hanging in the air like a dandelion seed, before gently blowing it away. There followed a brief and superfluous shuffling of some papers, before he released a smile of satisfaction. He was a skilled Old Bailey hack, well experienced in the art of conducting a jury.

Meanwhile, I'd quietly taken in a series of deep, shaky breaths, and had managed to force myself, and Lefevre, back into focus.

'And there is one final section of evidence that you may find very compelling indeed. For when the defendant was interviewed later that day, he admitted to police that he stabbed Miss Gunasekera, and pushed her over Beachy Head cliffs. Now, the Crown has to accept that the defendant's admissions are not entirely consistent with the forensic evidence, and this is where we will invite you to consider his mental condition. In any event, what is clear is that this interview took place in the presence of the defendant's solicitor, Mr Jim Harwood, who, I believe, is the gentleman sitting behind my learned friend Mr Douglas.'

'*Hell, don't look at me,*' I silently thought. I froze in my seat and stared at the blue counsel's notebook in front of me, desperately waiting for Lefevre to move on. I could feel many eyes inspecting me, with a cursory nod from the judge to boot. After what seemed like an age, Lefevre continued.

'It was therefore a full and frank admission, members of the jury, and one which the Crown says should help seal this case beyond any reasonable doubt. Now, with his Lordship's leave, I'll call the first witness... Mrs Rita Brandon, please.'

The velvet drapery was disturbed at the back of the court, as Mrs Brandon made her way towards the witness box. I was then that I caught a glimpse of one of Prosecution's photographs on Harry's bench, the one where Sarena's head is sticking out of the sack, with bits of seaweed providing decoration. A sickly feeling wrenched at my stomach, and a resin of culpability glued me further to my seat.

I couldn't help a strain of the neck and a further surreptitious glance at Elton in the dock. As I did so, Mrs Brandon took the Bible in her right hand, ready to swear the oath. Elton shot me another huge cheesy smile. In an instant I wanted to hold his hand, and run with him, bursting out through the Old Bailey walls onto Newgate Street.

Harry and Lefevre may have been in their usual theatre, but I had written the tragedy. I thought I could pull off the chief puppet-master role, but it needed a steady hand to pull their strings... one I suddenly felt I didn't have. I began to shake – vibrate, even. The pressure was reaching breaking point.

I'd been blocking it all out, cocooning myself in fact and fiction. I'd quashed all emotion, like I'd learned to do as a child, but Elton had just burst my bubble with his smile, and I was about to face up to the awful reality of what I'd done.

Just as Mrs Brandon uttered the words, 'I swear to tell the truth, the whole truth and...', I sprang to my feet impulsively, with a desire to confess to one and all.

CHAPTER 4

Distant lights twinkled in the background as a final vision of Sarena appeared on the car windscreen. It depicted her body, which had come to rest across the French oak flooring. One of her eyes was half open, and a small trickle of fresh blood bubbled from a nostril. It had been a solitary moment of hope, a brief betrayal of a sign of life.

The vision etched itself into the glass, before a dazzling light from the opposite carriageway blurred it beyond recognition.

I knew that everything about the case would suggest that both Loren and I were guilty of murder. It was this that had abruptly abducted the moment, as I'd sat with Loren in Sarena's flat, feeling alternate waves of terror and self-preservation forcing their way to the shore. There was no time for dithering. I couldn't afford her Albany Street flat to be a crime scene. A wholly different scenario would have to be conjured. Sarena had to be dumped, many miles away.

My hands tightened even further around the steering wheel, clinging onto it as if someone was trying to pull it from me. I only realised I was crying when I felt a tear slip off the end of my chin, and fall into my lap. Sarena had been my sensational succubus. I was hexed by that first glint of seduction in her eye. 'My' Sarena, my mesmeric mermaid. The girl who had reminded me of the beautiful Aqua Marina in Stingray.

Eventually I summoned up the will to overtake the Norbert Dentressangle lorry. I glanced further up the road, letting my eyes follow the trail of red lights right up to the brow of the hill. Which lane would take me to redemption? The inside, the central, the fast lane?

The rest of the journey was a blur of wet drops and refracted light, from the end of the M23, through South London, up over the river and heading past Marble Arch. I eventually reached Swiss Cottage and turned into the little drive behind my flat at precisely thirteen minutes to five.

I picked up the home phone and called Loren. I explained that I couldn't call earlier as the mobile had packed up. I told her that I had done all that was necessary. Loren kept asking me if I was sure everything had gone okay, and I told her that as far as I knew it had. The last thing I remembered doing was putting my solicitor's ID card into Elton's anorak pocket, as planned.

I told Loren I'd try and grab a few hours' sleep, and that I'd see her later. I sent my love. I heard Loren saying something about love as well, her comment marginally more disingenuous than mine, I feared. I took a huge dose of Night Nurse and followed it with a large Cognac.

I'd set my radio alarm for ten o'clock on that Monday morning, and woke to the gentle pulse of Morcheeba, singing 'Left my soul there, down by the sea'. I let the lyrics resonate for a beat before peeling away the duvet cover. What awful things had I done…? Poor Elton, rendered comatose in the fully reclined passenger seat of my car, and dumped in an Eastbourne beach hut with Sarena's blood splashed and smeared on his QPR football top.

Walking into the reception of Johnson Gower & Co., as I'd done umpteen times before, I imagined that the words 'Lying Murderous Bastard' were stamped on my head. Colleagues were there, saying 'good morning' and making superfluous sounds, but they had no faces.

I went straight up the stairs to Loren's office. I don't recall any conversation; I just remember her clinging onto me. We were still clasped together in pain when my secretary Nellie knocked and entered simultaneously.

'Sorry, Loren, it was Jim I was looking for... a phone call for you. A police station.'

It was just another day in the office for Nellie. I tried to pretend it was for me too.

'Thanks, Nel. Can you put it through here?'

As Nellie left I puffed out my cheeks in nervous anticipation. Loren wore a brief empathic smile in response, knowing the ordeal was far from over. The phone rang a few seconds later. I let my breath echo it for a moment, before picking it up.

'Jim Harwood… Yes, Elton Spears is my client. I see. Murder?... Holborn?... Okay, Sergeant, I'll be there within the hour.'

I put the phone down and looked at Loren.

'That was the custody officer at Holborn. What's Elton doing there?'

Loren mirrored my blank look. Elton's case was about to get underway, and right from the start it had thrown me off guard.

CHAPTER 5

I walked into Holborn police station and was introduced to DCI Litton. I was already on edge, as I'd been expecting a call from Eastbourne Police. Indeed, I'd been dreading the drive down there again.

I chose not to ask too many questions, constantly in fear of inadvertently blurting out things that I couldn't possibly know, like the precise time and location of death or anything at all about the murder victim. I was so nervous that Litton probably thought I was a murder case virgin.

Litton was in his early fifties. He had a hint of Huddersfield in his accent. He was dressed immaculately in a charcoal grey suit, and smelt of cigars. I concentrated on every single word that he said, though my head was throbbing with tiredness and fear. As Litton spoke, a drop of sweat dripped off my eyebrow and trickled down my nose. I imagined it splashing onto his shiny black shoes.

'He had your card on him, Mr Harwood. Old client, I presume?'

Litton was pleasant enough in tone.

'Yeah, I was with him at Acton nick last Thursday. I can't believe this. Murder... Elton?'

'We've had a preliminary from the path... fatal stab wound to the heart.'

I felt a lump of sick trying to reach my throat. 'Sarena, I adored you', I could hear my mind saying, and as it did so I could hear alter ego 'Ken' in my head, having a dig, as he was prone to do in times of stress.

-Now listen, Jim. Don't say anything silly.

-I won't.

-Don't tell him you were in love, will you?

-Ken, leave me alone, please. I'm trying to concentrate. Piss off, will you!

Ken had been my childhood friend – at least, that's the way he put it. I couldn't make sense of him when growing up. When I discovered that my peers didn't have a little mate in their heads, I realised it was prudent to keep him to myself. Occasionally he'd come out in a Tourettes rant, the condition that afflicted me until my first year at university. On other occasions he'd just appear from time to time, argue with me, say something trite, and then disappear for hours. I mustn't dismiss him, though, as he was often there for me, to help soothe the blow of Mum's death, and father's disappearance.

A fair few years had passed where Ken was nowhere to be seen or heard. I thought he had gone for good, but later came to realise that he'd only been dormant. Elton's case had somehow sparked him back to life.

Meanwhile, Litton was thrusting his hand into his inside jacket pocket. Despite the warning on the custody suite wall, he lit up one of his pencil-thin cigars. I declined his invitation, convinced that with one puff I'd throw up all over him.

'When did this happen, Mr Litton?'

'That I can't tell you. And I don't know yet whether she was already fatally wounded when she was pushed over the cliffs.'

'Of course she was dead,' I wanted to say, knowing full well that she'd been dead for hours when I'd kick-pushed her off Beachy Head.

Litton was handed some notes by a junior CID officer.

He took a moment to study them.

'What I *can* tell you is that your client was initially arrested at about half seven this morning, in a hotel in Eastbourne.'

'Eastbourne?'

I managed to convey the response with an element of surprise, then wondered if I'd done the right thing. But why shouldn't I be surprised that my client was arrested in Eastbourne, when he spends most of his life traipsing the streets of North London? I felt another drop of sweat leaving my armpit, as Litton studied his notes again.

'Arrested at zero seven thirty-two, at The Hotel De La Mare, in the kitchen. For theft of two chicken legs and a bag of croissants.'

'That sounds more like the Elton Spears I know.'

I was relieved to get some chit-chat in. Litton curled half a smile before continuing.

'He had bloodstains on his clothes. Initial tests show that it's the same blood group as the victim. We'll be running a DNA.'

'Who's the victim?'

I couldn't stop myself asking. I immediately wished I hadn't, inwardly chastising myself. Litton must have taken it as fairly routine.

'We believe she's a student. Found at the foot of the cliffs by a woman walking her dog. Her father's coming to identify the body. He's flying over from Sri Lanka.'

'*Is* he?'

'Why do you say it like that, Mr Harwood?'

'Oh, no, I just thought, long way, from Sri Lanka, you know…'

I tried to shut myself up, but I couldn't work it out. I just couldn't make sense of what I was hearing. How had they managed to ID Sarena so quickly? I'd left no documents on her. And how had they got hold of her father with such speed? Why the hell was DCI Litton dealing with the case anyway? Why not Sussex CID? Nothing made sense, and I was desperate to ask questions.

Litton, however, was taking everything in his stride.

'I'll be interviewing Spears later, when we get a few more facts together and a further word from the pathologist. In the meantime you're welcome to advise your client in the cells. Or we can arrange an interview room if you like?'

'No, the cells are fine. I expect somebody's made you aware of his psychiatric history?'

'Yes, and I've got the file from last week at Acton. Fifteen-year-old schoolgirl, I believe. An indecent assault.'

'I thought she was sixteen, but yes. He's… erm, he's not all there, Mr Litton.'

'So I gather. The quack's on his way,' he added, just so I knew all the correct procedures were being followed.

Litton led me to the custody area and left me in the hands of a constable who was acting as jailer. He looked like the magician Paul Daniels – very much like him, I remember thinking. I wanted to ask him if he could turn me into a rabbit, so I could hop out of the front door. I was feeling so drained that I was beginning to worry about my sanity – my overt sanity, I mean. Emotionally, physically, mentally – I was drained in every possible way. I'd taken some ProPlus and an extra caffeine boost to get through, and I was pulsing like a hill-top beacon. My fever was increasing, and I sensed I was hallucinating.

That's when a familiar old vision hit me, in which all sorts of childhood characters come hurtling at me along the Time Tunnel, spinning at me with menace. I momentarily stopped and rested. All the old ones were there...Wacky Races was playing a major part. Professor Pat Pending was back, stretching me to ridiculous proportions. Dastardly was setting up a road block. The Anthill Mob were all arguing... then lots of white horses were running through a village. The Dwarf from the Singing Ringing Tree was looking on. Robinson Crusoe took out a knife and cut open a pineapple. That music started again... that beautiful Robinson Crusoe TV theme. The robot from Lost in Space was waving its arms around again, shouting in manic tones, *'Danger, danger, liar approaching...'*

There was a slight earth tremor and all the characters shook. Shouldn't I be at school? Has it happened yet? How old am I? Has that horrible thing in the allotment actually happened yet? I needed to know. Was Dad still alive? Why did he kill my mum? Why wasn't he caught? Is that why I became a lawyer? Why not a detective? Who's asking me these questions? Help me, someone please help me.

I could hear a voice speaking to me – really speaking to me. He wasn't in the Time Tunnel. It was PC Paul Daniels.

'Are you all right, sir? Are you feeling all right?'

'Fine... sorry... flu...'

It was all I could concoct.

'Bit of a fever,' I then added, before accepting his offer of a plastic cup of water. I hadn't realised that I was sitting on the edge of the sergeant's desk.

My brain and body were in two different places. I tried to force them together, but they struggled to meet. They were behaving like two repelling magnets. When they did finally meet, they made a noise in my head like two train carriages shunting.

PC Paul Daniels then led me along the corridor and opened up the cell door, but my mind was still playing tricks – wicked and wanton tricks. It wasn't Elton sitting there, but Basil Brush. A giant Basil Brush… I'd been terrified of him as a child.

I was totally losing it. The officer shut the door, leaving me trapped. Brush was opening his mouth. It got wider and wider. It got so wide that the bottom jaw scraped the concrete floor. I could see fangs and huge serrated teeth. Brush was now coming towards me. He was going to eat me and was snapping his huge jaw open and shut. Then Brush laughed, that horrible cackly laugh. Then he finished it off with a *'Boom, boom'*, before disappearing into a mist that morphed into Elton.

I put my hand on the cell wall to stop myself from falling over. My fever was high, and it felt like the entire surface of my body was wet. Then I heard a familiar voice.

'Hello.'

The giant that was Elton looked so innocent in his white forensic boiler suit... too innocent, I thought, as paranoia began to set in. As I took a step into his cell, a wave of guilt gripped my chest, forcing me to snatch some air into my lungs.

PC Paul Daniels slammed the cell door behind me, making it echo with iron ferocity. When I looked at Elton he was morphing continuously, one second himself, the next Basil Brush.

I sat on the end of the solid wooden bench, pausing only to flick a small pile of his bitten nails onto the concrete floor. Elton stared at me as I deliberately scraped my knuckles against the grainy cell wall, to regain my focus, and to try get rid of the Basil Brush morph.

Elton was still staring at me, with an expression you might find on a naughty child.

'Been a bad boy,' he commented, quite earnestly.

'No, you haven't, Elton... well, yes, you have, actually.'

'Stole a chicken,' he added, as if that was all he'd been detained for.

I couldn't help but smile. There was a brief silence before Elton shot me a huge cheesy smile in return. I wanted to confess to him there and then. I wanted to tell him how badly 'care in the community' had let him down. I wanted to tell him that there was a method in my madness in framing him for murder. I didn't though. I stuck to plan, and started to sow seeds.

'What happened, Elton? What were you doing in Eastbourne?'

'Don't know.'

'How did you get there?'

'Don't know. Woke up in the sea.'

Another nervous smile bent my lips. I couldn't help it. I knew what he meant, but it was just the way that he said it.

'The policeman tells me that you stabbed someone,

Elton. Did you?'

Elton paused over the question, and then removed a bogey from his nostril. I wondered what he was going to say next, but he was just searching for a place to wipe his snot. He chose his leg.

'Stole a chicken... and ate it,' he added, as if the eating of it increased his culpability.

I had always enjoyed Elton's company, and often marvelled at his peculiar mind, but right then I had to keep my focus.

'Elton, I want you to listen to me very carefully. Last week you were arrested for indecently assaulting a young girl. Did that happen again, Elton? Did it go further this time?'

There was no response at all from Elton.

'Try and understand. If you listen to what I'm going to tell you, you might get some help. You might end up at St Vincent's in Epsom. You like it there, don't you?'

Elton nodded. He'd spent a brief period in St Vincent's psychiatric hospital and had told me he liked it better than prison.

'See, if you don't say anything, nobody will understand. You'll just go to prison again, for a long time.'

'In St Vincent's they let me have my telly.'

'Yes, I know they do.'

'Watch Scooby Doo.'

'Okay, Elton.'

'Scooby-dooby-doo!' Elton's impersonation was spot on.

'Please, Elton, listen and concentrate. I'm not interested in Scooby Doo right now, and you're not here for stealing a chicken, or eating it. You're here because of something very serious. Now, you met this girl. She was beautiful. You wanted her to be your girlfriend. You wanted to touch her, didn't you?'

Elton smiled again, but this time it was a smile I recognised. I knew exactly what he was going to say next.

'Do you want to see my pants?' he asked, almost gleefully. It was a question that Elton frequently asked, usually in the most inappropriate of circumstances.

'What colour are they today?' I had to oblige, knowing that if I failed to acknowledge the matter, Elton would get very cross. Elton then thrust his hand into the slit of his white forensic suit, trying to gain access to his groin area.

'I don't need to see them,' I quickly added.

Elton nodded, as if this was a perfectly normal conversation.

'Spiderman.'

I tried to ignore it. I knew Elton wanted to talk about the motif on his underwear. I decided to use the prompt.

'Is that what you asked the girl? Did you ask *her* if she wanted to see your pants?

Elton didn't respond.

'Sarena... the girl, the girl you stabbed.'

'No,' responded Elton, quite resolutely.

I took another huge intake of breath. I knew Elton's personality was as mad as it was malleable, and with a propensity for false confession. I had to persevere.

'You stabbed her, Elton. When you stabbed her, you hid her for a while. Then later, some hours later, you went back to where you'd hidden her.'

Elton let out a huff, one I couldn't read.

'You okay, Elton?'

'Hot.'

'It is rather hot in here, yeah. Tell me, Elton. Tell me about the girl. Did you want her to be your girlfriend?'

Elton stared at me with wobbly brown eyes. It was a battle of the loons, and I worried for a second that I might just be winning on points.

'My girlfriend,' Elton suddenly said, to my everlasting gratitude.

'Gorgeous, wasn't she? Sarena?'

'Salena,' Elton responded, not quite hearing the name correctly.

'Sarena. With an R. Sarena.'

'Salena,' he insisted.

'Guess that will do.'

'Tits.'

'Good.'

'My girlfriend.'

'Very good.'

And bit by bit, in a mix of probing and profanity, the story developed from there. Many years of dealing with Elton had taught me that if the seed is planted, the flower will grow.

By the end of the day Elton had told DCI Litton that he met his 'girlfriend'. Salena, he insisted on calling her. He touched her and he kissed her, and he stabbed her because she called him names. He didn't like people calling him names. He got in the bit about the sack, with prompting from Litton. He told him about his walk. He told him about his search for vegetables to eat and how he always carries a knife.

He didn't say a thing about the trip to Eastbourne, or genuinely seem to have any idea as to how he got there, or why he even went. Litton asked him about trains. He said he had been on a train once but that was a long time ago. He said enough to convince anyone that he was the madman who murdered poor, innocent Sarena. To cap it all, he even admitted touching the girl at the bus stop in Acton on the previous Thursday – a double whammy of admissions.

The reality was that although there were inconsistencies in Elton's version of events, his mental condition was an easy answer. Litton was swayed by the fact that Elton told him details that 'only the murderer could know', and for an old-school copper, there's still no bigger nail to ram into the coffin. Even without the forensic evidence he would have been in serious jeopardy, but with it, he hadn't a prayer.

I had represented Elton many times before, but never with such acute concentration. Despite nearly losing my mind, everything seemed to have gone to plan.

After the official interview, Litton wore a familiar smile of relief that said, '*Thank God we've got a confession. That'll make the job easier*'. I suppose the ultimate irony was that when Elton was finally charged with murder, DCI Litton took me to one side and earnestly told me that he was impressed how, unlike some lawyers, I hadn't advised him to remain silent or repeatedly spout 'no comment'. Litton thought I was doing the right thing. I cringed when he said it, but I wasn't about to argue the point.

CHAPTER 6

I'd been obsessed by her, caught in her full beams, and dazzled in delight. I will never be able to dismiss that flaming beauty from my mind.

It was early May 2011, a casual meeting in a High Holborn pub. I was having a post-conference drink with barrister Giles Derby, and he could bore for England. We were talking some nonsense about truth and justice when Sarena appeared, pausing in the doorway as if searching for a friend. A waft of warm summer air blew in behind her, gliding her in on the gentle breeze.

She was wearing a tightly fitting dress, patterned with seashells and clinging to her curves. There was definitely something of the mermaid about her. It even took me back to childhood, reminding me of that first subterranean encounter in 'Stingray' – the one where Troy Tempest first sets eyes on Aqua Marina, and that strange haunting song fills the air. I can hear it now: 'Sarena, Aqua Sarena, why do these strange enchantments appear whenever you're near…?'

Then Giles turned to see what I was gawping at. To my surprise Sarena threw a little wave, and approached our table.

Giles addressed her like an old friend.

'Sarena, hi. Oh, this is Jim... Jim, Sarena... Sarena, Jim.'

There was a knowing little smile from Giles, as if to say 'aren't I the lucky one?' Then off he went to the bar.

'Do you mind?' Sarena said, most politely.

Of course I didn't mind, and she sat down. I smiled and said the first moderately sensible thing that came into my head: 'You obviously know Giles?'

And there came the moderately sensible answer: 'I'm just getting work experience at his chambers.'

Then something unusual happened. I looked into her eyes and she looked into mine, and a smile cracked each face simultaneously. I'd caught the comforting heat of a welcoming log fire, and was overwhelmed by the radiance. I even sensed drops of sweet milky substances emitting from hidden pores. I immediately wanted to kiss those soft pink lips and talk mumbo-jumbo. I really was hexed from that moment on.

Giles returned with two pints of lager and a gin and soda. I watched and listened, and tried not to ogle. I thought I was learning the truth about her. Sarena was twenty-seven. She was on a six-month placement from her university in Perth, Australia. She had moved there from Sri Lanka due to some sort of death warrant on her father, something to do with the Tamil Tigers. She was planning to do her bar finals in Chancery Lane and wanted to join a set of chambers in Grays Inn. That's as much as I can remember, because every one of my senses was overloaded by this Aqua Marina of my youth.

When Giles had to nip off to the loo I took the plunge, and cleared the air.

'Are you good friends with Giles?'

'Well, he's acting as my chaperone, really.'

'Oh. You're not, erm…?'

Sarena's look was disapproving.

'No... no, it's nothing like that. Why do you ask?'

'I just wondered. He didn't ask you what you wanted to drink, when you first came in. Just went off to the bar and came back with a gin and soda.'

Sarena smiled. 'You lawyers, you don't miss much, do you?'

'You're a lawyer too.'

'Well... not yet.'

I couldn't resist the opportunity to look into those beguiling brown eyes. As Giles came back to the table, I placed my card in Sarena's hand, suggesting that she give me a call... so I could fill her in, on matters legal, of course.

Two days later I took her out for a drink and a Soho Chinese. She told me many things that night, about her likes and dislikes, her ambitions and desires, her childhood and her family. I took it all in with gusto. I was like a schoolboy sucking in the last drops of his melted ice-pop. Perhaps I should have known better, but Sarena was truly mesmerising. It wasn't just her beauty, it was that flaming chemistry... Bunsen burners or bust.

We had a few more dates and what I can euphemistically now recall as getting-to-know-you dinners. Then there was a hedonistic night of decadence at the Dorchester before we went away to the coast for a weekend, to Bournemouth. She said she'd barely heard of the place. She'd heard of London, Liverpool, Oxford, Cambridge, and for some reason, Melton Mowbray. It was something to do with her father's penchant for pork pies. She told me he used to have them specially flown over to Colombo. I remember conjuring up a picture. A smart little balding Sri Lankan relaxing on a crimson Chesterfield, pork pie in one hand, Bombay Sapphire in the other. Maybe a servant or two on call, and little Sarena, aged ten, kneeling by his side, listening to his Ceylonese anecdotes.

We walked for miles along the golden sands stretching away from Poole harbour. The girl seemed to have had an impeccable upbringing and a thorough education. She took me on face value. Jim, a reasonably successful lawyer, prone to wit and flippant speech.

We stayed in a local Bournemouth guest house, which was a bit of a come-down from the Dorchester the previous week. Sarena had insisted on going there, and I guess was trying to impress. Whatever, something was definitely amiss. She hadn't drunk that much before, and by the time we'd gone up to our room, she'd had three large Baileys with ice. She wanted to cuddle, but didn't want to make love.

I mentioned the scars in passing. They were light brown streaks on the darker background of her silky smooth back. Poor sausage had fallen off her pony. She'd told me the story before, while at the Dorchester, but this time things had changed. First time around she'd said she was eighteen, it was a hot, sticky afternoon, and the local gymkhana had ended in tears: a crushing fall at the parallel bars. In the second telling, she was still eighteen, still in Colombo, still approaching the parallel bars, but had missed the actual gymkhana due to her fall in practice. As I offered the same empathic smile, I knew she was lying. I remember puzzling to myself, what a strange thing to lie about.

I stared up at the ceiling as she fell asleep, her head buried into my chest, her gold chain momentarily tickling. It was nothing, surely. And anyhow, she was drunk... And yet that instinct that comes into play in the heat of court battle started to misbehave. I recognised a porkie pie when I heard one. And where there's a lie, there's a reason.

As I followed the cracks in the ceiling with my eyes, I started to recall other bits and pieces of our conversations over the preceding weeks. Little things, which on their own were easily dismissed, but with a touch more application were clearly untruths. Places, dates, names of friends, and even childhood pets… things that contradicted, thoughts loosened by alcohol and fatigue.

I guess I didn't so much smell a rat, more sniffed a hamster. I could almost feel someone stirring my brain, as if they'd opened up the top of my head and milled about with a small wooden spoon.

I waited a good while – waited until the heavy purring convinced me that she was Sleeping Beauty. Then I slipped silently out of bed, picked up her handbag and locked the bathroom door behind me.

There was the usual in the handbag, which was a mock crocodile job. I pulled out the hairbrush, the make-up bag, the tampons, the packet of gum, and finally the purse. I sat down on the toilet seat. There were a couple of credit cards in her name, eighty pounds in cash and some loose change. That seemed to be it. Then I slid back the zip pocket and took out a couple of bits of paper.

The credit card receipt was from the Dorchester. Our bill came to three hundred and fifty-two pounds. She'd paid for it, but on somebody else's card – a card in the name of Ms J. Srinath. And there was a football ticket: Chelsea East stand, Saturday last, their final home game of the season. She'd told me she'd been staying with a friend in Birmingham. She said she'd gone up on the train from Euston on Friday evening. I'd even dropped her off at the underground taxi point. She'd told me she got back on Sunday afternoon too. As I studied them further, a sickly feeling built up in my stomach.

I was still sat on the edge of the closed toilet seat, vexed and frustrated. I wondered why someone had squashed a snotty mess on the Van Gogh print. As I sat there a tear welled up, and my arms felt chilly.

I'd had these mad romantic images that Sarena might be the one, that after years of failed liaisons and time alone this extraordinary angel might have been sent down to save me. All those lies… I couldn't understand it. Maybe the little white ones were par for the course, but to lie about where she'd been for a whole weekend, and do it with such aplomb. Just what the hell was she doing at Stamford Bridge, and who did she go with?

CHAPTER 7

Elton had been remanded into custody, pending a 'directions' hearing at the Old Bailey. I deliberately waited a few weeks before seeing him, in the hope that his confession would have sunk in. There had been no application for bail. He wouldn't have stood a chance.

I parked up along a side street a few hundred yards from Wormwood Scrubs prison, where he was on remand. I was a touch early for the conference with Elton and the barrister I'd instructed on his behalf, Harry Douglas QC.

I sat in the car for a few minutes and took the opportunity to have a look at Elton's preliminary psychiatric report. Dr Audley knew Elton from his previous stays at St Vincent's, though Elton was never there long enough for anyone to really get to grips with his condition. I skimmed through the report, pausing on one particular paragraph:

'His history suggests that in periods of trauma and stress he is prone to fantasy. It is during these periods of delusion that Spears has committed the bulk of his offending. He often claims little or no knowledge of incidents which are known to have occurred. His disorder, as such, is complex, in that it is sporadic in its manifestation. Though there remain periods of reasonable stability and order, such is the ferocity of his delusions that they have become profoundly embedded within his psyche. In addition he has an extremely malleable and susceptible

personality, and, in my opinion, needs long-term assessment and care within a controlled environment…'

I was thinking about Elton as I walked around the corner from Du Cane Road, into the prison drive. I focused on the queue in the distance, where social and legal visits all milled together in a myriad of colours and shapes: three peroxide blondes, two lawyers in dark suits, four black youths in assorted hoods and logos, a balding probation officer in a corduroy jacket and two CID. I felt sorry for them, actually. The two CID guys were novices, I think, and doing their best to look like ordinary Scrubs visitors. Plain clothes or not, they were about as inconspicuous as a settee in a bicycle basket.

I joined the back of the queue and looked around to see if I could spot Harry Douglas QC. Harry was rarely late, but there was no sign of him. I fiddled about as the queue slowly dissolved. At the entrance stood the usual screw in uniform, who always looked thoroughly cheesed off, and rarely bothered to speak. He recognised me as a regular and just partially raised his right eyebrow. I said the magic words 'Spears D4574', and he nodded me in.

There was another queue in the security foyer, and I soon caught up with the same people as before. There was rarely any conversation, and usually a fairly sombre mood. The hoodies were doing their best to look cool and mean, although one of them seemed somewhat embarrassed when his Tupperware box was found to contain no more than a condom and a Snickers bar.

I handed over my bag for inspection and put the metal items into a little plastic box. More Tupperware. I wondered if they confiscated them from hip-hop lads? Then I walked through the security screen, like the ones they have in airports, and not for the first time the thing went off. Another screw then appeared with what looked like a black tennis racket with no strings. It began to make noises that Rolf Harris's Stylophone would be proud of. I removed the offending loose change, which had gone through a hole in my jacket lining, and soon found myself walking on through to the visits area.

It was ten o'clock, and the Scrubs was in full swing. I passed the large room used for social visits. As usual it was full of wives, lovers, mates and dodgy alibis, no doubt all contemplating their lot and working out the best moment to hand over the cellophane ball of skunk they'd just removed from some orifice or other. The screws pretend not to notice. They know that if there was no dope on the block the place would explode, but everyone has to put on some sort of a show.

I walked up to the old biddy's shop where a couple of ageing Dorothys were struggling with a scalding steel boiler, doing their best to produce tasteless cups of coffee. Then I sensed a presence behind me.

'Jim Harwood, I presume.'

'No, it's Stanley. You must be Livingstone?'

Harry smiled. We were both used to the banter.

'How about a cup of the dark continent's finest?'

'Thanks.'

'Sugar?'

'Two.'

I plopped two white lumps into the cup, shoved a plastic stirrer in, and handed the coffee to Mr Harry Douglas QC. We both walked on towards the legal visits area, pausing only to wait for a door to be unlocked by a screw who resembled a vodka junkie, with a nose like an overripe strawberry. He showed us through to 'boothland', a corridor of about twelve rooms, each with a table and four chairs.

We chose one of the larger rooms towards the end of the corridor. Harry dropped his briefcase onto the table, taking care not to spill the hot coffee as he did so. I sat across the far end of the table, looking at Harry as we waited for Elton to be brought from D-wing.

The early chit-chat had faded and the apprehension was building from within. Why on earth was I doing this to Harry, or to Elton for that matter? I could feel my head gently swaying from side to side as I wished I could be somewhere else.

Quite suddenly, a pulse of fear shot through me, causing my arm to jolt and spill coffee over the table. I'd just avoided staining Harry's brief, which was now uncurled with its red tape nestling beside it. As I dabbed away at the coffee spill with a tissue, I imagined the words 'Lying Murderous Bastard' were still stamped on my head. I had to leave the booth, and made some excuse to Harry about getting a coffee for Elton.

I asked one of the Dorothys for a large coffee, and grabbed a handful of cubed sugars to go with it. As I walked back along the corridor I had to rehearse the act again, and looked for distractions. I glanced at some of the lawyers and their remand prisoner clients occupying the other booths. There were a few faces I recognised in the booth next door. Barrington Brown QC was in conference with his client and solicitor. I still can't remember the solicitor's name, but he had a reputation for stealing other people's clients.

Barrington Brown is a crap QC. He's pompous, aloof, self-deluding and thoroughly convinced that he's God's gift to life, the universe and everything. Despite the high regard he has for himself, his advocacy skills are limited, and he has the intellectual reaction of a flu-ridden sloth. Quite why anyone would actually choose to instruct him is beyond me, and a number of his hapless clients have ended up in the Court of Appeal claiming that they weren't properly advised.

I sat back down and told Harry that Barrington Brown was next door. Harry cracked a little sneer. He didn't much like him either. I was once in court when Harry tore him to shreds.

Harry was dressed that morning in a dark blue suit with a yellow spotted tie. He could easily have passed for a cabinet minister. I studied him as he took out his oval-shaped glasses from a brown leather case. I pictured him in his robes and gown, then formed an entirely different picture of him at a party we'd attended together some years previously in

Belsize Park. It was a fancy-dress do. Harry had worn a denim waistcoat, green pantaloons and brown sandals. He had a Jimi Hendrix wig and couldn't resist a few puffs of black Lebanese magic. At one point he was standing on a pine table, playing air guitar to *All Along the Watchtower*. I later found him comatose in the spare bedroom, lying semi-naked next to 'Lulu'.

It never ceases to amaze me how attire can totally alter your projection. The legal world is really just a pantomime. Tear open the curtains prematurely and you'd catch them all with their pants down.

Three years later Harry became a QC, and word is he'll be sitting as a judge before long. He's sharp, is Harry. It wasn't just his analytical approach and cunning I admired, it was his ability to communicate with one and all, on both ends of the educational and intellectual scale. It's a skill to be applauded, and one that far too few barristers possess.

The diversions had worked, and momentarily at least, had distilled some of the guilt that had been setting in... but then it hit me again. I knew that at some point in the future our friendship might be tested to the hilt, and that same old sickly feeling washed over me.

Harry did that thing with his glasses, tilting his head down to look at me from over the top of them.

'Penny for your thoughts?' he enquired.

I answered straightaway, with a manic air. 'I haven't got any thoughts…'

Harry shot me a curious glance. He was used to me making slightly more meaningful comments.

'What about you, Harry? Any gut feelings?'

'Not really one for feeling my guts, Jim...'

Harry's retort was deliberate. Touché, I thought. In any event he was as relaxed as ever. This was just another case to him.

'…Spears's interview,' he continued. 'Have you heard it? I mean, since you were there. Have you actually listened to the tape?'

'I've re-read the transcript, that's all.'

I remembered that I hadn't actually covered Elton's second interview myself. I hadn't paid too much attention to it since, either, as there was nothing obvious that seemed to stick out. I told Harry as much.

'I was only present at Elton's first interview. My colleague Loren Granger covered the second.'

'Well, there's a hell of a pause before he admits to having a knife. He mumbles something... a few utterings that don't appear to be on the transcript, and I can't make it out. And in the second interview he seems to be mumbling something else – humming, I think. I suggest you get it tested. Get the tape sent to an acoustics expert.'

I briefly wondered what Elton had been mumbling, and why Harry felt it might be important, but all I said to Harry was a routine, 'Right. I'll get that done.'

Elton was then ushered into our booth. He was dressed in an all-in-one dungarees thing in chocolate brown. They'd actually called him out of the workshop where he'd been packing soft toys. He looked like he ought to be presenting a children's TV programme, something with cartoons and games. Elton sat down next to me, on the opposite side of the table to Harry. I told him the coffee was his and he grunted in reply, 'Yeah... six sugars.'

'I know. Here you are.'

I unfolded my palm and gave him the lumps. Elton grinned.

Harry let me have the first word. He was good like that. Solicitors have so much more contact with their clients than barristers. There are all sorts of arcane rules and mores governing the relationship between barristers and clients. It's all so unnecessarily complicated. Barristers have two clients: the solicitor, who's the professional client, and the defendant, the lay client, who's also your client... something very British, and something that in Elton's case I was happy to rely on.

I wondered then how much easier this awful charade

might have been if we'd adopted the American system of 'one lawyer advocate'. I could have framed Elton and physically conducted the trial myself. I shuddered at the very thought. I would have surely collapsed under the strain and made some dreadful error in front of the jury.

A smile of pure angst electrified me. Thank God for Harry, I thought. So, Elton had two lawyers. It was my job to start the ball rolling, go to the police station with him, advise him, prepare the case for trial, take statements from him and any defence witnesses, instruct experts that may be relevant to the evidence, and so on. Harry's job was to help advise me on all this, but above all else to physically do the advocacy at the Old Bailey trial – a sort of advocacy specialist, if you like.

The point is that solicitors *instruct* their barristers. Officially the solicitor is the governing party, and ultimately has conduct of the case. What's more, a solicitor spends many more hours with their clients than the barristers instructed for trial, and tend to know their clients best.

Elton was staring around at the walls, while playing with the straps on his dungarees. It was time to grab his attention.

'So, Elton. How's it going?'

'Packing toys for kids.'

'Good... right, this is Mr Douglas. I told you about him. He's going to be representing you at the Old Bailey. We want to talk to you about the case, get it sorted for you, okay?'

'Yeah.'

It was clear that the drugs Elton had been taking were having a calming effect, though the madness of Elton could still be detected, lurking beneath the surface. I smiled at him again. 'So, Elton, Mr Douglas is now going to go through a few things with you.'

'Yeah.'

Harry took over. He paused briefly to finish reading one of the prosecution statements.

'Elton, can I start with your interview with police? Now,

do you remember being taken to Eastbourne police station?'

'Yeah.'

'And after an hour or so there, some other officers arrived, and took you up to London, to Holborn police station.'

'Yeah, big Rover... big black Rover. Woof.'

Harry shot me a glance, unsure quite how the 'woof' was relevant. I raised my eyebrows a touch as if to say *'well, that's Elton. I did warn you!'* Harry smiled, before importing a more serious tone into his voice.

'Right, Elton, now listen. At Holborn police station one of those officers who'd been in the car asked you lots of questions, and it was tape recorded.'

'We went in a Rover.'

'Yes, I know...'

I think Harry was waiting for another 'woof', but Elton took a slurp of coffee instead. Harry continued, 'I'm going to just read a bit out to you... your interview with the police. The officer, Detective Chief Inspector Litton, said, "Tell me, Elton, why did you have a knife with you? Do you normally carry a knife?"'

Elton didn't respond. He stuck a finger up his nose. Harry tried again.

'Actually, that's two questions, really, isn't it? Let's take the second one first... "Do you normally carry a knife?"'

'In the kitchen... chop.'

'In the kitchen. Right. When you're not in the kitchen, do you ever carry a knife?'

'Yeah.'

'When's that?'

'Camp.'

'Camp?' Harry looked at me for an explanation.

'Maybe he means Scout camp. He was in the Scouts, his Dad told me. He only lasted a few weeks.'

'Yeah. Scout camp,' Elton confirmed.

Harry still looked confused, and I could hardly blame him. The thought of Elton doing the dyb-dyb-dybs and struggling with his woggle didn't bear thinking about. I could picture him in a little green cap, with his ten-yard swimming certificate peeling off... and wanted to cry. Harry ploughed on.

'But that was a long time ago, Elton. I mean since you've grown up. Have you ever carried a knife on the street?'

'No.'

'Right. So let's look at what you said to the police. You said, "yeah". Now why did you tell the police that you normally carry a knife?'

'Scout camp.'

'You meant when you were at the Scout camp. I see.'

Harry shuffled his papers again. I'd warned him about Elton, but you could see from his expression that he knew this was going to be hard work.

'So, let's go back to that first part of the question. Why did you have a knife with you? The officer means on that day… well, did you?'

Elton sniffed the air. He could detect the aroma of boiled beef coming from the kitchens.

'Food.'

Harry raised his voice a touch in response.

'Try and concentrate, Elton. It's only a few weeks ago. Did you have a knife with you?'

'No.'

Elton almost shouted the answer, but I wouldn't have been surprised if he'd shouted *'Yes!'* instead. Harry took it as a forward step.

'Good... good. Okay, now I know Mr Harwood – Jim – I know Jim's asked you this before, but try and think. What were you doing in Eastbourne, Elton? You were arrested there on the Monday morning. What on earth were you doing there?'

Elton stared directly at me, and was beginning to unnerve me. Then he slowly shook his head and my little internal guilty Geiger counter faded away. Harry scratched his ear and after a few seconds Elton scratched his, as if in an attempt to achieve synchronisation.

'Had you ever been to Eastbourne before?' Harry puzzled.

Elton stared blankly at Harry, before repeating his words, 'Had you ever been to Eastbourne before?'

'I'm asking *you,* Elton. It doesn't matter if *I've* been there.'

Elton didn't take kindly to Harry's stern tone. He blew out some snot from his nose and then wiped it with his sleeve. I watched on as Harry took a breath, figuring out how best to approach it all. He tried a more relaxed demeanour.

'All right, Elton, never mind that now. Back to the interview. The officer asked you some questions about your journey, about *when* you travelled down to Eastbourne. You said Sunday. Why did you say Sunday?'

Elton ignored the question and sniffed the air again. Then, just about audibly, he hummed something. I think it might have been the tune to *Food, Glorious Food.* Harry tried not to raise his tone, but couldn't disguise his frustration.

'Elton, please, try and think. This is important. When you were answering these questions, it was only a day or so after... well, after the incident, after you said you travelled down to Eastbourne. Now obviously you did, but can you think now, how you knew then that it was on the Sunday that you travelled down?'

Elton was lost for an answer and just looked blank again. Harry was finding it such tough going that I decided to chip in.

'Elton. Look at me... How did you get to Eastbourne?'

'Don't know.'

'Where did you sleep?'

'On the beach.'

Harry took over again, 'Ah. Good, so you remember that?'

'Woke up in the sea.'

That was a relief. I had to assume Elton wouldn't have a clue about anything that happened prior to that, but it was soothing to have it confirmed again.

'So, did you spend two nights on the beach, perhaps? Both the Saturday and the Sunday?' Harry continued.

'One night by the sea.'

'The Saturday, or the Sunday?'

'Day before I got nicked.'

'Well, that was the Monday. So you *are* saying that you didn't travel down to Eastbourne on the Saturday, but on the Sunday?'

Elton didn't reply. Days and times usually confused him. Harry scratched his ear again, and looked at me.

'Jim, this is crucial. Have we got anything from the bail hostel yet? We need to see their records.'

'I've checked. Their records are all over the shop. They just have a record of Elton being there, not of when he came and went.'

'That's ridiculous. These places...'

Harry was getting increasingly frustrated. He turned to Elton again.

'Elton, you remember you were on bail at the time... that weekend. You were at a bail hostel in Shepherd's Bush. Remember?'

'Saw Jim.'

'What do you mean, you saw Jim?'

Harry looked at me for an explanation. My guilty Geiger bleeped so loud I was sure Harry could hear it.

CHAPTER 8

I awoke with the sun bursting through the window, with its magnified rays boiling my head.

Sarena was still asleep, so I quietly slid out of the side of the duvet and slipped back the morning curtains. The guest house was perched on the cliff top, and our room afforded us a panoramic view of the coast. In the foreground was a monkey puzzle tree. Beyond was a winding path surrounded by rhododendrons, with blooms like the crescendo of a firework display. There were railings along the cliff top, which opened up to a narrow concrete stairway winding its way down to the beach.

As I surveyed the view from the window, I was desperate to try and cheer myself. I hoped for a few seconds that I had got it wrong, that I had dreamt my little excavation into her handbag, but the reality soon hit home again. As Sarena stirred, I covered my thoughts with a smile.

Sarena seemed reasonably bright, considering the night's imbibing, and was eager to get downstairs for breakfast. I wasn't hungry; the insecurity was eating into my appetite. What was this little beauty all about? What was driving her? Why was she lying to me? I kept my thoughts to myself for as long as I could, confining the breakfast conversation to things mundane.

All sorts were swirling around my mind as we made our way back to London. I wanted to cross-examine, but started out with a chit-chat approach.

'Nice weekend. You enjoy it?'

'Lovely, thank you.'

'We both chipped in, eh... unlike the Dorchester.'

'To be honest, Jim, I didn't actually pay for that.'

'Oh?'

'My father has a house in Hampstead, just off the heath. He rents it out to Japanese tourists and he includes a maid service.'

'Yeah? So?... What's all that got to do with the price of fish?'

Sarena then carried on talking without hesitation. Now maybe I was clutching at straws, but it struck me that a young Sri Lankan woman who'd been educated abroad and spent less than a football season in England wouldn't be familiar with such colloquial phrases as 'what's all that got to do with the price of fish'. I tried to argue it in my mind – well, maybe she might. I said nothing, and carried on listening.

'It's being refurbished this summer. The maid's gone off to work elsewhere. He gives her a credit card and pays off the bill in Colombo. Saves her paying tax, and saves him all sorts of red tape. So, he told me to collect her card and use it whenever I want. I just have to be a bit selective, that's all. It's not the money, Jim. I could have paid for this weekend too. It's just that too many hotel bills and Father will start asking all sorts of embarrassing questions, about boyfriends... you know.'

Sarena was talking fast, and with a liar's flair. If there was one thing my job had helped me with, it was to spot a liar at fifteen paces, let alone one sitting next to me. We flew past the M25 interchange, heading into London town.

'You mean about who you're staying with?' I enquired.

'Exactly… Javita Srinath's the maid. I use her card, just enter the PIN. Nobody actually looks at credit cards. They just put them into the machines. Anyway, it's all okay. Father pays the bill. He just helps me out, that's all. I'm not doing anything wrong.'

'I didn't say you were. Why did you tell me all that, anyway?'

'I didn't want you to think I was one of those... daddy girls... bimbos? Is that the word?'

I ignored the attempted diversion, realising by then that Sarena was a skilled liar.

'I meant, why did you tell me her name just then?'

'Whose name?'

'The maid. Srinath.'

'Don't know. I just did. Why?'

'Nothing.'

The tarmac turned into that pale concrete stuff with bitumen joints. There was a mile or so of rhythmic bumping. With every jolt, my mind jumped to a different thought. I imagined what her explanation for the Chelsea football ticket would be. I remember thinking, 'that'll be a good one, won't it Sarena? You were supposed to be in Birmingham'.

We went back to her apartment in Albany Street. She offered me a beer as I sat at the far end of her enormous four-seater sofa. It was almost pure white and looked like nobody had ever sat on it before. As I looked around the lounge I marvelled at all the expensive items: a beautiful Persian rug, top-of-the-range hi-fi, laptop, cinema-style TV... top-of-the-range everything, by the look of it. Sarena had even explained how the speakers were embedded in the four Monet prints on the walls.

Though I wasn't one to be impressed by such possessions, I was certainly curious. 'Dear Daddy', I quietly whispered to myself as she emerged from the kitchen, with a trendy beer glass and a bottle of Stella Artois.

On the one hand I sensed that Sarena did have some genuine feelings for me. I knew by then that she was living some sort of lie, but for the life of me I just couldn't understand it. Here was a beautiful and intelligent aspiring young lawyer who had the whole world in her hands. At least that's what she appeared to be.

It had been a warm weekend, and my perspiration had reacted with the black leather on the gear stick. Consequently I'd deposited a small black stain on her impressive sofa. I sheepishly pointed it out to Sarena and couldn't help smiling like a naughty child. She shrugged her shoulders, ripped the arm cover off and flung it towards the washing machine in the kitchen. Then she smiled back at me – a smile that briefly melted my resistance. I lay back on the sofa and admired what I saw.

'Sarena, you look great in those shorts. Really gorgeous.'

'Thank you.'

'Remind me, when did you come over from Sri Lanka?'

'I didn't. I came from Perth.'

'Oh yeah, I forgot. Sorry.'

Sarena sat next to me, brushing against me with a bare thigh.

'And I'm going back at the end of the month.'

'I know... I'm going to miss you.'

Sarena stroked my face with the back of her hand. I felt utterly paralysed, and shivered as if the temperature had dropped thirty degrees. She had this extraordinary presence: a powerful enigma that excited and scared the hell out of me at the same time. I knew then that if she pulled the imaginary strings she could make me dance like a marionette, and even though I knew it, I'd be powerless to do anything about it.

Imagine you wake up from the anaesthetic in the middle of surgery. Imagine you can see the consultant take out your heart and wave it around in front of you… and you can't do a thing about it.

I knew I was treading water, and tried to keep afloat. I took another mouthful of lager before I spoke.

'Why did you leave Colombo anyway?'

'I told you. Because my father thought it safer for us.'

'Us?'

'My brother and me.'

'So you both went to Perth?'

'Yes, to study. My father found us places at private schools.'

'It must hurt talking about your brother?'

'It was awful.'

I shook my head in dismay. She'd told me about the terrorist atrocity before, so skilfully that it had brought a tear to my eye.

'Unbelievable, being there when that bomb went off. That's horrible… I'm so sorry.'

Sarena wouldn't meet my look. She kept her eyes fixed on my glass as she filled it to the brim with some frothy Stella.

'What was he actually doing back in Colombo, your brother?' I prodded tentatively.

'Visiting Father.'

'And you didn't go with him?'

'Why the sudden interest?'

'Just wondered, that's all.'

Sarena paused. I knew exactly what she was thinking. She'd been chastised by her own tone, and aware perhaps that her accent had slipped a touch. It was the first time that I'd noticed. She forced herself to soften.

'I didn't go because I had exams coming up... at university.'

'I see... your poor brother...'

'Dinesh was only nineteen.'

'Dreadful... Your father must have been devastated. And you too... He must be very protective of you.'

'He is. He spoils me. Like the credit card... but I understand why, and I try not to abuse it.'

I took a large gulp of lager and smiled at Sarena. She was looking ridiculously radiant. My little mind was in turmoil. I could hear it saying, 'Oh, lie to me some more, you gorgeous creature...'

I looked at her again and marvelled. We shouldn't really take credit for such things as beauty. After all, it's very little to do with us. Yet somehow you can't help admiring someone like Sarena, as if it was the case that to be that overtly beautiful you must have somehow contributed to it yourself. I looked into those extraordinary brown eyes, and tried to throw her off guard, 'Who did you stay with last weekend?'

'Last weekend... I was in Birmingham. Why?'

'Just wondered what you did. I was dead bored at Newmarket on my own.'

'You didn't ask what I did. You asked who I stayed with.'

Sarena shot another of those blowtorch smiles, knowing full well that it would burn my face in adoration. Then she slowly shook her head as she said, with what I assumed must be mock concern, 'This wasn't supposed to happen, remember? We talked about this, about getting too close... I warned you... about getting upset.'

'Are you upset?'

Sarena paused before answering, 'Me?... Yes, I am. My time in the UK is nearly up, Jim. I don't want to leave you.'

I took hold of her and hugged her, this majestic mole, tunnelling up from her beastly burrow. We shared another beer, kissed and cuddled and christened her virgin white sofa.

CHAPTER 9

Elton's words were still resonating, while Harry's curious glance lurked for longer than was comfortable.

I could hear myself saying stay cool, and was expecting an interruption from my caustic alter-ego Ken any second. Before he could surface, I steeled and plucked up the straightest voice I could muster to Harry.

'He means, I dropped him there. I actually took him from Ealing Magistrates' Court to the hostel on that Friday morning when he got bail.'

Harry accepted the answer without a second thought... but then, why should he question me? How could he know what dastardly deeds were afoot? Harry carried on probing Elton.

'Yes, but after then, Elton... after that Friday... When did you go to Eastbourne? And why, for heaven's sake?'

Elton then blew his nose straight into the palm of his hand. He wiped his hand on his dungarees before drinking the rest of his coffee in one slurp. Harry was about to carry on but waited for Elton to stop playing about with the melted remains of the six sugar lumps in the bottom of his cup. The pause was a little unnerving, and I found myself involuntarily chipping in again.

'Trouble is, Harry, Elton's got a very limited grasp of

time. In fact, it's not really a concept he recognises.'

'I know. I've read Dr Audley's report. Just excuse us a minute, Elton. I want to talk about a few things with Jim.'

As Elton carried on swirling the dissolving sugar in the bottom of his polystyrene cup, Harry did that thing with his glasses again, and briefly looked into my eyes. Something about the prosecution case was bothering him.

'According to Stefanovic, the crown's pathologist, the victim died somewhere between twenty-four and thirty-six hours before the discovery of the body...'

'And...' I retorted, a touch shorter than I would normally address Harry, who carried on regardless.

'Well, the damage caused to the body from the cliff fall must also have happened about eight to twelve hours before the body was discovered, and without doubt, according to Stefanovic, at a time when she was already dead. Now, it wasn't discovered until about seven-thirty a.m. at the foot of the cliffs, on the Monday morning, 16th January. So, the victim must have died sometime between – and I'm being liberal here – say, mid-afternoon Saturday to seven thirtyish Sunday morning. Point is, she was dead by, say, seven thirtyish Sunday morning... must have been, on any account. Now, if Elton's saying he wasn't there until the Sunday, in the daytime, which I think is what he's saying... You see? This is crucial, Jim.'

I did see, but didn't want to face the issue there and then. I tried to put Harry off course.

'There isn't any *prosecution* evidence about how Elton got to Eastbourne, or when. So how does that help him?'

For a moment Harry genuinely appeared foxed. You could tell that he suspected something irregular about Elton's trip down to Eastbourne, but couldn't quite work out what it was. Harry raised his voice a good couple of notches, catching Elton's meandering attention as he did so.

'We've got to find out when Elton went to Eastbourne, why he went there, and how the hell he got there!'

Harry was beginning to frighten me. I wanted Elton to

have a fair crack, but there was a delicate balance going on. I was resting precariously on one of the scales held high on top of the Old Bailey. I could imagine Harry and Elton on one scale, and me on the other, being weighed down by the evidence. Harry addressed Elton again.

'Elton. Listen. You must understand how important this is. I'm going to summarise the prosecution case for you and then we'll come back to you. Now concentrate for me, please, and listen carefully: sometime between the Saturday afternoon and Sunday early hours, Miss Gunasekera was murdered. She was stabbed through the heart. The police say you did it.'

'I never.'

'I know, but you told them you did. Never mind, we'll come back to that. Just listen. Monday morning, a good 24 hours later, a woman walking her dog finds her body. It's found in a sack in a crevice at the foot of Beachy Head cliffs. That's a few miles along the coast from Eastbourne. Now whoever murdered her also dumped her over a cliff... but not at the same time. With me?'

'Yeah.'

He clearly wasn't, you could tell by the look in his eyes, but Harry struggled on. He gently loosened the knot on his tie and spoke with an air of puzzlement in his voice.

'We don't know *why* they should do such a thing, but they did. In any event, they must have actually killed her before say about seven thirty in the morning on the Sunday. Not necessarily dumped her over the cliff by then, but killed her – stabbed her. Forensics can tell us that. So if you're now saying that you didn't go to Eastbourne until daytime Sunday, then what you said to the police in interview must be wrong. Mustn't it?'

Elton rocked forwards and backwards and clearly hadn't followed a word of what Harry was saying. Nonetheless he replied, 'Not my girlfriend.'

'Sorry?'

Harry was looking for Elton to elaborate, but he didn't.

He looked to me instead.

'What does he mean, Jim?'

'I'm not sure. He said something in his interview about the victim being his girlfriend. He also said the same thing about the girl at the bus stop in Acton.'

'Yes, I seem to remember reading that. But now he's telling us that she's not his girlfriend.'

I shrugged in an effort to convey to Harry that I was just as confused. Harry moved on to something else.

'You don't drive, Elton, do you?'

'Yeah.'

'But you don't have a licence?'

'No.'

'Or a car?'

'No.'

'Have you ever driven a car before?'

'No.'

'But you've been in one, haven't you?'

'Yeah. Music car.'

'Sorry...?'

'Music in the car...'

As Harry tried to make sense of the answer, I started to panic. Might Elton actually remember being in my car, *the old Swedish thing* as I usually call it? Might he have somehow heard the CDs, despite the fact he was anaesthetised? Harry helped soothe my concern, and had clearly thought of some other angle.

'Ah... you mean like the ones they have at a fun fair?'

And Elton answered obligingly, 'Bashem car. Bang.'

Harry hadn't known Elton long enough to fully come to terms with how he communicated. As soon as Elton heard the term 'fun fair' he was thrown, and in trying to second-guess him Harry had only sent him further off track.

Harry continued to dig and prod and poke. He really did seem to have some sort of gut feeling about Elton, and you had to be impressed by his thoroughness and patience. But what else did I expect? I knew Harry as well as anyone. I could have instructed an ineffectual divot like Barrington Brown QC to conduct Elton's trial, and be safe in the knowledge that he'd go down for murder... but that wasn't the plan. The plan was that either Harry got Elton a manslaughter verdict, or, somewhat remotely, he might get him off altogether.

I thought a manslaughter verdict would be the best possible outcome. That way the crime would be 'solved', there'd be no need for any further investigation *and* Elton would get the help he so desperately needed. Manslaughter would open up alternative sentences for Elton, ones that involved long-term psychiatric care, whereas murder still demands a mandatory life sentence.

Either way the odds were stacked against him. There was the blood staining on his jacket with the DNA test stating categorically that it was Sarena's; there were fibres from her black velvet dress all over Elton's QPR football shirt; and to top it all, he even admitted to police, on tape, in front of his solicitor, that he had stabbed her, put her in a sack and pushed her over the cliff. Hey presto, get out of that.

It was obvious that his defence were going to raise issues like how did Elton get to Eastbourne? And how did he get the body to the top of the cliff? And such like... but that's just airy-fairy stuff in the world of hard fact and forensic reality.

Harry proceeded to take Elton through every single question and answer of his interviews with the police. I let him get on with it.

Eventually an older screw pushed open the door and told us that it was nearly time to 'sling our hooks'. He always said the same thing. Harry thanked Elton for his time – a rather odd thing to do in the circumstances, but he meant well. We both said goodbye to Elton, and off he went to pack a few more soft toys.

Harry had travelled down on the Tube and asked if I'd be good enough to give him a lift to his chambers in the Temple. He spoke to me from the passenger seat – the very same passenger seat that Elton had recently occupied. We were just about to approach the junction of Scrubs Lane and Du Cane Road.

'When I first got this brief I was thinking manslaughter.'

'Yeah, so was I.'

'He's not having it, though... *It wasn't me*, that's what he's saying.'

'It's not what he told the police.'

'But those are our instructions, Jim, and we're stuck with them. All or nothing.'

'But isn't manslaughter still a possibility?'

Harry paused for thought.

'We'll try at plea stage, of course we will, but I reckon this one's going to trial. Maybe things will develop from there. Anything could happen. The Crown might take a different view. I don't know.'

'I tell you what, Harry. I'd be chuffed if we got him manslaughter. I'd get into the secure unit at St Vincent's.'

'What did you just say?'

Harry was smiling. I didn't know why at first, until he explained.

'You said *'I'd'* get into the secure unit... *you're* not going mad, are you, Jim?'

'Ha, me? No... no...'

I glued a steely smile onto my face, and took a purposeful breath. Harry continued, 'I'm sure you're right... manslaughter is a possibility. We'll have to see how things go.'

Harry reassured me that nothing else in his diary would get in his way. He'd be representing Elton at the Old Bailey in a few months' time, come hell or high water. In the meantime he had some advice on preparing the case for trial, which he would later confirm in writing, but it was basically this:

To instruct an acoustics expert to listen to the tape-recorded interviews (to see if we can ascertain exactly what Elton is mumbling in the background). To check with the police to see if any tyre marks were recorded in the vicinity of the dump on Beachy Head cliffs. To instruct an expert on the DNA and bloodstaining evidence. To instruct an expert to assess how common the black fibres are from Sarena's dress, and to assess the fibre evidence generally. And to take detailed further instructions from Elton as to his movements between Saturday 14th January and his arrest on Monday 16th January, and, where applicable, to find evidence in support.

I was still the only person in Elton's life who had ever really tried to help him. Everyone else had just washed their hands of him. I'd been trying to get him decent psychiatric treatment for years, ever since I first represented him at Wembley nick. It's a bitter irony, and Joseph Heller would be proud of it. Truth was, unless Elton committed a really serious offence he would never get the attention he deserved. Okay, this was a bizarre gamble, and necessity is the mother of invention and all that, but this 'care in the community' stuff was just hopeless. As Elton had discovered, there was no 'care', and very little 'community' either.

CHAPTER 10

I spent the next couple of weeks trying to find her. It was as if Sarena had vanished into thin air.

When I'd left her flat after the Bournemouth weekend she'd promised to phone me in the week. She didn't, and when I tried to phone her at home all I could get was the answerphone. Phoning her mobile only prompted an irritating message stating that 'the number you have called is no longer available'.

I was numb with loss. Sarena, my stunning little cockatoo, had gone cold turkey. I felt like a junkie in need of a hit, desperate to have her running through my veins.

Fifteen days had passed before I received a text: 'Jim. Sorry not been in touch. Had to see to something urgent, for Father. *Had to bring my flight forward. Leaving from* Heathrow *tonight. Sarena'.*

I couldn't make sense of it. We'd laughed and played and loved, yet she'd disappeared as suddenly as a Sri Lankan sunset. When that text came through, I even thought about driving to Heathrow *to search for her. It seemed the only option left. Nothing made sense. The phone number she'd sent the text from was withheld, yet when she'd sent me texts previously the number had always been displayed. I even questioned whether the message was from Sarena at all.*

I was so close to getting into my car and driving to Heathrow*. I dared not though, not just because of that niggling fear that I might make a total fool of myself, but because I'd already downed the best part* *of a bottle of Merlot. I guess I could have hailed a cab, but somehow the option of opening another bottle and staying up until three in the morning, sharing misery with Morrissey, seemed like a less traumatic course.*

In the morning I was heavy-headed, and empty with loss. I could see Sarena's face everywhere: in the bathroom mirror, on the glass panelled drinks cabinet, even on the oven door.

I guess it was about then that I started to lose touch with reality. I would go to court in the mornings, then just aimlessly wander London's streets, hoping against hope that I might spot her in a crowd. Eventually my senses got the better of me and I kept telling myself that she was miles away – thousands and thousands of miles away.

I was a crumbling ruin. I started to take time off work and brief barristers to cover magistrates' court trials I could easily have done myself. There were days when I'd just sit in the park, or even stay at home and watch mind-numbing TV. I think that was what caused me to start reflecting on childhood, and I struggled like hell not to let it upset me.

I tried to ride the desire, like a smoker who's kicked the habit, and fought the cravings valiantly, but I just couldn't let it lie – or let her lie, to be more precise. So eventually I checked with Giles, the barrister who had first introduced us, and called him at his Grays Inn chambers.

I found out that Sarena had initially asked for four weeks' work experience at Giles's chambers. Her disappearance was no great mystery to him. She'd gone home, he guessed… why? What was the problem? I decided not to say what the problem was, but my mind was screaming, 'I love her, you idiot!' Looking back now, I recall Giles saying, 'If you do hear from her, let me know', but it was with such a casual air that I didn't attach any great significance to it at the time. Anyway, I was a determined little so-and-so, and I had to find out.

The Albany Street block was divided into four large mansion flats. I waited for someone to leave the main communal door before holding it open and sneaking in. As I climbed the stairs, I could hear the hollow thud of one of the big wooden doors from the flats upstairs, then quick tapping feet dancing down the steps until they hit the carpeted well. As I hid in the store cupboard with my nose far too close for comfort to an upturned broom, a bubble image of Sarena formed above my head.

I was imagining firing questions at her, on the slightest off-chance that she might still be there… How did she really get those scars? Where does she get her money from? Who is Javita Srinath? Did her brother really die in that Colombo bomb? Is this mystery father-figure a figment of her imagination? What about her studies? Well, she was going to court with barristers and learning the ropes, presumably just soaking it all up for later. She couldn't have faked that, surely? Anyway, why bother?

The tapping feet disappeared out of the communal door and I re-emerged onto the landing. Actually, I'm not sure what all the cloak-and-dagger stuff was about. I guess I just didn't want to be seen. I wasn't really sure what I was looking for, either, or even how I'd get in. I had this mad idea that I could somehow barge the door open, or fiddle about with a credit card like a second-rate TV detective... and the door would spring open. Truth was, these old mansion block flats were solidly built, and as impregnable as a castle keep. My only stroke of luck was that the little flap on the inside of the Chubb lock was stuck in the up position. That meant that if I lifted the outside flap I could see straight into Sarena's flat.

I bent down and peered in. The place looked spotless. I could just about make out pots and pans and crockery on the kitchen worktops, all laid out as if someone had done an inventory. Then the thought hit me: where the hell was the rest of the stuff? This was supposed to be one of 'Daddy's little London pads'.

I took it that Mr Gunasekera had access to a couple of London flats, including this one. Though from what Sarena said it was doubtful that he would ever venture out of Sri Lanka again. In any event, it didn't add up. Where was the expensive Persian rug, the porcelain, the antiques, the music system, etc. etc.?

As I went to walk away, I scuffed the outside doormat and caught a flash of something sticking out. On closer inspection it was a small blue card, like a calling card. I picked it up and studied it. There was an address in the top corner: Oasis Bar and Restaurant, Glasshouse Street, Piccadilly, London W1. I'd been there once myself, on a jolly with an old client. It was the sort of place that featured regularly in the celebrity gossip pages of many a magazine.

I made my way back to my 1990s Saab, my dear old Swedish

thing. I sat in the car and phoned Chelsea ticket office. I was concerned that my girlfriend's credit card had registered double the ticket price, something like that. I quoted the date and stand and seat number, which I'd written down in that Bournemouth loo. I was told that I must be mistaken. The ticket wasn't bought directly from Stamford Bridge. It had found its way to an agency in the West End.

The following morning, after a couple of minor matters to deal with at Westminster Mags, I took a stroll up past Buckingham Palace and through Green Park. I walked up Piccadilly, towards the circus, and crossed the busy interchange towards Boots. As I turned the corner from Regent Street, I could see a chalk board advertising 'West End tickets, Shows, Concerts, Premiership football, etc.', and realised it was just two units along from the entrance to the Oasis bar.

I wanted to investigate there and then, but I had pre-booked clients to see, and needed to get back to the office. I was still running through things in my mind as I walked into our reception, but I was immediately distracted.

There was Elton, large as life, sprawled out over the sofa with his bin liner full of worldly goods. He was about to take his first sip of Nescafé and six sugars from his favourite QPR football mug.

CHAPTER 11

I'd also instructed Elton's barrister, Harry Douglas QC, on the case of Matty Campbell. Matty was a steaming lump of Glaswegian blubber who was prone to robbing the odd bank. His case was also fixed for hearing on Monday 9th July 2012, the date scheduled for Elton's trial.

I recall sitting at my office desk, in realisation that I would no longer be able to instruct Harry Douglas QC to do both trials, and feeling a touch disappointed as a result. Then I thought, *why are you even thinking about Matty Campbell? If things go pear-shaped with Elton, you'll end up shafted.* At which point Nellie brought in a faxed report from Forensic Digest, a small outfit of ex-Home Office scientists who had set themselves up as independents. I'd been waiting for it for weeks.

I watched Nellie as she backtracked out of my office. I think she had a bit of an issue with the size of her derrière, and often removed herself from a room like a truck reversing from an awkward goods-in depot.

I'd always tried to put her at ease, and was very fond of her. She'd been my secretary for several years and we had developed a healthy mutual respect. I knew that she'd never forgive me if she ever discovered the truth. Nellie had always mollycoddled Elton. She'd regularly protected him from other clients, who liked nothing better than to wind him up in reception.

I'd instructed Forensic Digest on behalf of the defence, to review all aspects of the prosecution forensic evidence. They had only two conclusions of any significance. Firstly, that the DNA revealed that the blood on Elton's football top and anorak was Sarena's, and there was only a one in twenty-five million chance that it wasn't; and secondly, that the blood staining was consistent with smearing rather than from direct trauma. In other words, the blood had not spurted or dripped onto his jacket, but had come as a result of contact with blood already on Sarena's body or clothing. It would be, for example, consistent with Elton having picked up Sarena's body and placed it in a sack. What there wasn't, though, was any direct spray evidence suggesting that Elton was the knifeman.

The same outfit had dealt with the fibre evidence too, and the conclusions didn't help Elton at all. The black velvet dress Sarena was wearing was made of an unusual mix of three velvet fibres. The fibres themselves were not that uncommon, but the mix of the three much more so. The chance of Elton having come into contact with the same three fibres from separate and therefore innocent sources was 'very remote indeed'.

Further, Forensic Digest had examined the police procedure concerning the removal and analysis of both Elton's clothing and Sarena's, and had concluded that there was no suggestion of contamination. And finally, they commented that police had found numerous tyre tracks around the lay-by in the vicinity of the cliffs, but none were thought to be 'significant'. So the forensic evidence was rock-solid and suggested, quite forcefully, that Elton had direct contact with Sarena's bloodstained body and clothing.

I went back through Elton's file and reminded myself that I was still waiting for the acoustics report from JD

Sound and Vision. They were trying to ascertain what Elton might have been humming or mumbling in his tape-recorded interviews with police. As I was dictating a letter to them, one of the firm's paralegals, Gerry, popped his head in, coffee mug in hand.

'Want one?'

'God, you still here, Gerry?'

'Up to my eyeballs, Jim. You working on Spears?'

'Yeah, I am.'

'Tough case.'

'What would *you* know about it?'

I'd snapped it out, and immediately regretted it. Gerry answered a little defensively.

'Just that it's a difficult case, that's all.'

'Yeah... sorry.'

I was especially wary of Gerry, knowing for some time that he had a thing for Loren. He was forever asking her out to lunch, and though I doubted that Loren shared his enthusiasm, he was someone to keep an eye on.

I tried to tell myself not to make a big deal of the conversation, but as soon as anyone else started to poke their nose in, panic seemed to take over. And whenever I panicked I heard the theme tune to *Stingray* in my head. I wondered sometimes why the haunting TV reflections were so vivid. Maybe they were the first programmes I watched when I got back home as a kid...? After Mum had been stabbed.

It didn't take much to throw me off-kilter. Gerry was waiting for me to say something else. He was naturally curious, and unusually chatty. He suddenly piped up with, 'So, did erm... you know... did he *do* it?'

'Did *who* do *what*?' I said, to buy myself time to think. Then I worried. What if he already knew some of the answers?

'What's Loren told you?' I asked, in as polite a tone as I could muster.

Gerry seemed genuinely taken aback. '*Loren*? What's it got

to do with *her*?'

I felt stupid for asking. Gerry must have wondered what on earth Loren had to do with the case. I forced myself to focus on his original question.

'He says he didn't do it, Gerry... but that's not what he told the Old Bill, and the evidence is overwhelming. No, he's going down, I'm sure.'

I rambled on a bit to mask the Loren slip, still a little unsure whether Gerry knew more than he was letting on.

'Oh well, leave no stone unturned and all that,' he quipped.

'Yeah... of course.'

The conversation had really stumped me, and I was momentarily lost in thought. Gerry had prompted my mind to veer off at a tangent. I found myself talking out loud. 'I just wonder if I ought to find out a bit more about the victim?' I posed, rhetorically. Gerry took it as a prompt.

'The victim? Is she relevant? You know, to his guilt or innocence.'

I felt a touch queasy as I added, 'I don't know...'

'What is it you'd want to find out?' asked Gerry.

'Good question... very good question. La-di-dah, eh?'

'What?'

'La-di-bleedin'-dah... You know, I wish I wouldn't do that. Annie Hall, remember that? Woody Allen at his best.'

Gerry gave me a look, one I should have expected.

'Jim, excuse me saying so, but you seem quite... stressed. I hope you don't mind me saying, but you tend to ramble from one thing to another. You've been doing it a lot recently.'

'Have I...?'

I was fighting off horrible images again. Sarena, dead in her bath... Loren in a fit of tears.

'Why don't you go home, Jim, and get some rest...'

I couldn't tell Gerry, but all the time he was talking to me I could see Basil Brush. He was growing and growing, until he became the same size as the one I'd seen in Elton's cell.

These devilish hallucinations were crucifying me. If this was me coping then I perished at what I'd be like if I really started to panic. How would I cope with the trial? I hated to admit it, but I was going to need Loren more than ever. I thought I was learning to handle things, but truth was I was beginning to lose control.

Once Gerry had left, I noticed that Nellie had pinned a 'notice of additional evidence' on the outside of Elton's file. It contained a statement: that of Mr Jaya Gunasekera, Sarena's father. As I started to read it I knew instinctively that something was wrong... that something about Sarena didn't just fail to add up, but had a dangerous edge. As I continued to read the statement I could feel a wretched pain in my finger. I looked down and saw that I'd distractedly been forcing it back the wrong way.

CHAPTER 12

Nellie, my ever loyal and loving secretary, had just made Elton his super-sweet coffee. She gave me a knowing look.

'Elton's come to see you.'

'So I see.'

I shot Elton a warm smile.

'Hiya, Elton. How's it going?'

'They won't let me have a telly,' he moaned, without further reference.

'Who won't? What do you mean?'

I waited for him to explain, but he just took a huge gulp of coffee and then recoiled a touch as it was hot. Nellie filled in the blanks.

'His dad's chucked him out again. He's in a hostel. They reckon he smashed the television in the lounge. Here's his charge sheet – criminal damage.'

'Oh.'

I looked at the charge sheet, and then at Elton.

'Been nicked again, have you?'

'Yeah. Won't let me have a telly.'

Elton looked deeply pissed off as he slurped some more coffee. I just wanted to make sure I understood the situation correctly.

'So you thought nobody else ought to have one either?'

Elton didn't react.

'You broke the communal television in the lounge, did you?'

'Smashed it. Weakest Link. It's shit.'

I couldn't help but smile.

'Been nicked,' he then repeated, quite superfluously.

'I know... come on, let's go up to my office and sort it all out.'

What can I say about Elton Spears? To put it colloquially, something like a giant, cumbersome, gullible, unstable, delinquent loon... and probably my favourite ever client. I think 'a client with challenging issues' might be more the accepted modern parlance, but that wouldn't cover the half of it.

Elton always reminds me of the guy in 'The Crying Game', the black soldier whose 'girlfriend' has hidden talents. Forest Whitaker, that's who played him. Physically he reminds me of him, anyway. As for mentally... well, that's another story.

Elton's mother died when he was six. His dad brought him up, alone and incapable. Elton's dad was a man of very few words. On occasion he'd come to court when Elton was in trouble. In fact, on one particular occasion they were both on the same morning list at Marylebone – Elton for theft of a toy Dalek from WHSmith, and his dad for obstructing the police officer who came to arrest him. I can still remember Mr Spears Senior standing, in fact swaying, outside Marylebone Magistrates' Court with a can of Carlsberg Crucial Brew in his hand. He refused to enter the court until he'd finished it.

It must have been the same day that I asked him about how he'd come to choose Elton's name. A deep scar was embedded in his left cheek and a few rogue grey hairs sprouted from his nostrils as he said in a deep gravelly voice, 'I love Elton John.' I was stumped for a reply.

His latest criminal damage escapade was a pretty minor affair. Fact was, he was upset that someone at the hostel had switched over to the Weakest Link when he was happily watching Scooby Doo on one of the kids' channels, and I can't say I blame him. Anyway, in response he threw a vase of daffodils at Anne Robinson, causing her to explode into slivers. I eventually managed to get him a conditional discharge at Brent Magistrates' Court.

I have spent many years representing Elton, for an array of crimes and misdemeanours. The very first time I represented Elton, indeed my first ever encounter with him, was a bizarre shoplifting case, some years ago now, and also at Brent Mags. It was a cold December day and if I had to be pressed on the year I'd say it was either 1999 or 2000. I was on the duty solicitor shift and it seemed like just another routine call.

When I got to Wembley nick I was told that someone called Elton Spears had walked out of Woolworths with a pack of twenty-four giant-size Christmas crackers. He'd made no attempt to hide them apparently, not that you could. He'd allegedly just walked out with them, and unsurprisingly was swiftly approached by two security guards.

Unfortunately, Elton made a desperate attempt at escape, and managed to force his way out onto Wembley High Road, with one of the security guards still clinging onto him. Elton thrust him off, causing the security guard to collide with a Big Issue salesman, a guy who was later to be described in court as 'looking like a Gladiator who had gone to seed'. The security guard ended up with a broken arm, but fortunately the Big Issue salesman escaped unharmed.

Advising someone like Elton was almost impossible. This was my first meeting with him, before he became a regular – indeed a prolific – client. I can still recall entering the cells and speaking to him for the very first time...

'Hello, Elton? My name's Jim Harwood. I'm duty solicitor this evening.'

'Mirror. I'm in the mirror...'

I was instantly thrown, not having a clue as to what he meant. I tried to put him at ease, knowing that the particular custody officer on duty often allowed prisoners to have a sneaky smoke by the back gate.

'Shall I ask if we can have a cigarette?'

'Don't smoke.'

'Oh, okay. Well, I've spoken to the officer in the case, and he says you've been very quiet since being here. I just want to know how you are, if you're fit to be interviewed. Are you?'

Elton looked blank before repeating my last words, 'Are you?'

The sense that he wasn't quite all there was taking hold.

'Elton, do you know where you are?'

'Know where you are,' he repeated. I paused, thinking how do I play this one?

I tried again.

'We're at Wembley police station. You've been arrested for theft and assault. GBH, actually.'

'No, never.'

'All right, what happened then?'

'When?'

'This afternoon, in Woolworths.'

'Never been to Woolworths. Got a ciggy?'

I paused again – paused and puzzled – while passing Elton a cigarette, which he immediately put down his pants without so much as a word of explanation. What planet was this giant on? I pondered.

Elton stood up, revealing the fact that he'd been sitting on an old trilby 'pork-pie' hat. It was then that I noticed that Elton was fiddling with a miniature plastic mirror. It was a replica of a vanity mirror, and I immediately realised it must have come from one of the Christmas crackers. No doubt he'd pulled one himself and hid the contents somewhere the custody officer hadn't fancied searching.

Elton kept glancing into the mirror and smiling. I tried to refocus his attention.

'Listen, Elton. The police say you were arrested for leaving Woolworths with a box of Christmas crackers you didn't pay for...'

No response from Elton to that one.

'And that when you were stopped by security you lashed out at one of the guards...'

Still no response from Elton. I walked a few paces around the cell. Then Elton piped up.

'Christmas soon.'

'Yeah... So…?'

I wasn't quite sure of the relevance. Then he added, 'Jesus died.'

Elton then tried to punch his pork-pie hat back into shape. He kept doing so until eventually it was inside-out. He then briefly put it on, with the lining on the outside.

'Elton, do you understand why you're here?'

Elton took the hat off again, and deliberately sat on it. After a moment or two's silence he suddenly blurted out, 'I don't eat cheese.'

'I'm not interested in whether you eat cheese, Elton.'

I was already shaking my head in dismay... then it dawned on me.

'Oh… they're Christmas crackers, mate, not ones you eat.'

I had thought perhaps that we might finally be having a sensible dialogue, or at least a partially sensible one. Then Elton repeated again,

'Jesus died.'

'Yeah, okay. Just tell me this, Elton. Did you steal a box of crackers from Woolworths store?'

'I never.'

It was clearly a ludicrous denial, not least because Elton was still fiddling with the contents of one of the crackers when the officer fetched him from his cell for his interview. In any event, Elton insisted that he hadn't even been in Woolworths... even when he was shown a photo of himself from the CCTV, to which his response was, 'Jesus doesn't wear a hat.'

He seemed to have a vague understanding of all the concepts: arrest, interview, charge, etc. He was certainly weird, but not easily diagnosable.

I recall speaking to the officer in the case. He hadn't come across Elton before either, and seemed to think that Elton was fit for interview. He really couldn't have guessed what was to come. I can't now recall the interviewing officer's name. He was a young detective constable and I suspect that had it not been for the GBH allegation, uniform would have dealt with it themselves. The officer was all right. He seemed genuinely polite and upfront, not one of those coppers who thought that he was something special, or that all lawyers should be choked at birth.

I recall the hailstones attacking the windowpane in the interview room. Double-decker buses were passing through the storm outside, struggling on the High Road on their way to Harrow. An officer ushered Elton's large awkward frame into a chair, and I sat next to him. Following the formalities, the officer asked his opening question.

'Elton, you've given your date of birth as the ninth of September, but you seemed a bit unsure of the year.'

Elton replied quite resolutely, '1981. The year of our Lord.'

The officer continued, 'Okay… Right… So, earlier this afternoon, my colleagues were called to an incident at Woolworths in Wembley High Road. There, they were told by a member of Woolworths's security that you had been apprehended for leaving the store without paying for certain goods.'

Elton said nothing. I thought an interjection appropriate. Words like 'incident' and 'apprehended' seemed alien to him. I guessed he hadn't a clue what they meant. I spoke for the only time in that interview.

'Perhaps we should keep the language pretty basic?'

The officer briefly nodded at me in agreement.

'Fair enough,' he said, before turning to Elton again.

'Elton, did you steal a box of crackers from Woolworths?'

'Christmas soon. Jesus died.'

The officer looked to his colleague, who was equally devoid of a response and already looking to the heavens. Elton broke the silence by going into a mad ramble.

'Don't eat cheese. Eat sardines in oil. Sardines in oil. Sardines in oil...'

This got louder and louder, until Elton was shouting like a town crier. Soon he was standing, doing Nazi salutes. Rhythmically shouting.

'Sardines in oil. Sardines in oil.'

Then he stopped, quite suddenly, and sat down. Both officers looked at me, as if I ought to provide an explanation. I just sat there looking blank, before retorting somewhat sheepishly, 'I've never actually met Mr Spears before.'

Elton was seen by the police doctor and later charged with theft and assault. He was remanded into custody for his own good. By the time the case came up for trial, the quacks were agreed that Elton was fit to plead and stand trial. He did, was duly convicted, and placed on probation with a condition of attendance at a psychiatric hospital in Barnet. From then he drifted in and out of hospital and prison. He spent occasional periods in St Vincent's in Epsom, but was never there long enough for anyone to be sure what to do with him. Indeed, nobody seemed able, or bothered, to properly diagnose his condition at all.

Over the years I developed quite a soft spot for Elton. He's spent as much time in my office as he has anywhere else. He'd come in regularly for his coffee with six sugars and always knew that either Nellie or I would look after him. In any event, his Wembley arrest all those years ago was how I first came into contact with the madness of Elton.

CHAPTER 13

The day after I'd read the 'additional evidence' statement of Mr Jaya Gunasakera, I visited Elton.

I was a little late arriving at the Scrubs, and he'd already been brought out into the waiting area. As he was escorted into the little conference room I was feeling nervous, which often put me in a flippant mood.

I couldn't help thinking: *Today, Elton is wearing a British Heart Foundation dungarees in chocolate brown, with accessories from the Red Cross, jacket from Marie Curie, and shoes from SANE.*

I smiled at Elton as I said 'Good Morning.' To which his response was 'Yeah.'

In fact that was often Elton's response to such superfluous drivel as 'hello' or 'good morning'. I could feel my mind starting to slip, and fought to stay balanced.

'How are they treating you? Forget that, Elton. Stupid question. I know, how about this one...'

I paused, trying to fight it, but it was no use. Ken had taken control of my jaw.

'Why did you kill Sarena?... Mmm? She was too beautiful to die.'

Elton sat there for a second and looked into my eyes, with a focus, a thing he rarely did. He then put his left index finger into his nostril, and his thumb tried to join it. He pulled out a crusty bogey with a squidgy trail of green snot, and put it in his mouth. He started to chew.

I could feel a burning sensation in my eyes as I whispered, 'Why did you murder the gorgeous Sarena?'

My body started to convulse. A tear rolled down my cheek, lodging itself in the corner of my mouth. I could taste the bittersweet guilt.

For a brief moment Elton tilted his head to one side and looked at me with a puppy-dog devotion: with eyes of loving obedience. If I'd had a gun I'd have given it to my dear client Elton, and told him to shoot me dead. I couldn't believe I was actually doing this. I had to bite my lip hard, and concentrate.

The statement of Mr Jaya Gunasekera had caused me to panic, and set my mind reeling in examination. Apparently he had flown over from Colombo to identify the body, and provided the police with all their background information. He had confirmed that Sarena was staying in London to train to be a barrister. In fact, the statement specified all the things that Sarena had told me – things I suspected were untrue.

At first I thought, 'Well, perhaps that's what Sarena told her father too?' After all, even if he did know better himself, he's not going to tell the British police that his little girl was not all she appeared to be. I tried to justify the veracity of the statement, but something kept nagging away.

The same old questions started running around in my head. Just who did benefit from Sarena's death? Who collected her possessions? Where was the ten-grand music system, or that ridiculously expensive Persian rug? *Where, perhaps, is her real identity?*

I looked over at Elton. He was slowly rocking from side to side, and was humming something. I started to think aloud as I picked up the statement.

'See, Elton. This guy here. Jaya Gunasekera. What if he's not really Sarena's father? What if he *knew* who really did it, eh, Elton? Shit... I'd know, wouldn't I? Someone would have come forward by now, wouldn't they, Elton?'

Elton was staring at me with that same curious tilt to his head. I carried on thinking aloud, though to anyone in the corridor outside it would have just looked like I was talking normally to Elton.

'Perhaps he panics. He panics because Sarena is either a precious asset or a big risk. I'm not sure about that one... Right, so, pretend Dad reports his pretend daughter missing. He knows all the details, because they're details that were well rehearsed. So he phones in, pretending to be from Colombo. *'My daughter should have called me Saturday, but she didn't. Didn't call me Sunday either. It's Monday now and I'm worried, very worried about her safety...' 'Hold on a minute, sir... sir, I'm afraid I've got some rather bad information to pass on to you...'* Gurgle, gurgle, tears, tears... *'Oh, I'll fly to England straightaway.'* So, someone somewhere gets one of his Sri Lankan mates from Ealing to play the part. Sorted. Victim identified and not a single cause to doubt it. Accomplice then pays his man handsomely, collects all Sarena's worldly goods, keeps her real identity a secret and scarpers. You follow that, Elton?'

'Yeah.'

I don't know why Elton said '*yeah*'. I was barely following my own paranoid ramblings.

'We're losing control here, Elton...'

I petered out. I knew something was deeply disturbing, but I couldn't work out what it was. Then I saw another statement that Nellie had pinned to the file, from the Crown's forensic scientist. It stated that the sack Sarena was found in, at the bottom of Beachy Head cliffs, had a footprint on it... a size 8.

'Hell, you're size 10, mate, aren't you? We know that from your last case.'

Elton didn't respond.

'And we all know who's a size 8, don't we?'

Elton didn't answer that either.

'Right... Harry's not having that statement,' I said, as a quieter aside.

I lurched from one breath to another for a few moments,

as a tear fell and stained my notebook. By then Elton was staring at the wall, as if he hadn't a care in the world. After a good minute of catching my breath, I regained composure.

'Right... your barrister, Mr Douglas, wants me to prepare a timetable. You know, like bus timetables. Wants to know where you were every hour between Saturday midday and the following Monday morning at half seven, when you were nicked in Eastbourne.'

'There was music... da da da da di-da-da...'

'Music?'

Elton repeated the hummed song. I thought I half recognised it. He made the sort of noise people make when they are humming the riffs to their favourite guitar songs, and repeated it again. Hell's bells, I thought. I knew where he'd heard that... in the Swedish thing. The big teddy bear was conscious. He was bloody conscious. What part of his peculiar brain had that come from?

'What music, Elton?'

'Da didda di da di di da.'

'Right. That's on *Led Zep Four*.'

I flashed back to Elton's old man, Mr Spears Senior... standing there in a second-hand brown pinstripe, swaying in the breeze, Crucial Brew in hand, face as black as coal, grey hairs sticking out of his nostrils. A Mississippi blues man, if ever I saw one. I pictured the stale and rancid flat where Mr Spears Senior lived. I'd been there once to collect Elton for a court appearance.

It had a stack of broken furniture, empty cans of lager, one used as an ashtray, a one-bar electric fire, an old Philips stereo wired to one speaker, and in the corner leaning against the wall there they lay: Blind Lemon Jefferson, Robert Johnson, Leadbelly, History of the Blues, two scratched copies of *The Best of Elton John*, and *Led Zep bleedin' Four*! Maybe that was where he'd heard it, I hoped against hope. I knew, however, that there was an equally viable and horribly alternative explanation: that Elton had heard it in the old Swedish thing on the way down to Beachy Head... that he wasn't quite as comatose as I thought.

I pictured my face in horror, as if I was watching myself from the corridor outside. I could see my own worry brow lines bouncing up and down like my graphic equaliser at home. Elton had played a blinder. A forty-yard defence-splitting pass, stunning control by the centre forward, and a rasping volley into the roof of the net. A real graphic equaliser, if ever I saw one. I let out a nervous smile at Elton as I went into another mad ramble. As ever he returned the favour, with a huge cheesy grin.

I made my excuses and left Elton pretty sharpish, hurrying back out along Du Cane Road. I dialled JD Sound and Vision. Was their report ready yet? Sod two weeks, I told them, they could scan through a preliminary report tomorrow morning, otherwise I'd use someone else.

I couldn't sleep that night. I kept thinking that if he could remember the music in the car, then perhaps he could remember other parts of the journey as well. Perhaps the drugs had worn off before I dumped him in that beach hut?

CHAPTER 14

After Elton had turned up at the office to discuss his exploding TV episode, he left with a giant-size Snickers bar, provided by yours truly. I had got to know Elton well by then, and knew that he always got terribly excited by anything giant-sized, whether confectionery or Christmas crackers!

That particular day I was supposed to see a few more clients in the afternoon, but Nellie had a surprise for me, and not a particularly pleasant one either. She handed me a note and smiled. It was the same smile she always had when she knew I'd have to attend a police station, knowing as she did that it was something I was often keen to avoid.

Nellie never gave me time to read these notes. As soon as she handed them to me, she'd reveal the contents herself.

'One of your clients is at West End Central. He's been arrested for living off immoral earnings.'

'Aren't we all?'

'Speak for yourself.'

As Nellie trotted off towards reception, I read the note in full. Phil Reeves had been nicked. I couldn't think of anyone I'd less like to meet again, but there was no getting out of it. I had to go. I managed to persuade one of the firm's paralegals to see my pre-booked office clients. I decided to leave the Swedish thing where it was, and headed off with my briefcase towards Camden Town Tube.

On the walk to the station I kept thinking about all those mod cons that had disappeared from Sarena's flat. Perhaps she'd had them shipped over to Australia, with no expense spared? Whatever, I guessed she was probably sunning herself on Perth's Scarborough Beach. I really didn't want to go and advise some scumbag accused of living off immoral earnings; I wanted to make enquiries about the gorgeous Sarena.

Heading down the escalator, my mind started to veer. Why was it so difficult to shake her off? It was as if she'd smeared me with her sap, and I was a buzzing thing fatally attracted to her scent. The train doors closed. I started to perspire heavily. I heard a familiar voice in my ear. An unwelcome intruder... Ken.

-Gone all lovey-dovey, have you?

-I knew it. Just piss off and leave me alone.

-No, I won't... Jim?

-What?

-I'm going to shout a word in your ear... here it comes... Love... Love is for others. Sorry, Jimbo, but that's the way it is.

-Please go away. I'll stop thinking about Sarena. I won't think about her, I promise.

-'Course you will.

-Oh, leave me alone... Look, I'll read the adverts or something. Let's play that game... you know the one... The Tube map. Look, there's one. Let's play... Where's Cockfosters?...Where's Osterley?...Where's Theydon Bois?...

-Where's Sarena?

Sometimes Ken's intrusions are unbearable. He can rip me apart. The only other occupant in the carriage was an old woman. She looked at me with narrowed eyes. Ken doesn't have a compassionate side. He just carried on in the same vein.

-Not playing, then, Jimmy-Wimmy? So where is Sarena, then? Australia, or Theydon Bois?

-'Fuck off and leave me alone!'

I was horrified that I had actually said the last line out loud. The Tourettes hadn't surfaced since my teens, and shook me as much as it did the old lady on the opposite seat. It seemed to prompt her to get off at Goodge Street. I'm sure she didn't want to. I called out after her.

'Sorry.'

But it was too late.

Therapy as a teenager had given me the ability to control my angst, but at that moment it felt like I'd discovered a boil that I thought had long since been lanced. The only silver lining was that Ken had gone.

The Tube rumbled through the tunnel towards Tottenham Court Road. I tried to find a reality in my mind. Trusting was the problem. My father had seen to that.

Living with Aunt Marj wasn't as dreadful as it might have been, but it was mighty odd, and a constant reminder of the parents I'd lost. Trying to rationalise it as a kid wasn't easy. I wondered if I'd done something terribly wrong. Maybe I'd deserved such tragedy.

I was seven when it happened. Sitting on that Tube train brought something back. It was one of very few memories that managed to squeeze past the barriers Ken had so meticulously put in place. I remembered writing something down once. I think it was about four years later, when I was in my first year at Watford Grammar. I wrote out a mock letter during detention. It was to the editor of the Times:

Sir,

We get your newspaper in our school library. I know that some people write letters to you. Do they all start with 'Sir'? I wasn't sure, but thought I'd start that way too.

Well, I am writing to tell you that my best friend at junior school was a podgy girl called Christine Horrocks. My teacher used to say it was all right to say podgy instead of fat. Anyway, she never used to get picked for country dancing, and other kids called her smelly. She wasn't really. She was my friend. When we were six I showed her my willy. She told me she didn't have one. She wasn't lying. I know that now.

I used to talk to Christine about things. We used to go to the shed on the allotment. When we were seven we kissed once, but neither of us really liked it. Do you know Uxbridge? It was there that it happened.

I talked to Christine about what happened to my mum. I haven't talked to anyone else since then, except the cycologist man. I was seven and a half years old when my dad killed my mum. I wasn't supposed to find that out, but Christine heard her mum talking about it, and told me. It's something like my mum found things out about my dad and he didn't want Mum to tell on him. Like a grass. That's what some kids say in my class.

I am in detention now in the library. I was told off for talking in maths. I'm good at maths really. My teacher says that if I paid attention and didn't get distracted I'd be top of the class. I don't want to be top. If I'm top then everyone will see me.

I'm not sure what happened to Christine. She went to live somewhere else when she left junior school. I live with my aunt now. She's a Dutch aunt but she is not from Holland. I've got to go now, Mr Mead's coming.

Yours sincerely,
Jimmy Harwood. 1b.

Of course I never sent it, but I did keep it in the little drawer under my bed. It seems mighty odd now, but I had a real problem with maths and murder. My young mind kept linking the two.

When I look back now I realise what it was I hated about maths: its convergence, its destiny. It was taught as certainty, but still failed to explain the awful reality of what had happened. Yet somewhere inside I used to think mathematics was a fabulous thing, even though I pretended to be crap at it.

I felt uneasy discussing 'solutions.' After the tragedy – and that's the word everyone used – I was told that 'sorry, but there are no easy answers, Jimmy'. As a seven-and-a-half-year-old, this totally threw me. Some answers were easy. Six eights were forty-eight, I knew that. I felt annoyed that maths couldn't provide the solution to why Dad had killed Mum.

So I developed this sense as a kid that I shouldn't reach a destiny. I found solace in parallel lines. Every time I had to go to art class I would start off my sketch by drawing them. I knew it was a mock convergence. They looked beautiful. They looked like they were converging, but you could safely walk along them knowing that they never would. I found safety in that: the comfort that I'd never reach the end of the line… and that there'd be no-one there to meet me.

Over time I began to understand who I was afraid of meeting. My father was never caught. If he's alive now, he'll be seventy-one. I think he must have changed his name many times to survive. I never used to allow myself to think about him.

That day, on that short, dark, bumpy ride down to Tottenham Court Road, it all started to come flooding back. That day I felt resigned to the fact that I struggled to love and be loved. It was all right having those senses stimulated by Sarena. There was nothing wrong with my chemistry and instincts, but I couldn't fit all my feelings properly into place.

When the old lady got off at Goodge Street, a busker took her place, standing in the door-well of the carriage. His guitar was covered with bright yellow stickers. He started to sing a song that Aunt Marj used to have on vinyl, but I wasn't sure who had sung it: 'I can love, I can really love, I can really love… In a trance, whilst the lonely mingle with circumstance…'

My Tourettes started a few months after the tragedy, and lasted into my teens. With help I managed to overcome the more extreme elements and fortunately it began to fade away. I was left with what the child psychologist called 'mild episodes', a number of which still, on very rare occasions, manifest themselves in public. Fortunately the affliction doesn't always result in sudden and unprompted profanity. Sometimes I just say silly things out loud, or deliver excruciating faux-pas, or laugh inappropriately. Whatever it is, it's beyond my own field of understanding.

Yet despite those manifestations, I had still managed to achieve so much 'normality' – at least on the surface, anyway. I'd passed exams, flown through interviews, and to the outside world was just another professional going about his business. I'd managed to hold a job down since my first post as an articled clerk.

As long as I had my havens, I was okay. Somewhere to go, and be alone when required, and lose myself. Somewhere to recharge, and rehearse the self I was struggling to project. Sometimes my haven was the courtroom, but unbeknown to others it was also the bookies. As a result, and despite a very reasonable income, I was heavily in debt. I bet to create a thrill, to create a focus – win or invariably lose.

I eventually got off at Tottenham Court Road. With jealous visions of Sarena gallivanting with another man at Stamford Bridge, I entered West End Central to set about my business.

When I got to the police station I found that I had two clients to represent, not just the insipid Phil Reeves, but his girlfriend Debbie Ward. I'd been asked by the senior partner Graeme Gower to look for opportunities to give Loren more experience of serious criminal cases, and in particular experience of police station attendance and advice. This seemed like the ideal case. It would take thirty minutes or so for her to get down from Camden, if the Tube was running properly.

As it happened, the case petered out. Without going into too much detail, there emerged what is known as a 'conflict of interest' in their instructions. In other words, Reeves blamed Ward, and vice-versa. It was a mess, and even though I could have carried on and represented Reeves alone I decided to withdraw altogether. The truth was that Phil Reeves was a pain in the backside, and made my skin crawl. What I didn't know at the time was that the case would turn into one of London's major murder trials.

Reeves was eventually charged with the murder of three prostitutes, and Debbie Ward would end up as the Crown's key witness. When the case hit the news, I read how Reeves had allegedly dumped the bodies in bin-liners in the river Thames.

As the opportunity to help Loren with her police station procedure had gone, I offered to buy her lunch instead. She wasn't sure if she should at first, so we compromised on coffee.

I took Loren to a little alleyway off Savile Row, where Romello produces the best cappuccino in town. I told her all about Phil Reeves, and that he was a nasty piece of work who ran a few seedy brothels. I also explained about the conflict of interest. Loren wondered why anyone would want to be his girlfriend, to which I commented that I doubted Debbie Ward was a 'girlfriend' in the traditional sense.

'He probably pumps what he pimps,' I told her. Loren let out an 'urgh', before adding, 'Actually, that sounded quite poetic.'

It was at that moment that I sensed a morsel of attraction from Loren. Something undetectable to the naked eye, but something nonetheless. I could also tell from her look that she knew I was thinking along the same lines. It was the catalyst, that's for sure – the very moment when you suddenly realise there might be more to a liaison than meets the eye. When we finished our coffee there was an awkward pause, as if one of us ought to prolong the encounter.

'Come on, Loren, Why don't me and you go for lunch? I know a nice little place up the road.'

Loren was tempted, but still a touch wary.

'Have we got time?'

'I'll vouch for you, if that's what you're worried about.'

Loren smiled in return.

'Let me just check with Nellie, to see if one of the paras can still do my office appointments, then we can go. If you want to have lunch, that is?'

Loren released another half smile.

'Is that what you call them?'

'What?'

'Paras... paralegals.'

'Yeah, why?'

'Makes them sound like the SAS.'

'Can you imagine Boney M in the SAS?'

Loren couldn't help but dribble the last drop of cappuccino down her chin. She had a raucous laugh, one you simply wouldn't have expected from someone so seemingly demure.

Boney M was the nickname of Mark Benham, one of the firm's three paralegals, whose role it was to help solicitors prepare their cases for trial. Mark was a stick-insect of a man with an unfortunate whiny voice. Just to complete the stereotype, he also wore very old-fashioned half-moon glasses. Loren was still laughing at the prospect of him scaling walls and ambushing the Taliban.

Despite the frivolity, it still hadn't escaped me that Loren had yet to answer my question.

'So... Lunch? What do you think...?'

'Okay, then, why not. Thanks.'

Loren and I walked through the doors of the Oasis Bar and Restaurant at precisely one o'clock. The entrance was on street level, off Glasshouse Street. You had to go down some stairs, where you'd be greeted by reception and asked if you wanted the bar, the restaurant, or both.

Once we'd been at our table for a quarter of an hour or so, and had ordered lunch, I made a 'nature calls' excuse. We had passed the ticket outlet on the way to the restaurant, and my curiosity was getting the better of me.

I quickly popped up to street level and walked a few paces along the narrow Piccadilly street. The ticket kiosk was about the size of a kitchenette. The scruffy little guy in a baseball cap stared at me as I fired questions at him. It didn't take long. The Chelsea seat, and the one next to it, were bought two months ago. The scruffy man was getting quite shirty. Perhaps he suspected me of being a journalist looking into ticket touting or something? Anyway, the seats were paid for in cash and that was all he was prepared to say. I showed him a photo of Sarena. He shook his head, more in a gesture of 'piss off' than 'I've never seen her'.

I'd only been gone from the table for a few minutes. I wanted to show the photo of Sarena to the staff at the Oasis too, but couldn't find an opportunity to do so without Loren being there. At the time I thought it best to keep Sarena's disappearance to myself, and didn't want Loren cross-examining me with all sorts of questions.

We both had salmon with a dill sauce, and shared a bottle of house white. Then an Irish coffee and a liqueur or two, and before we knew it, it was mid-afternoon and we were half cut. The last thing I remember talking about was our top five films of all time. Loren's number one was 'Ghostbusters', mine was 'Fargo'. We'd got on great.

Loren's flat was a few minutes' walk from Camden Road station, up towards Holloway, and just past the dirty-looking bridge. I'd agreed to have a coffee before returning to the office. After all, we could hardly turn up drunk at four in the afternoon. Johnson would have kittens. Looking back now, we must have been out of our heads.

Her flat was surprisingly scruffy. It was clean but disorganised, and I remember thinking that I should learn from the experience. It's easy to misjudge people sometimes, and it's dangerous to think you're any good at it. I'd have taken odds that Loren would be the fastidious type. I'd pictured bits of old twigs sticking out of large brown pots, and cream canvas blinds, and a terracotta floor, and a little mat to put your shoes on when you entered.

Instead of that, there were all sorts randomly spread around. I did notice a Beatrix Potter theme, though. There was a collection of hardbacks, which looked like a full set, and various little stuffed animals on shelves – Flopsy bunnies and Tiggywinkles and the like.

There were bits of the Sunday Times scattered liberally across the floor. There was a cat litter tray in the corner by the kitchen, but no cat. As I was sadly informed, 'Randolph' had been flattened by a John Lewis delivery driver only three weeks earlier. Loren said she couldn't face getting rid of the litter tray, so I offered to do it for her. She also swore on oath that she'd never shop at John Lewis again, even if it wasn't the driver's fault.

The lounge had a large crescent bay window that looked out onto a little green. There were three swings and a roundabout in view. It must have had double-glazing, because you couldn't hear the children playing.

Loren was wearing a black cotton skirt and a sort of cardigan thing. Green, deep green it was, with lighter green buttons. She had no tights on. I guessed that underneath the cardigan there was only a bra, and my alcohol-soaked mind thought it might be fun to find out. She returned with two large red mugs and put them on the table in front of her.

Loren smiled and pulled her cardigan across her chest in a very old-fashioned sort of way.

'I'm not just saying this, Jim, but I really admire you.'

'Me? Why?'

'I don't know... your work. You seem to really give it everything. You really care about your clients.'

'I try to, yeah.'

'I haven't done that much crime, done a bit. I just... I sometimes wonder how you do some of those really nasty cases. You know, the murders, the rapes. I mean, if you really think somebody has murdered somebody, and they're fighting it, doesn't it make you, you know...'

'Feel guilty?'

'Well, yes. I mean, what if it was some guy accused of molesting a child, and murdering him. And you knew he did it. Would you represent him?'

'Come on, Loren. What do you mean, you knew he did it? Has he

told you?'

'Okay, yes.'

'Then he's given you instructions that he's guilty and has to plead guilty, or you can't represent him.'

'What if you know yourself but he doesn't say anything?'

'What I know, or think I know, isn't an issue.'

'Not even a moral one?'

'Moral? What's that got to do with it? We're lawyers, for heaven's sake.'

We were both slurring our words and enjoying the provocation. Pissed arguments, you can't beat them. I was pretty blotto and could have said anything, but it was Loren who spoke next:

'Anyway, why did you become a lawyer?'

A moment's silence followed, as I reflected on the fact that Loren's question was one that had already been circling around in my mind, and for some time too. I think I knew the answer, but it would open up too many old wounds to explain it to Loren there and then.

I sensed Loren shuffling nervously on the sofa. I slowly moved towards her and cupped my hands around her face. I kissed her and made an exaggerated kissy noise. The sort of noise Penelope Pitstop would have made. I think I did so in order that I could make light of things if Loren took my move the wrong way, but she was smiling and clearly enjoying the moment, and so was I. Just for an interlude, life was simple.

I put my arm around her. Within seconds we were locked in a semi-drunken snog, all tongues and lips and slush. Before long I was undoing those green buttons, kissing her neck and shoulders, and holding tight on the rollercoaster… and then I realised I had to pee.

As I made my awkward excuses with Loren, I started to question what I was doing. My little mind was in turmoil... This is Loren, your work colleague. You're pissed, she's pissed. How on earth is she going to feel tomorrow, or even later today? Won't she respect you that much more if you make your excuses? After all, you can get back to starting position any time you choose, if that's what you both want...

I sprayed Loren's Armitage Shanks logo with a determined jet. Sod it, I thought. I strolled out of the bathroom with a false air of bravado. Let's have a little fun and frolic.

I focused in on the sofa. I wanted to see Loren laying there, seductively opening up a green button or two and metaphorically licking her lips in anticipation. She wasn't. She was looking in the hall mirror, adjusting herself and straightening her skirt. Her cardigan was done up, her breasts were back in hibernation, and her shoes were on. She'd just finished with the lip liner and was looking at herself and licking her lips, but not at me. She popped an extra-strong mint in, and spoke as if she had a mouthful of cotton wool.

'We better get back. It's all right for you, I'll get in trouble if Johnson finds out. What do I say if he asks me where I've been?'

Loren had thrown me off-scent.

'Erm... yeah, I was just thinking that myself. Nellie will cover for us, say we were at the nick... It's Gerry you're worried about, isn't it?'

'No. Why did you mention Gerry?'

I thought Loren had been having a fling with one of our other paralegals, Gerry Robinson. She was surprised that I had suddenly thrown up the name. In any event, it put her off-balance for a beat, but only for a beat. Pissed or not, Loren was regaining control.

'Don't worry about Gerry, if that's what you're thinking. I know what I'm doing.'

Loren knew I wanted to make love, and the very fact that I'd shown I wanted to was good enough for our Ms Granger. This girl was cute. If I learned nothing else that day, I learned that.

Chapter 15

The following morning I double-checked the report from JD Sound and Vision. Elton was mumbling the same tune on the tape. He must have heard it in the car on the way down to Beachy Head, when I had him comatose, stretched almost horizontally over the passenger seat. Sarena was in the boot... wonder if she heard it, too? Don't be silly, she was dead. Perhaps she'll really come back and haunt me, I thought? My mind was on fast spin... but Elton was tranquillised to the hilt. Anyway, how on earth?... Ken was chipping in.

-Jim? Stop panicking. This is ridiculous. So what if anyone notices? How could it be linked to you?

It was there, in black and white. Elton's interview with DCI Litton, the bits where he rambles on and on. The bits Harry Douglas was referring to. He was even repeating the lyrics. Elton always repeats things. I'd never noticed this particular example before, because I didn't attend that second interview at Holborn nick, just the first – the one when he admitted everything.

Elton had got a couple of the words the wrong way round, but... Hang on, I panicked, Harry's been in my car. He knows every CD in that contraption – at least the two that always get stuck. Oh, yes. He knows the *Doors Greatest*

Hits backwards, and he knows *Led Zep Four* as well.

Okay, I was telling myself. Okay, don't panic. What I'll do is retype the acoustics report and send it to Harry, suitably amended. I was reminded again that there was good reason to have two lawyers. Harry only gets what I send him. He didn't need to know about Elton's ramblings either.

So, JD Sound and Vision had concluded that it wasn't possible to make out what Elton was humming and mumbling. That was all Harry needed to know. That would be the end of that little line of enquiry. Or would it? Ken wanted an argument.

-Jim?

-What?

-Stop being completely fucking paranoid.

-I'm not...

-I mean, Harry Douglas isn't going to put two and two together and come up with *Led Zep Four*, is he?

-No? ...No... 'Course he's not.

-Eh? What's the problem, Jimbo? You think old Harry's going to say, 'Jim, I've listened again to the tape and I've re-read Elton's interview with the police. It's quite clear that he is reciting the tune of a song called Black Dog, which is on Led Zeppelin's fourth album. Now, you know as well as I do that he must have heard that song while lying semi-comatose on the passenger seat in your car, while you were in the process of framing him for murder.'

-Shut up, Ken.

-No, you shut up. It's ridiculous. Stop being paranoid, man.

I sat there and shook, hoping that I hadn't been talking out loud. I couldn't tell if I was just thinking something or actually saying it. I was rescued by the telephone. I knew it was an internal call because of its longer tone. It was Loren.

'Can I see you after work tonight? Over the road?'

'Yeah, yeah sure. Half five, I'll knock off early. Love you, Loren.'

I wasn't too sure why I'd said it. Insecurity, probably. I

put the phone down and it rang immediately. It was an external call this time.

'Jim. Know who this is?'

'Yeah... yes, I do.'

I recognised the voice immediately, but had to wait a couple of beats for my mind to come up with a name. Then it clicked.

'Sammy. Sammy Todd. Or should I call you Dennis Banks? You're out, then?'

'Yeah, listen. I want a chat.'

'There aren't any problems, are there?'

'I want a word, that's all.'

'Sammy, I'm really up to my eyeballs at the moment. Got a heavy case on.'

'I'll be in touch.'

The call was a little unnerving. Sammy was a professional gangster with a hold over me... and I'd long since regretted becoming involved.

CHAPTER 16

A fortnight or so before I first met Sarena, I was called out to a police station by a guy calling himself Dennis Banks.

His real name was Sammy Todd – Samuel Arthur Todd, to be precise. A fifty-something businessman, and long-time acquaintance of mine. He'd been detained at Harrow Road nick on suspicion of fraud.

Sammy was an antiques dealer, or so he claimed. True, he owned a shop in Portobello, and one near Camden Market too, but bric-a-brac would have been a more accurate description of what was on view. He had a couple of convictions for cultivating marijuana, and for being involved in a mortgage fraud. He is what I call a 'tip of the iceberg' client. It's fairly obvious that a sizeable chunk of criminality lies beneath the surface, and seldom gets exposed.

I'd first represented him some years back, when he went down on the mortgage fraud. However, I'd secured him an excellent barrister who really hit home with his mitigation. Sammy ended up with a twelve-month suspended sentence. It was then that we became friends – or acquaintances, at least.

Sammy shared my love of horse racing, and on occasion we'd go to the races together. But Sammy wasn't just a punter, he was an owner too. He had four horses in training and would always let me in on when they were up for the job. I guess it wasn't the most prudent of relationships for a defence lawyer to have, but Sammy was an infectious personality, and a laugh to boot. I knew he could be as hard as a diamond when he wanted to be, but as I'd done him a few favours in the past he'd always been sweetness and light to me.

So when I bumped into him again at Harrow Road nick, I was a little taken aback to discover that he had metamorphosed into 'Dennis Banks.'

As the custody officer led me through into his holding cell, 'Dennis' poked his head out from behind his Daily Telegraph. Sensing that the custody officer was still in earshot, I muffled the surprise...

'Ah... Dennis. Hello. Let me just check the door… Right, we're in the clear... Samuel bleedin' Arthur Todd, you old sod.'

'Reckon you could do with a new suit, Jim.'

'Yeah... so what's happening?'

'Spot of fraud.'

'Really? You do surprise me.'

'Don't take the piss, Jim. I'm in the shit.'

I could sense that underneath the epidermis was a deeply troubled soul.

'I see... So that's what the 'Dennis Banks' is all about, I suppose?'

'The donkeys have swallowed it. Least, they have for the time being.'

Sammy always called the police 'donkeys'. He was persistently trying to get one over on them, and 'take them for a ride', and to be fair, most of the time he succeeded. I listened on.

'As far as they know, Dennis Banks is a man of good character with a chain of auction houses to run.'

'Eh, maybe you should have used Robin instead of Dennis?'

Sammy looked nonplussed.

'Robin Banks… It's a joke name.'

'I know it is. I'm not in the mood, Jim. Just listen.'

I'd been chastised by his tone and thought I better come up with something a bit more serious, and formal.

'Anyway, even if you have fooled them with Dennis Banks, they'll take your prints, and find out who you really are. You've got form, haven't you?'

'Only when they charge me, Jim. That's when they'll take my dabs. It will be too late by then.'

'What will? I'm not following. You know I can't act for you – well,

not if you're calling yourself Dennis Banks.'

'I know you can't represent me under an alias. Do I look stupid?'

I tried my best to wear the blandest of looks, and gently shook my head. Sammy continued.

'Just listen. As far as the donkeys know, Dennis Banks has been pulled in on a stolen credit card. One used at an art gallery in Stratford.'

'Upon-Avon?'

'Well, not bloody East London. Listen, it's a big purchase on a gold card – six grand's worth of painting. The Met's donkey sanctuary reckon the card was stolen from some mansion block in Maida Vale. They've got some scruffy little arse down at Paddington. But they want to know how I got hold of it. You with me?'

'Erm, sort of… well, no… not really.'

I realised I ought to concentrate harder, and listened some more.

'I don't give a shit about this card. I'll put my hands up to a bit of deception. But this is the biggest racket of all time.'

'What is?'

Sammy lowered his voice.

'Jim. I've got access to every fucking gold card application that comes in. See, the card I used wasn't the original. It's a copy, a clone. We've got a few days on each card before the real owner uses it for the first time. Then the shit hits the fan, and they realise they're up to their credit limit before they've even signed the thing.'

'So there's someone on the inside?' I was trying to keep up to speed.

'My partner's a fucking whizz-kid with computers. Don't ask me, I know bugger all about the things. I want you to go and see him for me.'

For some reason Sammy decided to fold his Daily Telegraph up into a neat rectangle. Then he got up from the cell bench and paced about, pausing by the wicket of the cell door to make sure he wasn't being overheard.

'Right. Now this block in Maida Vale gets fucking burgled. It's just an unfortunate fucking coincidence. The old boy who lives there assumes that his gold card's been nicked. Well, he doesn't assume it; he just raises the possibility. Tells the donkeys he's ordered one and for all he knows it might have been delivered the very fucking morning the

burglary takes place. And fuck me, it was.'

Sometimes following Sammy's train of thought was tough, not least because I tended to get distracted every time he swore. And the more irate he became, the more sullied were his words.

'So, the little bleeder who's nicked the real card must have picked up his PIN too, because he uses it at some fucking poxy mini-mart in Paddington to buy two hundred fags and a bottle of Glenfiddich. And guess what? This is timed at eleven minutes before the card's also supposed to have been used in Stratford-upon-Avon, a hundred miles away. Now, the old donkeys think, hang on, how can you get from London to Stratford in eleven minutes? Fuck me, Great Western struggle to get there in eleven hours.'

I couldn't help but laugh at Sammy's joke. I think it just flew out of his lips unintentionally. He soon reverted to a more austere look. In any event, this was complex stuff and I wanted to understand him correctly.

'So they know there's a clone, then?'

'They know there must be, yeah. They can't work it out though... they'd stroke my cock to find out.'

I reeled at Sammy's words.

'You always were a charmer.'

Sammy had a habit of stopping you in your tracks with his tawdry ways. He wanted me to listen carefully to what he was saying, though, and sported a look that I had come to recognise as 'shut up and listen'.

'Right, the local donkeys start to dig – fucking dig, dig, dig like the fucking seven dwarfs – and they find out that the organised crime squad have been after a gang of fraudsters for over two years. They suspect I might know something about this gang. So I get pulled in. Now, I don't mind a bit of deception, a one-off, but I don't want them thinking I'm the fucking brains… So, that's why I need you to see someone for me.'

'See someone?' I posed, circumspectly.

'Yeah, I'm offering you a big wad, Jim, a fucking big wad, just to do a little chore.... a little favour... for me?'

I tried to ignore the bribe, moulding a recalcitrant look, as if whatever it was he wanted me to do, I wasn't going to do it. Sammy was persistent.

'All you've got to do is pass a little message on, before they find out

who I really am. I can't risk contacting him from here. And if they bail me I'll be tagged, the mobile will be tapped, everything. This is my only chance, Jim. You're my only fucking chance.'

All the time Sammy was talking I was thinking, 'No way, mate. Are you crazy?' I knew somewhere along the line there was bait to be dangled, but my ears still sprang forward a touch as he said, 'Anyway, there's forty grand waiting for you, in cash. Straight up.'

My mouth dropped like a dead weight.

'You'll be saving me five years at least. I reckon eight grand per annum's not a bad return for that... Anyway, we've got the same bookie.'

As Sammy shot me another of his looks, a pulse sprinted through my veins. He knew I was in debt. Twenty years of gambling had taken its toll, and Sammy had done his homework.

'You're in the shit, aren't you, Jim?'

I didn't answer. He knew I was. Then he carried on as if somehow it was just a matter of trust.

'I'm allowed a legal visit, and this is it. They don't know that I know you, and they don't know that I'm going to sack you in about ten minutes either.'

'Oh, cheers.'

'Seriously, Jim. I'll get some local lawyer from up the road to do this deception case. I'm not worried about that. I just need to get a message out. I need you. I really do, mate, and you need the money...'

And there I was, being offered an enormous wad of money to drive up to the Cotswolds and pass on a message. I suppose the harsh truth was that had I not been so heavily in debt I would never have even considered it. And maybe, if I'm honest, not necessarily for strong moral reasons either, but because I knew I'd be scared. Shit-scared of anyone ever finding out.

I was trembling like a tambourine as I pulled off the M40, heading for the Cotswold hills. I met up with this guy who Sammy said I should call 'Mr Bamber'. I guessed it was some code or other so he'd know I was a bona fide mate of Sammy's. Whatever, we met in a small stone-clad village in Gloucestershire, not far from Bourton-on-the-Water.

It was just after one o'clock when I arrived. Bamber lived in a sprawling bungalow, a five-bedroom affair made from pure Cotswold stone. In fact, I doubt he actually lived there; I suspect that Sammy had rented it out as a base for their little operation. Most of the rooms were full of what looked like junk. On closer inspection I saw the cards, the magnetic strips, the embossing machines, and the computers. Every wall seemed to have telephone sockets linked up to computers, and computers linked up to each other.

He seemed to be expecting bad news about Sammy. He spoke in monotone, a sort of military monotone. He listened to what I had to say and told me he'd get on with it right away, as if he was a sergeant taking orders from a captain.

As it transpired I had to say very little. As soon as I asked if he was 'Mr Bamber' his look suggested that a message of a different type was being conveyed. He went to an old fashioned writing bureau and removed a small metal key from an inside drawer. He then thanked me and handed me the key. He didn't say much else, just rushed me along as if he had something terribly urgent to do. All he actually said was that I would have to wait until three o'clock before using the key. He wrote down an address on a post it note, finally reminding me again, 'not before three'.

The key fitted a locker in a sports club changing room in Evesham. I got there at about twenty past three, opened locker 217, collected the Adidas bag from within, and drove back to London, with forty grand in cash on the passenger seat. Simple as that.

CHAPTER 17

Half past five came and went, and I'd forgotten about the drink with Loren. More often than not, if something comes into my mind I have to follow it up immediately, and Sammy's phone call was one of those things. So I made a call to the Crown Court at Warwick, and was told that Sammy had pleaded guilty to one count of fraud on the art gallery in Stratford-upon-Avon. He got two years, so with time taken off I guessed he'd probably only just been released.

As I was thinking this, Loren appeared at my office door, coat in hand. We went over the road to the Black Horse, a pub that was bearable before nine but a den of iniquity by eleven. I noticed that the ceiling had been repainted and the old yellowing stains were now pristine white. I got myself a pint of ice-cold lager and Loren a white wine spritzer. She sat down next to me and took hold of my hand. She squeezed it tight and stroked it.

'Jim, talk to me.'

'What about?'

'You know... You've been really *odd* recently. What's going on? Has something gone wrong?'

I shot her a nervy smile. I was tapping the table with my thumbs, like a drum machine.

'Elton was conscious. He heard the CD.'

'What do you mean?'

'He heard the CD! He knows what was playing. He's been humming tunes in the Scrubs. He was humming it in the interview, the one you covered for me.'

'I don't remember that.'

'I don't expect you to, or to have taken any notice of it. But he was... why now? That's what I can't get over, why remember it now? It's like part of his brain has just been reactivated.'

'But that doesn't mean you're in trouble, does it?'

'No? What if he remembers other things as well? How the hell do I know what's in that mangled brain of his?'

'Calm down, Jim.'

I couldn't. Those little tremors were building.

'What if he goes on the stand and suddenly says, 'It wasn't me, it was my solicitor. He framed me'...?'

'Don't be ridiculous!'

'What? It could happen.'

'But Mr Douglas wouldn't call him anyway.'

'I know, but... but what if he did? What if he *had* to? Sometimes, Loren, it's just the last throw of the dice, especially if the trial's not going your way. You just think, 'Oh, sod it, I'll call the silly bugger anyway.''

'Jim. It will be all right.'

Loren stroked my arm, trying to reassure me.

'You've got to keep yourself together. It's not long, it will all be over soon. Anyway, who would ever listen to a nutcase like Elton?'

I sat there with Loren clinging onto me like a limpet. Did she care that deeply, or was her main concern for herself? If I crumbled, she'd cop it too – at least, she probably saw it that way. In any event, we shared a moment and just sat silently together for a few minutes, sipping at our drinks. Of course my mind refused to play ball and relaxation was out of the question.

I drifted back to that day, the day that horrible thing happened in childhood. The day of death.

My immune system was broken, my antibodies overstretched, like an army line unable to cover the ground. Gaps were appearing, and little pockets of enemy troops were seeping in. They joined forces, well behind my ranks. I knew then that I was about to be savaged from within... as certainly as night follows day.

What had Mum found out? What was it that made him kill? I'd always doubted it was just the adultery, to clear a path for his other woman. Mum must have found out he'd been embezzling money, and was planning to run off into the sunset with his lover. He could never have loved Mum. I knew that. Never.

That he got away has always haunted me. He had access to so much ill-gotten cash that he was able to wriggle free, and change his abode and his shape and his face. At least that's what I'd always reckoned. And one thing was for sure: he'd never made contact with me. Never tried, not even once. I didn't know whether to be grateful or desperate. I didn't know what to feel, and that's when my emotions started to misbehave, and take no entry paths, and pick up penalty points, and cause me hell… And Mum was unlawfully killed, said the coroner. And Dad was unlawfully at large. And nobody was ever convicted, and the law had failed… and for some stupid reason many years later I thought I could put it right.

I got through the Aunt Marj stage. I got my A-levels at Watford Grammar. I studied in London and learned the law. I had a desire to prosecute back then, to work for the Crown, to catch the purveyors of misdeeds.

I searched high and low for titbits of information. I checked every statement the police had taken years before. I followed every avenue, as had they, but it all led into a horrible black void. I found nothing. Nothing except the discovery that a vagrant had once been brought in for questioning, and was actually charged. He had come across the body shortly after I had run screaming down Goldington Street, which ran away from the allotment towards home. He had blood on his clothing, and fibres from Mum's coat on his sleeve.

His name was Kenneth Walsey, of no fixed abode. His solicitor had got him off at committal proceedings at Uxbridge Mags. There was no case to answer. He wasn't her murderer; he was just a drunken old scavenger who stole money from a dead woman's purse.

It wasn't until the mid eighties that I found out. I was twenty and had just finished my second year at university. It was then that I realised I no longer had a desire to prosecute. I wanted to defend. I wanted to *test* the evidence. I wanted to work things out for myself.

My thoughts were weakening, my picture fading, my own troops had regained lost ground... I felt someone brush me from the side. Loren sat down and put another pint of ice-cold golden liquid in front of me. I hadn't realised I'd drunk the first one, or that she'd gone back to the bar. I tensed and squeezed and just about forced my barriers back into place. I hadn't even realised that Gerry had joined us and was sitting opposite us at the table.

CHAPTER 18

After my first thwarted attempts at passion with Loren, a couple of weeks went by where nothing much happened. To be fair, that's a pretty cheap way of saying that I hardly spoke to her. I didn't like myself for ignoring her, though, and to be honest I quite craved her company for a while.

By this time I guessed that Sarena had been back in Perth for a couple of months. I'd convinced myself that there was little point chasing up the football ticket thing any further, or going back to the Oasis. I was trying to come to terms with the fact that it was possible to fall passionately in love with someone who didn't give a toss about you. I guess the liaison with Loren had been a welcome break, but I knew she could never fill the gaping gap that Sarena had left behind.

In early August I happened to be in Piccadilly again. I've got the date here in my diary: Friday 5th August 2011. I'd been to one of the central London magistrates' courts to do a shoplifting trial, which had turned into an unexpected plea. I had some time on my hands, a potentially dangerous thing at the time.

Shortly before midday I found myself strolling down Carnaby Street, enjoying the summer breeze. I was reminiscing over a trip down the Thames a couple of months previously, when I'd fallen head over heels with my very own Aqua Marina, my little stingray.

I was ambling past an art shop, admiring the window display, conjuring up memories of Sarena, when I accidentally bumped into a bizarre-looking guy who briefly reminded me of Boy George. He was wearing a black T-shirt with a fading logo, and wearing trousers that looked as if they'd been made from aluminium foil. There were splatters of make-up and small silver stars stuck to his forehead. It was as if he'd walked out of a time warp from the early eighties. I recall his sunglasses falling to the concrete paving stones below. I bent down to pick them up, and apologised.

'I'm sorry, that was my fault.'

I picked up his sunglasses and handed them back. It was my carelessness that caused the collision, I'm sure it was. The man was still slowly getting to his feet. I expanded on the apology, 'I wasn't looking where I was going. Too busy staring at that.'

I glanced towards the abstract piece in the window. The man didn't say a word. I noticed that he had a nose stud, and that it had caused a festering reaction on his skin. His eyes were grey and pink, the wrong colour for eyes.

As he pulled his T-shirt down and adjusted his clothing, I couldn't help but notice the outline of breasts and erect nipples sticking out through his T-shirt. The he was a she.

'My fault,' she barely mumbled, as she took a few unsteady steps along Carnaby Street. I could see she was about to fall and managed to catch up with her just in time. I rested her back against a shop-front and she slowly slid down until her bum reached the pavement. Her hands were rougher than mine, and covered with fine cuts.

I asked if she was okay, but got nothing in response. I noticed that the shop was one of those that looked like it been hastily rented out, as if it was only a matter of time before the shopfitters arrived and decked it out properly for a high street chain. I think it was being used as a temporary base for a squatting entrepreneur, selling British paraphernalia and the like. I bent down next to the girl. I remember looking into those haunted eyes and thinking, 'she's a junkie and a half'.

A drop of thick, pinkish liquid dribbled from a cut ear. I thought I ought to get her some help. As I turned around I noticed an American couple looking like they'd seen a ghost. The girl was now sprawled out across the shop entrance, and the Americans decided to shop elsewhere. This had obviously been seen by the shop owner, or someone I took to be the shop owner, who came out in a rage.

He was a large-framed man wearing a Union Jack waistcoat, denim cut-offs and large lace-up boots. He just stood there at first, muttering something at the girl, as if he knew her. In fact, I asked him as much.

'Do you know this girl?'

'Yeah, I'll sort it,' he replied in a gruff tone.

I carried on for a few yards, then heard a commotion and turned around.

'I told you to fuck off, slag.'

The man then threw her across the street. Literally picked her up and threw her with all his might. She collided with a trendy lamppost and bounced off it with great force. There was a weird crunching thud, and she slid to the ground, her body twisted, her right arm distorted and bent back the wrong way. The man then kicked her in the face. She screamed out in pain. I felt sick with anger.

The man was fuming with rage as he headed back into his shop. I couldn't believe what I'd just seen. I went straight into the hairdresser's opposite and without even asking picked up their reception phone and dialled 999.

The girl was now lying silently on the pavement. As I walked back out, a woman with bright orange hair emerged from the hairdresser's, pushed past me and went over to her. I think she'd been watching the incident from the window. She knelt down by her side, then looked up at me. She didn't speak. I thought she wanted to say, 'I think she's dead.' I wanted to say, 'She's probably just unconscious', but neither of us actually said anything.

I must have had an adrenaline high, because I can't imagine doing this again. I went into Mr Bullyboy's shop and spoke to him.

'What on earth were you doing?'

'What?'

'Throwing her like that? Kicking her.'

'Who the fuck are you?'

'Do you think you're going to get away with this?'

Bullyboy slammed a fist on the counter.

'Just fuck off, mate. You don't know what you're on about. That slag's been nickin' things, jackin' up outside and everythin'.'

Bullyboy twitched and jerked his head to one side. I thought he was going to punch me. Just as he made a move towards me, two police officers arrived in a cloud of dust and radio static.

I backed out of the shop and saw the paramedics carefully lifting the girl onto a stretcher. As they moved her, one of the paramedics unknowingly kicked a small stone in my direction. At least, I thought it was a stone. I crouched down and could see a tooth, a complete tooth, root and all, attached to a small piece of gum. The officers were still dealing with Bullyboy. I looked through the window and saw him remonstrating with them, no doubt pleading his innocence. I stared at him through the glass, peeking in between the one-armed mannequin and the life-size cardboard cut-out of Winston Churchill.

If my little street urchin needed a witness, then she had one. I thought out loud, 'The tooth, the whole tooth, and nothing but the tooth, so help me God.'

I got out the packet of mints that were in my trouser pocket. I peeled off some paper, and picked the tooth up. I held it in my hand as one of the officers approached me.

'Excuse me, sir, did you see what happened?'

'Yes, I did actually.'

'What's your name please, sir?'

'Do you want to know what happened?'

'Sure, but will you just give me your name, please?'

I huffed, 'Not at the moment, no. Do you want to know what happened?'

'What happened then, sir?'

'The man who runs this shop – owns this shop, whatever – he saw two potential customers, American tourists, I think. He saw them turn their noses up at something just as they were about to enter his shop. He came out and saw the girl lying across his shop front. He just went up to her, picked her up by the scruff of the neck and threw her into that lamppost. She cried out in pain and had clearly broken her arm, and then he just marched up to her and kicked her. Unbelievable. Oh, and this is probably hers too.'

'What is it?'

I opened up the paper.

'It's a tooth.'

The officer took it, studying it as he said, 'Anything else you remember, sir?'

'Yes. When he threw her he shouted 'fuck off, you slag'. I'm pretty sure that's what he said.'

'Did anyone else see this?'

I looked over to the woman with orange hair.

'That woman might have done. Somebody else must have done. There are enough people around.'

'I have to ask you for a name and address, sir. And I'll have to ask you for a statement.'

'Not now. Look, you're PC344. Where from, West End Central?'

'Yes.'

'Okay, I'll phone you later. See how the girl is. If she wants to press charges I'll make a statement. Promise. My name's Jim Harwood. I'll call you later.'

'But...'

'It's all right. I'll make my notes as soon as I'm back at the canteen.'

The officer half smiled before returning to a puzzled expression. I didn't want to be awkward, I just knew from experience that you can waste a lot of time on these things, and I wasn't sure whether the girl would want to press charges. If she did, I was going to help her, there was no doubt about that.

I could almost hear the officer writing the words, 'he went off in a southerly direction' in his notebook. I turned right at the end of Carnaby Street, walked over to Regent Street, then down to Piccadilly. I kept having visions of the girl's head bouncing off the lamppost. It had upset me. The bullyboy really did throw her hard. He should be punished, I remember thinking, he should be punished.

I went in search of a café to calm down. It was then, at almost precisely midday, that I found myself passing the Oasis again. I still had the picture of that vicious assault in my mind, and decided that maybe a soothing alcoholic drink was a more satisfying tonic.

The waitress recognised me from my après-midi session with Loren a few weeks earlier. After all, we had left the sort of tip that only drunks can leave. She had the same name badge on: Claire. I asked her for an ice-cold lager.

Ten minutes or so later she came to collect my empty glass. On a whim I took out the photo of Sarena – the one of her on the pleasure boat with the Houses of Parliament in the background, and her jet-black hair caught in the breeze. She could have been posing for Vogue.

'Can I just ask you, Claire. Have you ever seen this woman before?'

'This sounds exciting.'

'It isn't really... have you?'

She looked at the photo and puzzled. To my surprise, she slowly started to nod her head.

'Yeah… Yes, I have, actually. A couple of times.'

'You sure?'

'Yeah, I've seen her. Pretty girl.'

'You must have a good memory for faces.'

'Not really. She's been here quite a few times in the last couple of months. She was here last Saturday.'

It might have been early August, but it felt like a raw Arctic wind had chilled my whole body. A hollow pain immediately lodged itself deep in my gut. Suddenly the beer residue in my mouth tasted like malt vinegar. Claire was no longer Claire; she was now Cruella de Vil. Mutley laughed and hissed in my ear. Suffen ruffen guffen, Dick Dastardly, hee hee hee...

'You what? Pardon?'

'Saturday night, I'm sure. Let's have another look... Yes, definitely.'

'Definitely.' A word I hate. I won't go on about maths again. Suffice to say there was no mistake, no doubt about it. Cruella de Vil was certain. The gorgeous Sarena had 'definitely' stabbed me in the back.

The same empty feeling I had when Sarena had left so suddenly hit me again, pounding me like a stoning. I couldn't face life on my own. I took the plunge and phoned Loren at the office. I didn't know what I was doing, but I had to speak to someone. I needed someone.

Loren's mobile was switched off. I knew that she must be with a client. I had to phone the office. I didn't want senior partner Johnson suspecting anything, so I spoke to our receptionist and put on a disguised voice and a thick 'street' accent.

'Loren Granger, urgent. I've been arrested.'

The line went dead for a few seconds. I'm glad to say Johnson Gower & Co. hadn't succumbed to the temptation of playing irritating music. I heard Loren answer the call and couldn't control my hyper mood.

'Loren, it's me. I'm sorry, but... well, I just wondered if you wanted a drink later?'

There was a silent pause. You could almost hear the disbelief. Loren then spoke.

'Jim, I'm with a client!'

'Please, Loren. Just meet me in Piccadilly later. I'll explain then. You remember the Oasis? Can you be here, say half six? Please? Cheers, Loren.'

I hadn't given Loren a chance to say no. I kept the phone in my hand and dialled a different number.

'West End Central? PC344, please... Is he? I don't know his name. About an incident in Carnaby Street this afternoon. No, it's all right. I'll call later.'

I walked towards Golden Square. I was in a daze. I'd been through it with Claire three times. She didn't know her name. She'd been in Saturday with a couple of guys. Rich types, according to Claire. Left about midnight, and called a minicab to take them to the Victoria casino on Edgware Road.

I sat on a bench on the garden square. It had a little silver plaque saying 'Audrey's Bench - She Loved to Sit Here'. I said a little silent 'hello' to Audrey in my mind as I wiped something from my eye.

I could feel my pulse thumping and could actually see the skin on my wrist bouncing up and down. I wanted, more than anything, for Cruella de Vil to have got it wrong. Oh, Sarena, if only you knew what you'd done to me. I hated the thought of her with someone else. I hated the fact that she had the power to crucify me. I'd thought I might be over her, but who was I kidding?

I lumbered from one place to another, even ended up in Burger King, a place I'd never previously had the inclination to venture into. I stared out of the window, looking out towards Eros, while holding my hands around an ice-cold regular Coke, for what seemed like hours.

Burger King was jammed full of tourists. There was a group of Spanish girls with thick black eyebrows, giggling and looking excited. An old guy in ripped clothes came in and sat at the next table. His hair was matted into ropes, his face cut and torn. A tall man in a security uniform swore at him and told him to leave. Okay, there was a bit of a whiff, but the guy was doing no harm. He didn't deserve to treated like a piece of shit. He might have been an ex-lawyer for all I know. There but for the grace of God and all that.

I could feel the venom circulating again, looking for an escape route. 'Burger King security,' I mouthed to myself. I wanted to confront him, this plonker in the ridiculous uniform. How dare you work for Burger King security? How dare such a thing exist?

After marching the streets again I went back to the Oasis to wait for Loren. I couldn't relax at first and felt uneasy about being there. Loren told me she was supposed to go to the pictures with Gerry.

'Why didn't you, then?'

'Because you asked me to come here, that's why.'

'But why didn't you say on the phone?'

'I was with a client, for God's sake. What is wrong with you, Jim?'

'Nothing.'

'Oh, right, nothing. Great.'

Claire smiled at me and winked. She'd obviously jumped to some wrong conclusion or other. I soon realised what a dick-head I must be in Loren's eyes, and slowly shook my head.

'I'm sorry.'

Loren shot me a well-deserved look, before bemoaning, 'I don't know why I just don't get up and go.'

I could barely force myself to talk about Sarena, and garbled, 'Listen. I don't know where to start…'

'You've practically ignored me this last couple of weeks.'

Loren, as was becoming her wont, got straight to the point.

'Yeah... I'm sorry. I… I wasn't sure what to do. You know, Gerry and that. I didn't know if you liked me or you were just pissed, or what.'

'Why not just speak to me? Did you think of that? Why not ask Loren how she feels? You're a partner, for God's sake.'

'A junior one, yeah.'

'So? You still have to make the moves.'

Loren saw the world in pyramid shape.

'I didn't think of it like that.'

One of those awkward silences followed, where neither of us was sure what best to say. What I did finally come up with was a little left-field.

'Why don't you tell me about yourself?'

'What do you mean?'

'Anything… I know, why did you decide to become a lawyer?'

Loren baulked a touch, then looked like she was about to get up and leave. To my surprise she collected her drink from Claire, and launched into a monologue. It was a touch scathing in its reflection, but I knew that it was the least I deserved.

'Right. Loren Granger, twenty-nine next March. I've got a mum and a dad and a brother called Simon. Dad's a consultant anaesthetist; Mum's a care assistant. Oh, and Simon's a bum. I'm a solicitor at Johnson Gower. Been there just over a year. Before that worked for London Transport as part of their legal team. Got bored with it. Wanted to go into private practice. I'm ambitious; I want to be a partner at Johnson Gower. I want to run my own firm eventually. I want to have children too. I want to have a nice home and a husband who loves me. There you are, simple.'

I smiled at her in return, but Loren hadn't quite finished. She added, 'Actually, I'm not sure about the husband bit. It seems to go with the children, that's all.'

I smiled again and briefly clasped her hand.

'Sorry, Loren. I'm calming down now. Really.'

'From what?'

I tried to speak, but I felt myself welling up over Sarena. I even surprised myself that I was so smitten. Loren took offence at the pause.

'This is ridiculous. It really is. I've spoken to you lots of times. I've made you tea. I've gone to police stations and courts with you. You've never even hinted that you fancy me, then a few weeks ago you get me pissed and want to make love to me. Then you ignore me. Now you want to get to know me. Is that it?'

'Yeah. That's about it.'

Loren smiled, more in incredulity than anything else.

'Look, if you must know, Gerry's not important. He's just a friend, really. He thinks there's more to it than that, but I don't.'

'Perhaps you should tell him.'

'I will.'

'Good.'

There was another awkward silence. Claire was looking over and mouthed something to her colleague. I guess she thought I was involved in some sort of love triangle. I finally managed to spit it out to Loren.

'Loren, listen. I've been going out with a girl called Sarena.'

'Oh…'

Loren tried not to look deflated. She took a small make-up bag out of her handbag. A vanity mirror then emerged and she studied her left eye with it. Not sure what that was all about. I think perhaps she wanted to appear cool. Maybe she just had something in her eye. I don't know. Eventually she said, 'So?'

'I met her in a pub in Holborn. She's from Sri Lanka, but lives in Perth, Australia, so she tells me. Anyway, to cut a long story short, she told me she was going back there a couple of months ago.'

'So you've got a girlfriend?'

'No. That's not what this is about.'

'Well, what is it about, then? You've got one minute to explain, otherwise I'm leaving.'

'You want to see Gerry, don't you?'

'You've got fifty-five seconds left.'

I pointed over towards Claire.

'See that waitress over there? Well, a little while ago I showed her a photo of Sarena. And she said that she was in here last Saturday.'

'Yeah. So?'

'Well, she never went away. I mean, I'm sure she didn't.'

'How do you know?'

'She made out like she was going for months. Not only that, she did the same thing before. Lied about a weekend away in Birmingham, when she never even went there.'

'And why do you care so much about it?'

I didn't really want to answer that, and fumbled around for some words.

'Look, I know this can't make much sense, but...'

As I tailed off, Loren looked me straight in the eye.

'You're in love with her, aren't you?'

'No…'

'Yes, you are.'

There was another silent beat, before the first thing that came into my head spewed out.

'Shall we get something to eat? Then maybe go to a casino.'

'Casino?'

'Yeah. That's where the trail leads. I'll explain…'

We carried on talking about Sarena, and I said enough to convince Loren that there was a genuine intrigue. I explained to Loren, quite candidly, that I needed a female perspective. I wanted to know if she could throw any light on why Sarena had been lying to me... perhaps even guess what it was that she was trying to cover. I knew that I was taking advantage of the fact that Loren fancied me, or at least fancied a liaison with a 'junior partner' in the firm.

Once I'd explained to Loren about how Sarena and I had met, and the mystery of her disappearance, etc., she seemed genuinely intrigued. In fact, having been hooked by the scent, she wanted to know all the gory details.

Loren had her lawyer's brain in gear. I guess she thought it might be worth analysing the opposition, if that's what Sarena was. Anyway, I held back on a few things, but said enough to lure her in. That evening I needed her – needed her clear thought and her ingenuity, just like she'd needed my advances a few weeks ago. It wasn't the most conventional way to fulfil each other's needs, but it's how things got going.

Having dined together at the Oasis, we took a cab up to Edgware Road. We tried to talk our way into the casino, but you had to be members to get in. Loren spoke to one of the doormen with a little spiel about wanting to suss the place out before actually committing to membership. It was while this conversation was going on that I showed the other doorman the photo of Sarena.

It was obvious from his reaction that he recognised her. He then pointed out this guy who was just passing through, showing his membership as he did so.

'Mr Norton might tell you more.'

'Really?' I replied.

Then I think he thought better of saying anything further, as Norton went up the stairs. I noticed he had a distinct limp.

A few seconds later the doorman's mobile rang and we found ourselves being politely escorted out of the vestibule. But, boy, was Loren sharp. On hearing 'my' doorman's words, she'd focused her own mobile on him, and had a picture of Norton frozen on her screen.

As we loitered outside, I asked Loren what 'her' doorman had told her. Apparently he'd also recognised the photo and mentioned something about Sarena being there the previous weekend, 'with a fella who used to be on the telly.' I asked Loren for further and better particulars, and she started to mimic the doorman's words.

'Ooh, aah, ooh, who is it? What's-his-face, you know… that old quiz thing. Not Mastermind, the other one.'

And that's about as far as we got. Sarena had been with a bloke with a limp called 'Norton' and 'a fella who used to be on the telly'. Looking back now, I guess that Loren was as curious about me as I was about Sarena. I was churned up and so emotionally confused that I never really stopped to think about it. When we left the casino that night, Loren asked me if I wanted to come back to her flat for coffee.

The previous rumpy-pumpy foreplay with Loren had served its purpose. There was little embarrassing fumbling around, and Loren made love as if she'd just been reading the text book. She had this sexual confidence that I found quite unnerving. I could almost imagine her drawing a little sketch and taking me through each and every stage of development. At one point I thought she might phone the local council and ask for planning permission before laying down her foundations. That's not to say that it wasn't an enjoyable experience – it was, of sorts, but if there was a male equivalent of a faked orgasm then I might well have gone for it. I suppose it reminded me of those dreary chemistry lessons at school. We used to crowd around the specially designed 'experiment cupboard' and watch through toughened glass waiting for the reaction. And what a let-down they so often turned out to be.

Despite the lack of fusion, which only Sarena seemed able to spark in me, there was something very comforting about Loren. I wasn't used to being wanted, and I'd had too many kicks in the teeth to reject an offer of consolation. I really wanted to tell Loren that I didn't fancy her, but that I admired and respected her. But I couldn't do that. She wouldn't want to hear that. At least, that's what Ken was assuring me.

That night I dreamed about the poor junkie girl. The details, I struggle to recall, but as soon as I woke up that Saturday morning, in Loren's bed, I picked up my mobile and dialled.

I called PC344, an officer who went by the name of Tony Trent. It sounded to me like one of those contrived stage names. I asked how the girl was and offered to make a statement against the bullyboy. All the time I was listening to him on the phone, I had this mental picture of some dreadful club act from Birmingham: 'Ladies and gentleman, put your hands together for the top of the bill, all the way from Perry Barr, it's Toneeee Trent…' Anyway, the junkie girl had a broken arm and some facial injuries. The shop owner bullyboy was one Derek Clements. He'd been arrested for grievous bodily harm, but they needed my statement to make the charge stick. I was to be the Crown's chief eyewitness in the case of Regina versus Clements. I was going to be on the Queen's side for a change. I remember thinking that Aunt Marj would have been pleased about that.

CHAPTER 19

With Harry Douglas being booked in to do Elton's trial, I had to get another barrister to represent Matty Campbell. I'd instructed a barrister called Jessica Strong. She's a 'good egg', as those types like to say, a no-nonsense, get-on-with-it advocate, who seems to relish battles with big, burly, bronzed flying squad officers.

Unlike Elton, Matty was languishing in HMP Brixton. I'd turned up to see him during a thunderstorm. It was hot and sweaty and depressingly humid. Migraine weather, and I was struggling to keep one at bay. I waited in the little booth until one of the screws collected Matty and brought him to the door.

'Matty. How are you doing?'

'Fuckin' shite in this jungle. Can't theys open the windows in here?'

I shot him a look. It didn't register, so I had to explain.

'Is that one of your little funnies, Matty? Windows? Crawl out, escape, nudge, nudge.'

It wasn't. Matty was as saturnine as he was sullen, and in no mood to jest. As I spoke to him he was giving me his best Glaswegian stare.

'It's just me and you for a few minutes. The barrister's a little late.'

'When's my trial?'

'July. Monday 9th July. Not long. Anyway, that's what I wanted to talk about. I'm afraid there's been...'

At that moment there was a knock on the door. A little man with round glasses entered, tray in hand. He wanted to know if we wanted tea or coffee. I could have done without the interruption, because I was about to get onto a delicate subject with Matty. But what made matters worse was that the little man had an exaggerated feminine demeanour, and Matty just wasn't in the mood.

'Doos I want what? Yous fuckin' little shite!'

Matty had clearly declined the invitation, and I thought it best to follow suit.

'I won't have one either, thanks.'

The door was shut, and the little bespectacled man minced his way down the aisle. Poor sod. I wanted to shout out 'sorry!', but Matty was already bellowing in my ear.

'So what's fuckin' wrong?'

'Harry Douglas won't be able to do your trial. He's booked.'

'What? Fuck. He's my man. Why not?'

'He's... erm, he's doing a murder trial. He's already spoken for. I'm sorry.'

I daren't tell him that it was actually my fault that Harry couldn't represent him, and just said that he wasn't available. Matty wasn't too pleased.

'Great. Any other good fuckin' news? Eh? Shite... So who's doin' my case?'

'Listen. I've got the best there is... honestly, a real fighter. A very experienced barrister who won't let you down, I promise.'

'Who is he?'

'She... she's Jessica Strong, and she's brilliant.'

'A bird! A fuckin' bird! No way!'

'Now listen, Matty...'

'No fuckin' way is a bird doin' my case.'

I managed to calm Matty down, and at least persuade him

that he ought to judge Jessica after he'd spoken to her and not before. He wasn't happy, though. Matty lived in his caveman's world, where women had their roles... and representing him wasn't one of them.

I could see Jessica arriving in the legal visits area, and nodded towards her through the meshed glass. I spoke quietly to Matty.

'Here she is. Please behave.'

Matty was already breathing fire.

'Just give her a chance,' I pleaded, as Jessica was shown into the booth.

Matty, sporting a plain, pale-blue T-shirt with the words *Celtic Are Fucking Shite* written in black biro, stared at the door as Jessica entered. She was dressed in a black trouser suit, and smelled like a Paris perfumery. She offered Matty a genteel hand of introduction. Matty turned his nose up and made an exaggerated grunt.

Jessica had a confident 'Roedean' voice, and folks often misjudged her as a result. I just sat there and listened.

'Mr Campbell. My name's Jessica Strong, and I'm going to be representing you at the Old Bailey. Now, what shall I call you? Matthew? Matt?'

'Call me what yous fuckin' like, darlin'.'

'Okay, then. Matty the Fatty, how about that?'

'What?... Yous... Hey, Jim? She can't...'

Matty blew hot and cold for a few seconds. I stared rigidly at him but couldn't hide the smirk that was eagerly forming. Matty finally smiled.

'All right. Matty. Call me Matty.'

'I had anticipated that you might be a little hostile towards me, Matty. I'm well aware that Mr Douglas was your first choice. That was just my own brand of humour, that's all.'

'Aye, well...'

'And don't call me 'darling' again. Is that clear?'

Jessica had dramatically changed tone, making it sound like a scolding. After looking at me, Matty eventually nodded like an obedient schoolboy as Jessica took over.

'Right... Matty... Let's have a look at the evidence, shall we? Well, we've got this holdall that Detective Inspector Yallop says was found under your bed. And inside, according to him, was a spent cartridge from a shotgun, two-bore. Now there were no shots fired at this attempted robbery, were there?'

'Not at all,' Matty replied, with some authority.

I had to cover a smile. Matty had answered the question as if he'd been there himself. His instructions, however, suggested he had an alibi to confirm he'd been many miles away from the scene.

'No shots fired,' repeated Jessica, deep in thought, before adding, 'So what's the relevance of the spent cartridge case...?'

'Um, don't know, luv.'

'No, you don't, luv, do you?'

Matty wasn't too sure how to react. Jessica continued:

'Well, I'll tell you: nothing. It's out as far as I'm concerned... nothing to do with the actual offence. I'll argue it out in court, inadmissible, prejudicial, out. So, that leaves us with this security photo. Now, Matty, Jim's probably told you this already, thorough as he is, but let me just recap. The prosecution say that this is you. You say it isn't. Now they've instructed an expert, so-called, to say that in his opinion the robber is you. He reckons that the shape of the robber's nose, and the bottom of his ear, the bits sticking out under the hat that you can see in the picture, are identical to yours.'

'Shite.'

'Yes... well, Jim's instructed a man called Dr Franks. He's an expert too, but he says there are some irregularities between the facial features of the robber and your own. And what's more, I think that we can show that he's more qualified to give an opinion. The other chap – Leonard, Professor Leonard – well, he's not really given a scientific view. You see, he's well known for putting faces back together, and having a stab at what people look like from dental records, skulls, that sort of thing. You know, they find a skull in some Godforsaken place and then he pops in to build a face around it. They then use his likeness to trigger people's memories. Do you know this girl, went missing in Cornwall in 1985, etc.? With me, Matty?'

'Aye.'

'And our Dr Franks here is a scientist. He measures things. You see, Matty, the difference is, you can test what Dr Franks has done. You can go over it, do it again. You can't do that with Leonard. Now, in my submission, Franks is an expert witness and Leonard isn't. He's more of an artist, I'd say. Now if we win that battle, then you're halfway there.'

'Aye.'

Matty started to lap it up. He didn't understand everything Jessica was saying, but he understood enough. He understood that this woman knew what she was talking about, that she was up for the fight. The whole thing was really quite surreal, Matty being the centre of scientific argument, and I have to say, it did look awfully like his features in that security photograph.

After the conference I had coffee with Jessica at a place fondly known as the *Digger's Caff*, just off Brixton Hill. I think we were the only ones not wearing bright orange jackets with builder's logos. Anyway, she was great company for the afternoon, and an oh-so-welcome respite from the horror of Elton's case.

CHAPTER 20

Loren had always received a fair bit of attention from men, and knew how to use her overt charms. We had an odd relationship back then. The mutual admiration was clearly evident, but so was the lack of effervescence.

We were never going to reach the heights of passion, but there were plenty of other distractions. She would plan our evenings out, and I showed willing in going along with them. Sarena had left a feeling of emptiness in me, and anything to fill the void was a welcome release from the loss.

Loren always wanted to know a little more: about me, about Sarena, and about her partnership prospects. In fact I was becoming increasingly suspicious that hanging around with a junior partner was probably seen as a sensible move in Ms Granger's eyes. I told her that I thought she was a pretty ace lawyer and that she was Johnson's golden girl, and I meant it too.

So, Loren and I were getting on okay; we'll leave it as blandly as that. We found out that Norton went to the casino a fair bit, but we also discovered that the realities of tailing someone are not quite what the silver screen portrays them to be.

Norton would exit from the underground car park into the night, and that would be it. We did make a ridiculous attempt at tailing him in my old Swedish thing, but lost him within seconds at the Marylebone lights.

We made one last trip to the Victoria casino. It was more a detour after a night out than a planned escapade, but in any event we managed to find the same doorman again – the one Loren had spoken to. On prompting his memory with the photo of Sarena, there was more of the same.

'She's been back, yeah, with that chap. Ooh, that chap from... ooh, you know. They had to press buzzers and sat on top of each other.'

Loren laughed, and so did the doorman. Anyway, we put the quizmaster mystery to one side at the time, and concentrated instead on Norton. We'd learned that he was a trader in the City. The doorman thought he was a banker, but might have been a City lawyer. He wasn't sure.

I tried a few City firms and showed them the photo Loren had printed off from her mobile. I discovered that he was a trader who spent half his time here and the rest out of the country. But that's about all I discovered. It wasn't until a month or so later, after another Grays Inn conference, that I saw him emerging from Chancery Lane station, and limp his way east.

It was much easier tailing on foot, and Norton was hardly going to outrun me. As I followed him I left a message for Loren to join me. I knew she was on a legal conference that evening too, down at the Temple in Goldsmith Buildings. According to my diary this was Thursday September 22nd 2011, in the year of our Lord, as Elton would say. About six thirty-eight p.m. as I would.

I met Loren outside a trendy café/bar in Hatton Garden – the same place Norton had entered half an hour previously. Loren recognised him immediately.

'Jim, grab that table over there. He's sitting the other side of the glass partition.'

'Yeah, I know. He's talking to someone.'

Loren suddenly piped up with, 'Not Jeremy Paxman, is it?'

I shot Loren a puzzled glance, before she explained.

'Well, I was thinking about what that doorman said at the casino. Quiz show, they used to sit on top of each other. I reckon he meant University Challenge.'

'Yeah... yeah, you could be right. So maybe Sarena knows someone who looks like Jeremy Paxman?'

Loren piped up again, 'They don't really sit on top of each other, you know. It's just the camera playing tricks.'

'Is it?'

I held Loren's stunned look in response, then let out a little smile as I added, 'Well, well, you learn something every day.'

'Yeah, right.'

We enjoyed the odd sarcastic spar, I guess. In fact, it was that as much as anything else that kept us together during those late summer months.

Loren didn't want an alcoholic drink so we both ended up having a frothy coffee. We carried on talking mumbo-jumbo and kept glancing over at Norton. He was a good-looking sort of guy, tanned, with a semi-chiselled face, striking blue eyes and a very expensive suit. Loren thought he looked a bit like John Travolta, and she wasn't far off. As for the guy with him, well, he was as far removed from Jeremy Paxman as you could imagine: short and blond with a full and rather piggish face.

As I picked up the accent in his speech I formed the impression he'd sailed round the Monopoly board of life. I thought he'd probably gone from the Angel Islington to Park Lane, and probably without going to jail.

I glanced back at Norton again, and as I did so, quite out of the blue, alter-ego Ken squeezed my knee, making me jolt.

-He must have touched her, you know, old John Travolta... and maybe danced with her, and kissed her too... your little stingray.

I begged Ken to go away, and to my surprise he did, but when I turned to face Loren again all I could see were Sarena's exotic eyes. Eventually concentration took over again and Loren and I were back in tune. We began to listen to some more snippets of conversation, but talk about dull! They just droned on about stocks and indexes and pensions and derivatives.

No key words sprang out, so Loren said she'd try another approach. When she came back from the ladies', she paused to grab Norton's attention, smiling at him as she did so. I listened on.

'Hello... We've met before, haven't we?'

'Erm, I don't think so.'

There then followed an awkward lull on Loren's part, before she covered, quickly thinking on her feet.

'You were with an Indian girl.'

'Was I?'

'Sri Lankan, I think.'

'I'm sorry, I don't…'

Norton was perplexed. I sat there thinking, 'what the hell are you doing Loren, you idiot!', when suddenly Norton said, 'Was that Egan's in the Haymarket?'

To which, to my surprise, Loren replied, 'Yeah, that was it.'

'Must have been Javita,' Norton uttered to his mate.

Loren surprised me by carrying on the conversation.

'Yeah… lovely girl. Do say hello.'

I could sense that Norton couldn't quite fit things together in his brain. Loren had stirred some suspicion or other, and his brow went from a puzzled curiosity to a troubled glare.

Loren carried on, nodding towards the partitioned booth as she said, 'We're next door, actually. This is my husband Ronnie.'

After freezing for a second, I popped up from behind the frosted glass with a smile, looking as much like a 'Ronnie' as I could muster.

'Hi.'

'If you don't you mind, we're having a meeting.' Norton's tone had totally changed.

Loren stepped in again, 'Oh, sorry. Come on, Ronnie, film starts in fifteen minutes. I hate missing the beginning, don't you? Bye Mr... er...?'

There was a stony silence as Norton looked at his mate, then at me, then at Loren. It wasn't a pleasant look, either. I got the final menacing stare as I imagined Norton mulling, 'I didn't give you my name'.

I grabbed hold of Loren's elbow and ushered her out. It was Norton's look that shook me. Mind you, I had to admire Loren's gall. She had never even been to Egan's in the Haymarket.

In any event, something about Norton was mighty disturbing and I got the impression that Sarena or Javita or whatever she wanted to call herself had really got under his skin. It just made me all the more intrigued to find out why.

We walked briskly along the street and turned the first corner we came to. I looked for a black cab, but it had started to rain heavily and

I knew there was no chance of finding one. We both sheltered under Loren's large colourful umbrella, with the words 'Legal and General' printed on it. As I looked down at the paving slabs I could see Loren's boots. She was clicking her heels rhythmically along the pavement.

A downpour was getting into full swing. Soon it was raining cats and dogs, and amongst the cacophony you could almost hear the meows and the barks. I lost my cool, no doubt unnerved by the whole Sarena/Javita thing. I stared at the water splashes in the gutter as I snapped at Loren.

'Well, that didn't go too well, did it?'

'Oh, thanks for trying Loren. Thanks for making the effort.'

Loren wasn't amused by my lack of gratitude. Understandably, I guess, but I was on edge.

'And what's with calling me Ronnie?'

'It was the first name that came into my head. Anyway, she calls herself Javita, at least you've found out that.'

'That doesn't surprise me. It was the name on that credit card receipt. She knew I'd found it all right.'

'What credit card receipt?'

'It doesn't matter.'

A few steps further, a few more lashings of rain, and Loren's mood altered.

'Tell you the truth, Jim, I'm getting fed up with all this. I think we should leave it.'

'What do you mean, leave it? No, hang on. What do you mean, 'we'? You leave it if you want to.'

Loren looked like she was about to launch a tirade, but held it back. She shook some rain off the umbrella. before pleading at me, 'That bloke turned nasty. I don't like it, Jim.'

'So? You don't have to get involved.'

Loren then snapped in reply, 'You still love her, don't you?'

I shivered, just like I'd done when Sarena had stroked my face with the back of her hand.

'I don't love anyone. Shut up and change the record.'

Loren cocked me a look and strutted off up the road. Though the rain was still loud, I could just make out her words: 'Oh, get stuffed.'

Loren's Legal and General brolly disappeared around the corner. I ran to catch up with her but she turned around and shouted at the top of her voice.

'Just leave me alone, Jim! I mean it. Leave me alone!'

I watched as Loren veered off towards Chancery Lane station.

I didn't want to take the Tube. I'd always tried to avoid it whenever possible, and had been disturbed by the incident with the woman at Goodge Street some weeks before, when Loren and I had first got to properly know each other. I felt so brittle that night that I was sure a return to the Underground would have brought out some caustic words from alter ego Ken... and possibly an unwelcome return of what I thought was dormant Tourettes.

I got drowned as a rat instead, walking for miles through the city streets. I walked along Holborn, then up Gower Street over the Euston Road, up past St Pancras and Mornington Crescent, through part of Camden, over the canal, past Chalk Farm and up towards Adelaide Road. That's where I live. By the time I got home it was well into the early hours.

I tried to sleep, but Sarena was still in my brain. Ken was up for an argument, and he just wouldn't let me rest.

-So, is Loren right? Do you love Sarena?

-I had a feeling you were going to show your ugly mug again. I'd like to sleep if that's okay with you.

-Look, Jim. Dim Jim. Just stop all this nonsense and be a bit kinder to Loren, will you.

-But I want Sarena. Don't you understand? I want her to touch me again. I want to feel something.

After what seemed like half the night I threw Ken out of bed and finally fell into sleep... a wicked and restless sleep.

CHAPTER 21

With only a fortnight to go until Elton's trial, I was stumped by Loren's announcement:

'I've done it, Jim.'

'Done what?'

'Got a last-minute jolly on the net. Tunisia.'

Loren had been leafing through a few travel brochures and making the odd comment about how lovely this or that hotel looked, but I'd never thought she was seriously considering a break. There must have been a good few seconds' silence, which I eventually broke:

'I thought you were joking. I mean it. I really thought you were joking about going away.'

'Why should I be joking?'

'I don't know. I just can't imagine you not being here. I can't imagine being able to relax, for one thing.'

'Well, that's why I'm going.'

There was another period of silence, before I finally mused, 'In your dreams, you've been to Tunisia...'

'Uh?'

Loren gave me a funny look.

'It was an old advert on TV, years ago...'

Loren ignored me.

'You didn't want to come, you said.'

'I know... you *know* I can't. It's only a fortnight until the trial.'

'Is there anything I can do?'

'No... nothing...'

I couldn't even say our relationship was hot and cold. It seemed permanently lukewarm. I wanted to say something along the lines of, 'I thought we might stay together to support each other', but it didn't seem worthwhile.

'So when are you off?' I asked, a touch forlornly.

'Next Tuesday... back the following Tuesday.'

'Well, enjoy it. It will be hot... bloody hot.'

'I just have to have a break, Jim.'

Looking back now, some of this period before Elton's trial is a mysterious blank. I remember that there was a further conference scheduled with Elton, but as Harry had the flu, we had to postpone it at the last minute. He seemed confident enough that we'd have sufficient time to talk to Elton at court, before the trial properly got underway.

Every day was a battle, though, I can remember that. I tried to keep up to date on my other cases, but such was the pull of Elton's case, and the potential for disaster, that it was hard to concentrate. I used Nellie as a defensive shield, to keep me away from unnecessary demands on my time: irritating clients and the like.

Of particular concern was Sammy Todd. He'd started to bug me more regularly, leaving messages on my answerphone and even writing notes when Nellie lied to him, telling him that I was away or off sick. One such note was more than a little disturbing:

"Jim, I've been trying to get in touch. You're never in. Are you avoiding me or something? We've got to talk, and soon. Don't avoid me and everything will be alright."

I recall Nellie handing me the note and telling me that Sammy was downstairs in reception. It was the day she had told him that I was away in Cardiff, on a Crown Court trial.

'He won't go away. He's just planted himself in reception,' she said, seeming annoyed rather than concerned.

She hadn't meant it in terms of 'he won't go away now', more that he kept coming back. She told me that this was the third time he'd been in that week.

'What does he want?' I asked.

'I don't know... *you.*'

Nellie wasn't one for expansive replies.

'Thanks, you're such an efficient secretary.'

Nellie was used to the banter, but she proceeded to unnerve me.

'I think he said something about being stitched up.'

'What?'

'Or something like that.'

'What do you mean *something like that*?'

'Hang on, it's coming back to me... stitching someone up, is he? That's what he said.'

'Are you sure?'

'I think so. I thought it was a joke at first, but he had a face on.'

What might have been confusing to some was dead plain to me. When Nellie said that, I knew exactly what she meant, and Sammy wasn't one to get on the wrong side of. Nellie picked up the note she'd given me seconds earlier and started to read it.

'So why *are* you avoiding him?' she asked, nosily.

I took the note from her grasp.

'I'm not.... well, I am, but not just him. It's Elton's case. It's getting to me.'

'Don't I know it...' Nellie cocked a look, more aware than anyone how on edge I'd been.

As Nellie left my office I started to worry about Sammy. It had been well over a year since I'd compromised myself and done the unthinkable. I reckoned I'd got away with it, too. I searched for a reason as to why Sammy might be disgruntled with me. What had I done wrong in his eyes? I'd tipped the guy off in the Cotswolds, as asked. I'd collected my reward, as promised. He'd got a pretty light sentence considering what he'd really been up to, and I'd never uttered a word to a living soul either.

I couldn't understand what he meant, in his note or in his discourse with Nellie. I knew at some point I'd have to confront Sammy and find out what was concerning him, but I hoped that I could get Elton's case done and dusted first.

I continued to keep a low profile, and counted the hours. Loren went away and returned, and it was the weekend before the actual trial before I spoke to her again at any length.

It was on the Sunday – the day before 'twelve good men and true' would begin to hear the evidence. Though, as it transpired, it would be seven good men, and five good women. It was they whose duty it was to decide if Elton Spears was going to spend the rest of his life behind prison bars, in a mental health institution, or back on the streets of London.

I woke up about nine that day and went out to buy a Sunday paper. Loren came round at eleven, with two hundred fags and a bottle of Rémy Martin, my gifts from Tunisia, or more likely Gatwick.

She was itching for me to comment on her tan. I told her it looked less like a tan, and more like her freckles had expanded and merged. She wasn't amused, and I wasn't chatty enough to cover the awkward banter. I felt a real urge to spend the day alone, but thought it best not to say or do any more to upset her. I still had the feeling that she had to be 'kept' on my side, that she might not naturally rest there.

We sat at my table eating croissants, drinking coffee, and desperately thinking of something to say. My mind was so on edge it felt like it was cutting its way out of my skull. As Loren read the colour supplements, I looked at her, and thought: I'd known her some eighteen months or so. Is she a wolf in sheep's clothing? Can you trust her? *Do* you trust her? Does she have an agenda of her own?

How she could go on holiday the week before Elton's trial? I'd been a bundle of nerves all week, barely surviving on a diet of codeine and Cognac. Maybe that's why she'd bought me the Rémy Martin. Perhaps she wanted me to overdose. At least then I wouldn't be able to cock the whole thing up.

Loren turned a page, oblivious to my increasing paranoia. A big photograph of Robbie Williams appeared before me, with a headline about how he'd spend his 'perfect Sunday.' I remember seeing it fleetingly, as it prompted me to drift back to childhood....

...I was normally stuck indoors with dotty Aunt Marj on a Sunday, one of thousands of sad, bored children watching *The Champions* or *Lost in Space*, though they were far more of an escape to me than many others, I'm sure. I didn't so much watch TV, as it watched me, or watched over me, to be more precise. Television was once my saviour, before turning tormentor.

Black Beauty would turn up at about five in the afternoon while Marj served buttered crumpets for tea. If Marj felt really depressed, she'd sit in front of *Songs of Praise* and weep. I can remember her singing and crying at the same time, and it used to be an odd cacophony indeed: 'All good gifts around us are sent from heaven above, so thank the Lord, yes thank the Lord, for all-all-all his love'... Yeah, thanks, Lord, I thought. Thanks for killing my mum, and giving me a father who was rotten to the core.

Marj wasn't a real aunt. I realise now that after the demise of my mum, some jiggery-pokery took place with the social services. Some people once referred to her as a 'Dutch aunt', which totally threw me. When I was a teenager we at least managed a joke about it. I told her she ought to start wearing orange clogs or smoking joints. Anyway, truth is, so many things had gone on behind my back that I still haven't a clue where the truth lies. I could go back in time, seek out a few official reports from social services, that sort of thing. I *could*, but I never have.

When I did finally check up on that awful day, it was solely to do with the facts of the case. I was obsessed by what had *happened*. And the journey, the actual finding out what had happened, proved to be an unlikely shield from the very pain it had caused. It wasn't the last time I was to bury myself in the facts of a case.

Suddenly you have no parents. They've gone. It seems pat to even say it now, but that's the way it was. One day Mum and Dad were at home, albeit constantly arguing, and the next day I was alone. Suddenly your whole life is turned upside down and your seven years of experience on the planet is supposed to rationalise it.

I was too scared to ask Aunt Marj the questions that needed asking. Not scared of her, just of the questions. In fact, I was more scared of the questions than what the answers might be. I needed a touch of experience and a layer of leather before I was able to find out for myself.

Marj told me that I was a lucky boy. I never used to understand what she meant, but I think I have an inkling now. I wondered whether Dad had worried that I had actually seen him commit the deed, and that I needed to be silenced too.

I shot back from the thought just as Loren got up from the table to get some milk out of my fridge.

That's when the Big Ben chimes alerted me to a text message. 'CALL ME ASAP. SAMMY.' I turned the phone off in frustration. I just couldn't cope with Sammy, on top of everything else.

At that precise moment all I wanted to do was hibernate. I wanted to resurface next spring, to discover that my whole life has been directed by David Lynch. I wanted someone to tell me it had all been staged for somebody else's entertainment.

Perhaps I can start again without the baggage, I thought, as I let my mind wander again. Tell me I don't have to go to the Old Bailey tomorrow. Can't I stay at home and watch *Crown Court* and *Paint Along With Nancy*? Just like I used to...

Loren put a cup of coffee in front of me.

'Are you okay?'

'Yeah.'

'You were sort of half asleep, mumbling something... Aunt Marj or something?'

'Was I?

'Then you snorted, like a sudden snore, and shouted 'Nancy.''

'No, I didn't.'

I realised immediately that I must have done, but the denial was spontaneous.

'Who's Nancy anyway?'

'*Paint Along With Nancy...*'

'What's that?'

'It used to be on when I was a little kid.'

Loren couldn't find anything worthwhile in response, apart from 'oh'.

'I used to be good at art... used to draw parallel lines.'

'Really... how odd.'

Loren tried to cover her look. She might as well have said, 'what are you on about now?'. I smiled at her – a nervous, desperate smile.

'I was good at maths too.'

'Shouldn't you be thinking about tomorrow's trial? And Elton?'

Ken was desperate to shout 'fuck off' at full volume. In fact, 'fuck off, you freckle-faced tart' almost came out. I had to do that thing again where I force my thumbnail into my skin to keep control.

'I don't really want to talk about it today, Lol. If that's okay? Let's go out somewhere shall we... anywhere.'

We decided to go for a walk in Hampstead. We went from pub to coffee bar to restaurant. I read all the papers. I even read my horoscope in the *Mail on Sunday*. Apparently I was going to have to make a difficult choice. I was also likely to undergo a change in surroundings. Oh great, I thought, so I'm going to the Scrubs then. That's it. I'm going to be found out, tried and convicted for murder and incarcerated with the likes of Matty Campbell.

As the day progressed, we found ourselves drifting

towards Loren's flat. That evening we ended up in the Swan, her local pub. At about half eight, sitting in the beer garden, I decided to turn my mobile back on, and give Harry one final call. As I did so I could feel my nerves twanging like a Duane Eddy guitar.

It seemed to take an age for Harry to answer his home phone.

'Harry? Jim. Nothing much, really, just wondered if there'd been any last-minute developments on Elton's case?'

'No, not that I know of. We're in Court Two. Judge Llewelyn-Davies.'

'Right... what's he like?'

'LD? He's a lamb.'

I didn't know whether that was good or bad, or why I'd even asked. Harry seemed up for it.

'We'll give it our best shot, Jim. I'll see you in the cells at half nine. We'll have a chance to talk then.'

'Okay. Sorry to bother you, Harry.'

'No problem... you're pretty uptight about this one, aren't you? Don't know why. You've done all you can. Nobody could have done more for Elton than you.'

'Yeah. Thanks.'

I turned my mobile off again and suggested to Loren that we went our separate ways. By then I *needed* to be on my own. I was just about to reach the pinnacle of guilt, and I didn't want Loren to see me crying.

CHAPTER 22

After the argument with Loren over the Norton conversation, when we'd clashed outside the bar, we had another one of those 'awkward' periods at work. We avoided eye contact, and exchanged morning pleasantries like political opponents.

She was pissed off with me, and wanted me to know it. I desperately wanted to explain, but knew that the more I mentioned Sarena the more it would hurt her. So we went through the motions and I hated it. Truth was, I needed her and she needed me, but neither of us would budge.

Meanwhile I gathered all the facts and tried to piece it all together. Who was Norton? Who was the piggy-faced man? Who was Jeremy Paxman? And who on earth was Sarena? What was all the training as a barrister and getting work experience all about? Why all the lying and the false identities? I just couldn't work it out, and not knowing was eating away at me.

Eventually, after weeks of puzzling over what to do next, I went to Grays Inn Court to see Giles Derby, the barrister who had first introduced us some months previously. I hadn't spoken to him for ages, since I made that initial enquiry over Sarena's disappearance, when he'd told me, quite unsurprisingly, that her return to Australia was because her work experience had ended. Of course, by that time, I knew that the closest she'd been to Australia was probably the Walkabout bar in Piccadilly.

Giles's clerk was a guy called Billen Andersen, one of the few foreign head clerks in the whole of Grays Inn. They often called him 'Billen the Swede'. His father was a Swedish lawyer who'd married a Scottish woman who was a clerk in Grays Inn. So like many such positions, it was all kept in the family. I'd dealt with him a fair bit back then, as I used to instruct that set of chambers quite frequently.

Billen was quite an earnest type. Every time I phoned him up I used to ask to speak to 'Ben'. There would always be a slight pause before he answered, quite straight-faced, 'It's Billen speaking. We have no Ben'. He didn't get the joke at first, until the other clerks explained it to him. Then he decided to play along. Anyway, as I walked in he was sat at his desk.

'Hi Ben, how's it going?'

'Busy… busy, busy,' Billen answered from behind a mountain of briefs. I asked if Giles was in, and was a little taken aback by his reply.

'Giles? No, he left us a couple of months back. He's set up his own business.'

'What, as an advocate?'

'Oh no, he's finished with the law.'

After a little more probing I found out what Giles was up to. He'd had a total change of scene. To my great surprise Billen told me that Giles had invested in a couple of video karaoke outfits – little shopping-mall booths where you can record your own version of your favourite song and take it home on DVD. He had a shop in Guildford and one in Reading.

By the time I caught up with him in Reading he'd begun to claw back some of his investment. Of course, I told Giles it was just a chance meeting, as I spotted him talking to one of the security men outside his shop.

'Good God! If it isn't old Giles.'

'Jim!... Less of the old, please. How are you?'

I'd half forgotten his accent: posh Yorkshire, I suppose you'd call it.

'I'm fine, thanks.'

'What brings you to these parts?'

'Just passing through. Been visiting a client in Reading jail... so this is yours, is it? The karaoke set-up.'

'Yes, all mine. Want a go?'

It was the last thing I wanted.

'Might do. So I heard you'd left Grays Inn?'

'Yes... yes.'

Giles wasn't forthcoming at first.

'I'm sure last time we met we were in some pub in Holborn.'

'Yes, that's probably right.'

'You were with an Indian woman. Nice-looking girl, if I remember rightly.'

Giles paused before answering. He looked up at the roof of the shopping mall and scanned around it with his eyes. He made out that he was going to sneeze, and then apologised for not doing so.

'Sorry. She was Sri Lankan, actually.. and I wasn't with her. Well, not exactly.'

I felt a punch in the solar plexus. I must have instinctively known where this conversation was going.

'Yeah? What does that mean, then?' I asked, not really wanting to hear an answer.

'Actually, she ignored me half the night so you wouldn't think we were bothering.'

'Bothering?'

I knew what he meant but pretended not to, as much for my own pride as anything else. Giles took it at face value.

'I forgot. You're a southern softie, aren't you? Are ya botherin', lad? You know, going out, seeing each other.'

'You were seeing each other?'

I'd tried to cover my horror, but failed dismally. Giles of course had no idea that Sarena meant anything to me.

'Tell you the truth, Jim, I wish I'd never set eyes on her.'

'Tell me.'

I'd said that far too enthusiastically. My little pumping organ was working overtime and blood was racing around my circuit. What was Giles trying to tell me? That he and Sarena had...? I prayed not, and tried my best to look nonchalant. Giles finally answered:

'I suppose it doesn't matter now. I can trust you, I guess.'

I forced my brain back into gear.

'Giles, of course you can... trust me with what, anyway?' I added

tentatively.

Giles took a moment to make sure he wasn't going to sneeze again.

'Listen, I'll let Jenny take charge, and we'll have a spot of lunch.'

'I've eaten... have half a lager, though. Who's Jenny?'

'Not bad, eh?'

I glanced over to the shop or whatever it was and focused on Jenny. She, apparently, was his assistant – a giggling twenty-something with green stripes in her hair. It was clear from his inference that she and Giles shared extracurricular activities.

'So, what happened to...?' I couldn't remember his wife's name.

'Mrs Giles?' he offered.

I instantly remembered that he often used to call her that.

'Daphne. Mmmm,' he mused, before adding, 'we've separated. In a way it's all part of the story.'

On the one hand I was itching to find out about Giles and Sarena, while on the other I was dreading it. Giles led me over to a ridiculously trendy Mexican bar, bucking horse and all. I sat there on an upturned barrel, self-consciously trying to get a decent-sized gulp of lager down my throat. Not easy when some jerk of a barman has stuck half a lime in the top of the bottle, and not even given me a glass. I ignored the trendy inconvenience and listened intently.

'Sarena and I had a bit of a fling, for a few weeks. Anyway, cut a long story short, the bitch copied all the details from my wife's credit cards and ran up about ten grand on them.'

'She never!'

'She did. Daphne had gone to stay with her mother in Harrogate for a fortnight.'

'That's dreadful,' I whimpered. Though of course what was really dreadful was the awful image I had in my mind of Giles kissing Sarena.

'That's not all. She tried to blackmail me. I had to make out like the card had been stolen. If I'd reported her to the police she'd have told Daphne about our little fling.'

'I'm sorry, Giles.'

He shot me a look as if he was the most hurt soul in Berkshire. If only he'd known. Then he released a phlegmatic breath, and blew into the top of his lager bottle.

'Anyway, all in the past now. I let it be, got the insurance cover on the card, so... God, you won't say anything, will you?'

'Giles, please.'

'No, sorry. Course you won't. Mrs Giles and I are kaput, but she still doesn't know the truth.'

Sometimes following Giles wasn't easy, but I tried to take in all the information that had been relayed. Then he said, quite suddenly, as if the thought had just hit him, 'You never saw her again, did you?'

I tried to cover the blow with a look.

'Me? No. Not at all.'

Giles then puzzled, squinting his eyes a touch as he said, 'Didn't you call me about her a few months ago?'

'Yeah... yeah I did.'

I could feel myself squirming and came up with the best lie I could muster.

'It was about a niece of mine who wanted work experience, and I wondered if you had any vacancies. With that girl leaving, you know.'

Giles seemed to accept this, though I wasn't convinced it would rest that easily. I added to cover, 'Anyway, do you still keep in touch with any of the old cronies?'

'Not really. I moved out to Swindon. My old clerk still sends out the odd check that filters in, but apart from that, me and the world of law are a million miles apart.'

I conjured up a smile, as if my only concern was for Giles.

'Would you Adam and Eve it, eh?'

I'd managed to convey a light but dismayed inflection. I wanted to try and steer clear of any more chat about Sarena, but there were things I just had to ask.

'So, was she doing work experience, or...?'

'She was supposed to be...'

Giles then lowered his tone, conspiratorially.

'You remember our head clerk, Billen the Swede?'

'Billen-Ben, yeah.'

'Checked out her letter of introduction. Sarena's letter. A dodo. And her referee.'

'Don't tell me, offside,' I mused out loud.

'Amazing, isn't it? You would have thought butter wouldn't melt.

Billen's still head clerk and sworn to secrecy. Bad for business.'

I nodded at Giles emptily, 'Right... I see.'

I made the effort to ramble on to Giles about all sorts of other things, just to disguise the Sarena conversation. It was tough going. I wanted to rant and rave about Sarena. I wanted to say things like, 'I knew she was a fraud, the cow', but I couldn't. I concentrated hard and played the game.

Giles was well into his new vocation and would have sulked if I hadn't had a go. I didn't really have much choice, so I went back over to the shop and picked a track out at random. I ended up doing a karaoke of 'Everlasting Love': 'Open up your eyes, then you realise…'

CHAPTER 23

On Monday 9th July 2012, at eight minutes past nine, I walked through the revolving doors of the Old Bailey, as prepared as I could be for Elton's trial. I recall Harry waiting by the entrance to the cell door, where we exchanged good mornings.

It was just another day at the office for Harry. He must have spent half of his life in that place. He then proceeded to unnerve me.

'Jim, first off we must have a word about the expert evidence. Something's been bugging me.'

'Right.'

I was already dreading the conversation, which was just routine to Harry.

'Mind you, I doubt we'll be on much before lunchtime.'

'No? Why?'

'Judge has got a couple of other matters listed before we're on, sentences I think. Anyway, I'll be asking for an hour or so to speak to the Crown... got a few things to talk about.'

'Like what?'

'Procedural matters... are you *okay*?'

'Yeah. Yeah, I'm fine.'

'You seem edgy.'

'Oh, just... not been sleeping.'

'Well, come on. Let's see our man.'

We headed for the cells to see Elton. I stood there and pressed the buzzer, waiting for the screw to open up. As I did so I stared at the decaying wooden gate, which had been kept as a memento of days gone by... when murderers were sent to the gallows in Newgate Jail. I swallowed a lump of nothing.

One of the jailers then answered the main door and showed us through to reception. Then another jailer asked for our names, even though he knew them. He wrote them down in the visitors' book. He looked a touch irritated by the disturbance, having been preoccupied by a taxing crossword clue in the *Sun*, which was spread out on the desk in front of him.

As usual there were a number of newspaper articles pinned up on the wall. There was a play-on-words headline about bringing back hanging, which the screws seemed to find amusing. There was also a score chart on the wall. It was keeping tabs on some sort of gambling game. All the top QCs were listed in a vertical column. There were marks next to their names.

I discovered that each barrister would get three points for a not-guilty, two for a hung jury and one for a guilty verdict on a lesser charge. So if your client went down for manslaughter instead of murder, it would be one point. If he got off altogether it would be three points, etc.

It was a sort of 'fantasy barrister league', and I could see Harry's name on the list. He was in second place behind Kieran Daly QC, who was top with twenty-two points. Harry had nineteen. Then I noticed that Barrington Brown QC was bottom with five points... after twelve matches! Relegation was looming.

One of the screws recognised Harry and smiled at him. He crossed out his odds of 2-1 and wrote 7-4 instead. Harry was now clear second-favourite to win the Old Bailey champion hurdle.

Just for a minute I lost myself in the perverse joviality of it all. I had to jolt myself back into focus. I kept telling myself that I must stay fine-tuned, and try and keep Ken at bay. We waited a few minutes before being led along one of the cavernous corridors that lead to the conference rooms. The sounds of keys clanging in the distance could be heard, along with distant echoing voices.

I swapped glances with Harry as we traversed the corridor. I didn't know what he was thinking, but I couldn't get one particular thought out of my head: there I was, about to meet my client – a client who was accused of a murder I knew he hadn't committed because...

Once again I had to scrape my fist against the corridor wall, allowing the grainy brick to break the skin on my knuckles. Then I took my place with Harry in the little conference booth and waited for Elton to appear. As I sat on one of the moulded plastic seats that were secured to the floor, I could see the white paint from the brick on my hand.

We waited in deathly silence. After a couple of minutes I got up restlessly and popped my head out of the door, to see if Elton was on his way. Harry kept wondering why I was so jumpy, but I couldn't give him a meaningful reply.

Further along the corridor I could see Loren with Jessica Strong. Loren was clerking the Matty Campbell trial in court five. There was no way she wasn't going to be there, and the fixing of Matty and Elton's case on the same day was a perfect excuse for her attendance.

Jessica looked as regal as ever. She was too far away to say hello to, but my nostrils twitched as her perfume greeted me. She waved at me from the along the corridor. I waved back. If she knew? If Harry knew? It just didn't bear thinking about.

I sat back down around the table with Harry, who was silently concentrating on the case papers. I wanted him to break the eerie stillness. I was about to shuffle nervously back out into the corridor when Elton appeared at the door with two burly screws. They escorted him in to our little private room and closed the door behind them.

Elton was dolled up in a new suit. Well, new to him. His dad must have bought it from a charity shop. Bless him. I wanted to cuddle him again, the giant teddy bear.

Elton sat down. I decided to leave things to Harry. I'd done all I could to prepare the case for trial. At least, that's the way it was supposed to look.

Harry was expecting me to have the first word because he knew Elton and I went back a long way. I just smiled at Harry, and nodded, and let him take over. I couldn't physically speak. Harry obliged and addressed Elton directly:

'So, Elton, how are you feeling this morning?'

'Yeah.'

'Not too nervous?'

'Was watching telly.'

'In Brixton Prison?'

'Yeah. Scooby-doo. Woof. Scooby-dooby-doo.'

Harry smiled at him.

'Right. Well, let me just take you through what's going to happen today. Now, we probably won't be up in court for a couple of hours or so. When we do, there'll be a bit of legal argument between me and the barrister who'll be representing the prosecution. I won't bother you with all that, shouldn't take long. Then the jury will be sworn in. You must remain silent while all that is taking place, unless you actually know any of them of course, which is most unlikely. Anyway, then the clerk will read out the charge and you'll say 'not guilty' and sit down. Then we'll get on with it. Okay?'

Elton didn't answer. He smiled at me instead. I've no idea why. Harry continued.

'You've provided Jim with your best recollection of your weekend. You know what I'm talking about?'

'Yeah.'

'Eastbourne, right. Now is there anything else you've remembered since you last saw Jim?'

'Yeah.'

My heart sank. There was a worm wriggling around in my

stomach – a grass snake, more precisely. My guilty Geiger counter was bleeping like a car alarm. This is what I had feared. What was the giant teddy bear going to say? Harry asked him:

'What else do you remember, then, Elton?'

'Smell.'

'Smell? What do you mean?'

'Smell in the car.'

'What car?'

'Car.'

I put on a vacant expression, as if someone had stuffed an imaginary pear in my mouth. Harry was looking at me.

'Jim? Have you heard this before?'

I shook my head with my mouth still open and took out a packet of chewing gum. I wanted to shoot Elton. I wanted to fire point-blank into his peculiar brain. Harry prodded a bit more.

'Elton. Listen to me very carefully. Are you saying somebody gave you a lift to Eastbourne? Is that what you are now saying?'

'Car. Smelly car.'

'Why didn't you tell me this before?'

'Don't remember.'

'Okay... okay, so you've just remembered. Or remembered recently... Jim, when did you last see Elton?'

'Not long ago. Not a mention of this.'

Harry accepted my answer as fact, but then why shouldn't he? He turned to Elton again:

'All right. Elton, what sort of car?'

'Don't know.'

'Thank fuck,' Ken nearly said out loud.

Please don't say anymore, Ken, I begged. A brief battle for supremacy raged in my mind. Ken was fighting for space, but I managed to shove him aside.

Meanwhile, Harry had released a weary sigh at Elton's 'don't know' answer, while fiddling about with the red ribbon that had tied his brief. He pulled out a copy of

Elton's statement, the one I had forwarded to Harry – my client's instructions. Before Harry could say anything else, Elton suddenly piped up again.

'Smelly car.'

'What sort of smell? An engine smell? An unpleasant smell?'

'Like the girl.'

'He's looking at you, Jim. What does he mean like the girl?'

I had no option but to join in. I had to take control. I knew Elton better than anyone, at least I thought I did. I had to take the lead.

'Elton. Look at me. Which girl?'

'Girl at the bus stop.'

I shot Harry a blank look, before saying, 'I think I know what he means. Elton, you mean the young girl in Acton, outside the amusement arcade? You mean her?'

'Smelled like her.'

'Harry. This is the case I was telling you about.'

'The indecent assault in Acton?'

'Yeah. They've put it on hold depending on the outcome of this. It was the Thursday before he was nicked in Eastbourne. It's why he was already at the bail hostel.'

'Yes, I know. You've shown me the papers.'

'Of course I have. Sorry...'

'But what's this got to do with it? He must mean perfume or something?'

Harry turned to Elton again. He took his glasses off and smiled reassuringly.

'Elton, you remember the day Jim saw you in Acton police station? That day... you're talking about that day and that young girl?'

Elton looked genuinely puzzled, as if his own memory was playing tricks. Harry tried again.

'Or do you mean a car you travelled down to Eastbourne in a few days later?'

'Yeah. Perfume, yeah.'

Harry was on the scent now, pardon the pun. And once he'd got the scent…

'Would you recognise it again? The smell?'

'Yeah.'

'Good. Well, that's something. So the car's aroma was that of perfume.' Harry muttered the last section to himself as he made a written note on his typed instructions. Harry then turned to me, looking genuinely excited.

'This is good stuff, Jim. If Elton can remember a car, one that he might have travelled down to Eastbourne in, then we've got another suspect... an alternative for the jury.'

'Have we?' I asked, feeling a sudden sore throat as I swallowed.

'Well, it's *something*, isn't it? The jury will have *something* to think about at least. They're not going to think he was the driver, surely? I wouldn't have thought they'd rate his chances of negotiating a trolley around a supermarket, let alone driving a car down to the south coast!'

Harry's quip made me smile, albeit with a nervous disposition. He prompted Elton a little further.

'Anything else? Anything else you remember?'

'No.'

'Whose car was it?'

Elton looked blank.

'Who *drove* it?'

Elton looked blank again. It was time for him to start rummaging into his nose. He yanked away at a stubborn bogey. Harry either didn't notice or didn't care. He was still asking questions, and with a more purposeful voice.

'Do you know who else was in this car? Try and think, Elton.'

Elton slowly shook his head. Thank you, I silently thought. Enjoy your bogey, you deserve it. Then Elton suddenly started humming, and playing air guitar.

'Da da di da di da da da da da da...'

Shit! He was doing *Black Dog* again from *Led Zep Four...* and doing it well. I couldn't look Harry in the eye.

'Music? There was music in the car? Well, we are making progress, Jim.'

I had to say something, and managed a weak, 'Yeah.'

Harry was getting increasingly excited.

'Do that again, Elton. That song.'

'La da di da di da da da di di da da...'

My eyes darted from Elton to Harry and back again. Then I tried to look as blank as Elton, but I think I probably looked terrified. Harry started to repeat Elton's humming under his breath.

'I'm not sure who's going mad here, Jim. You know, I think I half recognise that.'

'Really?' I barely managed.

'Well, don't *you*?' Harry asked.

'No. Don't think so...'

I could hear Ken shouting in my ear.

-Liar!

Ken's intrusions were unbearable. One minute he was warning me not to say anything stupid, the next he was mocking me. Meanwhile, Harry patted Elton on the arm.

'Good Elton. Keep thinking. This is good. The music and the perfume. At least that adds credence to your account of a car. What else? What else, Elton? Anything else you remember?'

'Music...'

'Music, yes. Anything else?'

'No. Was asleep.'

'Asleep?'

'Dreaming.'

Harry then looked a little disconsolate. He shot me a glance, expecting me to share the disappointment. His voice was now forlorn.

'Oh, please don't tell me you're dreaming all this. Elton?... Elton?'

Elton went strangely quiet. He probably couldn't make much sense of it himself. He probably had a subconscious memory, perhaps of a brief period when he might have woken up. He probably thought he was dreaming, at least those were the hopes I was clinging onto. Then he started to roll his eyes around and was playing the part to perfection. I needed to build on the moment and turned to Harry.

'It could just be Elton's mind playing tricks.'

'I guess it could. We'll move onto something else, but I need more time with him, Jim. What's all this about a car?'

'No idea.'

'Has he got friends who drive him about? Associates?'

'Not that I know of.'

'Well, if necessary I'll have to explain to the judge and ask for more time. I've got to make sure one way or the other. Because if it *is* reality, any of it, we've got to pull our fingers out.'

I sat there trying not to show my feelings, though I doubt if there was enough room on my face to express them. Ken was fighting his way through to the front again.

-It's no good going back, Jimbo. It's happening, 'right here, right now' as Fat Boy Slim might say.

-Not now, Ken. Go away!

-You created this monster, Jimbo. You have to keep control of him. Can't have him bursting out of the dungeon and scaring the good townspeople.

Harry was using the break to re-read one of the prosecution statements. I remember looking at him, and thinking: Oh, Harry, what have I done? I love Elton. I've spent years looking after him, finding him homes, keeping him out of trouble. I've made him countless cups of coffee, each with six heaped teaspoons of sugar. I've even let him sleep in the office when he's been homeless. I've blamed the police, probation, social services, medics, the law makers, anyone and everyone who's stood in the way of getting this guy the help he needs. Now Jim Harwood, criminal lawyer of no little regard, is letting down the very client who has placed such trust in him.

My body was damp and rotting. I could see my carefully crafted veneer peeling away.

CHAPTER 24

On Christmas Eve 2011 I received a postcard. It was postmarked Perth, Western Australia. She gave me her flight number and the estimated time of her arrival at Heathrow in a fortnight's time. The postcard ended, 'I might be able to arrange transport, but if I can't, and of course if you don't mind, I might ask if you can pick me up. I'll email you. I've still got your email address. Bye, see you in the New Year. Love, Sarena.'

I didn't know what to make of it. Perhaps she had really been in Australia? How had she faked the postmark? What was the point in all the artifice? Then it dawned on me that I'd never given her my email address. Where had she got that from? I felt a pulse of anger at her, for hurting me, but it was washed away by the notion that it was still the best Christmas present imaginable. I was going to see Sarena again. The tingle went all the way down to my toes.

The actual Christmas period of 2011 was horrid. Try as I might, I just couldn't get Sarena out of my head. I ached to be with her, and just wanted each day to zoom by on fast forward.

Loren had badgered me that it wasn't the done thing to spend Christmas Day alone. So I had Christmas lunch with Loren's mum and dad in Reigate. It was pleasant enough. Loren's parents were okay, and her brother wasn't quite the bum she had painted him to be. He did cheat at Trivial Pursuit, though, and would furtively glance at answers when he thought nobody was looking.

After lunch we went for a walk in the woods with their family dog Jake, who was a Basset hound with a pleasing demeanour and ridiculously large ears. Loren told me that her mum thought I was quiet and withdrawn over dinner. I tried to argue, saying that at least I'd put on the silly paper hat from the Christmas cracker. Truth was, I was withdrawn and thoroughly preoccupied, but couldn't admit as to why.

When the subject had cropped up, as it inevitably did, I had to skirt around the issue of family. I told them that my mum had died when I was seven and that my father couldn't cope and had left me with an aunt. I felt awkward as hell. I really wanted to tell them that my father had killed my mother, then ran off with another woman and the proceeds of his crimes, but I wasn't sure that would rest well on top of two tons of turkey and Christmas pud.

On Boxing Day I went home and stared at Sky Sports for hours on end. I don't even know what I watched, and did so in some sort of inane trance. The following day I went into work. I even worked the next weekend and then every single day right through to Wednesday 4th January 2012, when I was expecting to see Sarena. I caught up on all the time I'd lost, and was so up to date that for the first time ever I actually had no backlog of work.

I wished then that I hadn't erased Sarena's old mobile number from my phone. Mind you, it seemed defunct anyway and the number she'd left that text on, the day she was supposed to fly out to Australia, was sent from a blocked phone. After that, all I ever got was that one email, confirming all her 'return' travel details. Of course I wrote back, but never got a reply.

On the drive to Heathrow I hated myself for going, for taking part in the whole charade. I waited for ages in the arrivals lounge. The place was crammed. There were the usual assembly of folk holding names written on boards, waiting patiently for their passengers. Sarena was supposed to be arriving on a stopover flight from Perth. Supposed to be…

I was in the process of poking my head about, trying to spot her coming through arrivals, when I felt a tap on the shoulder.

'Jim. Didn't you see me coming through?'

I smiled, because I knew she'd have to say something like that.

'No, obviously not.'

Sarena kissed my lips with a gentle peck. I tried not to let it affect me, but it was if someone had gently brushed my face with a silk scarf.

'How are you?' she enthused.

'Yeah, fine thanks. Here, I'll take that, you must be tired. Long flight?

'Don't ask. I need a bed and about two days' sleep. Come here, Jim. Hug me, hug me hard, please.'

I hugged her hard. I wrapped my arms around her and kissed the back of her neck. She was wearing a patterned silky dress with big sunflowers on it, which finished just above the knee. She had skin as smooth as glass, big shiny brown eyes, a smile made in heaven (or hell), a hint of pinkish lipstick, and a caramel perfume with a deliciously sublime scent.

I had to admit, she looked just about as beautiful as a young woman could. Not bad, I silently jested, not after a flight of some twenty hours or more.

As I drove through the Heathrow tunnel and headed into London town, I kept glancing across at the girl. I had to pinch myself that she was really there. I had to admire her, this hostess of inveiglement. She was a true professional, not one of those uninspiring little farts I come across day after day. No, she was an immaculate little beauty who could charm the pants off a born-again Christian. One sworn to celibacy too.

I wondered what she planned to do to me. What did I have? A good job, a half-decent salary, and not a lot else really. Mind you, Giles wasn't exactly wealthy, and he was conned out of a few grand. Someone like Norton, though, could easily be a millionaire, so why bother with small fry? Shame I couldn't ask her really. Why couldn't I? Because I wanted to find out for myself. I wanted to see how it all unfolded, and didn't want to rely on Sarena's lies… and of course I wanted her, in all her glib and garrulous glory.

Anyway, what could be worse than stopping a race a furlong from the line and being told who the winner was? Where was the fun in that? And how could you trust the bastard who told you?

I guessed that Sarena had dug a little deeper than normal.

Whatever her plans to rip me off, I felt that she was genuinely pleased to see me. Genuinely pleased to kiss me and touch me and just be with me. Okay, so if we'd been spiders she'd have made love to me and eaten me, but she'd have done so with relish, I'm sure.

As we flew up Shepherd's Bush Road, Sarena was looking gaspingly gorgeous. She was just sitting there with her luggage on the back seat, playing the part of the international traveller to perfection. I guess she thought that Giles wouldn't be stupid enough to say anything about their little escapade, and in any event, as far as she knew, Giles was just a another barrister, just someone I happened to have a case conference with on the day we met, someone no longer connected to the legal hinterland.

As we turned onto the Marylebone Road I asked about her plans.

'So, what's on the agenda now?'

'I'm starting my course soon. Father's paying for me to do my final exam.'

'And after that?'

'What do you mean?'

'What are you going to do with yourself?'

'Father's rented out Albany Street for me.'

It was hardly an answer, but I let it go.

I paused at the Baker Street lights, looked into her eyes, and smiled. She no doubt took it that I was admiring her beauty. I was, but I was also marvelling at her instant responses, and her ability to deceive with such aplomb.

'So what about your stuff? You know, furniture, and bits and pieces. Have you kept it all?'

Sarena paused before answering.

'Everything I had before? It's been in storage. One of Father's friends has fitted it all out again.'

Another wonderful lie, I felt, but didn't dare betray as much.

'Very nice... very nice, I'm sure. We're not going to have too much time together, are we?'

Sarena's look suggested that she hadn't followed my drift.

'If you've got studies to do, I mean.'

'But we can still see each other...'

The prospect cheered me, though I doubted that even Sarena could keep the prevailing pretence blowing for long. Quite spontaneously I came up with a plan.

'Why don't we go out for dinner tomorrow?'

'I can't.'

'Friday?

'I can't, Jim.'

'Oh,' was as much as I could manage in disappointment. Sarena seemed distracted, apprehensive even.

'What's wrong?'

'Nothing.'

'Sarena, I've been a criminal lawyer for twenty years. Don't tell me nothing's wrong.'

'Next weekend, maybe...'

'What? You'll see me next weekend?'

'If I can.'

'Okay...'

I'd been planning my next announcement for some time.

'How about we go to the Oasis?'

Sarena looked at me and then quickly looked away again, as if she hadn't time to form the correct expression. I deliberately stayed silent, waiting for her to speak.

'What do you wanna go there for?' she said, in a manner that momentarily betrayed her cover.

It wasn't quite as posh as her other lines. I'd never thought it strange before, because she had this sort of international accent. There was a base, albeit a thin one, of the sub-continent – a slight twang that could have been Australian or South African – and a gloss of Queen's English. Every now and then there was the slightest of slips, as if she'd forgotten who she was speaking to, but you had to have a very acute ear to detect it. I have to say that had I not actually met Sarena I would have doubted that such a chameleonic creature could exist.

By the time I was helping Harriet Houdini and her luggage up the stairs of her Albany Street flat (although neither of them had been anywhere near thirty thousand feet), I knew I was getting hooked again, like the bait I was. I was the maggot, the little grub on the end of the line, and I'd put myself there by choice.

There was one slight blemish though: she'd forgotten the labels.

She'd put on address labels, but not made the ones the checking-in staff stick over your handles, good old LHR. I wanted to point it out to her, should she make the same mistake again, with Norton or whoever. Anyway, what a palaver it was. I must have been mad, but within seconds of setting eyes on Sarena again I was more excited than a child on Christmas morning.

That's how I renewed acquaintance with Sarena again. Only, of course by this time life was a little more complicated: Loren was on the scene.

CHAPTER 25

After the worrying conference with Elton in the cells, I went to the canteen, in need of a coffee. I was happy to take in as much caffeine as I dare, to get me through the day. Harry was just finishing a chat with the prosecution barrister, Raymond Lefevre. That little session with Elton had really disturbed me. I knew that I was in for one hell of a battle.

Harry walked over. He told me that Prosecution weren't objecting to the interview being played to the jury. The audio tape, that is. They normally just have the transcript read out. Harry was smiling, as he told me how Lefevre found it odd that the Defence wanted the jury to listen intently to an interview in which their client fully confesses to a brutal murder. Well, it was odd, but I knew there must have been a method in Harry's brand of madness.

Harry went to see Judge Llewelyn-Davies in his chambers, to explain that he needed more time with his client. The judge agreed to put the case back to two o'clock. I asked Harry if he'd like to have coffee. He said he would, and a chat too.

I fetched a couple of coffees from the canteen and we went off in search of an empty conference room. On the way, we passed Loren and Jessica. Harry and Jessica knew each other well, but I assumed he'd never met Loren before.

'Harry, this is my colleague Loren. She's covering a case for me in Court Five.'

'Pleasure to meet you, Loren.'

'Pleasure to meet you, too, Mr Douglas.'

Loren smiled. She had a look to accompany it too, but it was one I couldn't quite fathom.

'Anything interesting?' added Harry, who was as polite as ever. Loren smiled back at him again.

'Attempted armed robbery. Yes, it is actually, all about ID and facial mapping.'

'Sounds intriguing,' quipped Harry.

Jessica then chipped in with her two-penny's worth.

'We've got a battle of the experts, and may the best man win.'

Harry smiled at Jessica's 'jolly hockey sticks' approach. He then checked a message on his mobile, as Loren glanced at me, quietly enquiring, 'How's it going?'

'Fine, yeah. We're put back 'till two o'clock.'

Loren nodded in response, by which time Harry had finished checking his text message.

'See you later, then. Nice to meet you, Mr Douglas.' Loren was chirpy but polite in tone.

Loren and Jessica moved off towards the lifts. I walked on with Harry, along the corridor from the new part of the building to the old. I couldn't believe just how cool Loren was. I wanted to say, 'Oh, by the way, Harry, that was one of the real murderers, only it was an accident, you see.'

Harry and I eventually found an empty conference room on the first floor. I had genuine respect for the man, and couldn't quite believe that I'd got him involved in all this. I held on to the hope that if anyone could wangle a manslaughter verdict, it would be Harry. He still had that air of concern in his voice.

'There's *something* about this case, Jim...'

Harry paused for reflection. I joined in with, 'Yeah, I

know...'

Then Harry let out a few of his thoughts.

'We might be able to have a go at the forensics. There's an argument to be had about the spray of blood, or lack of it. You'd expect Elton's clothes to have a spray of blood, not just a smear, if he was the knifeman. That's always bugged me. What else?... The journey, of course. How the hell he is supposed to have got down to Beachy Head, heaven knows...'

I smiled in response, barely interrupting Harry, who was in full flow.

'...The Crown are going to get his arrest in, on the Thursday before, when you went down to Acton with him. The indecent assault allegation is a killer. The jury are going to love that!'

'It doesn't help, does it?' I offered.

'No, and I'll *try* and keep it out, but I reckon Lefevre's got me on that one. It goes towards motive, a possible sexual assault... and in any event they're going to have to know that he was staying at the bail hostel over that weekend.'

'Yes, I know. Doesn't look good, does it?'

'The knife's never been found. That's something the prosecution will have to deal with. You know?'

Harry was deep in thought. Whenever he said 'you know' and then stared right through you, he was in very deep thought.

'What is it?' I asked reticently.

'What was *she* doing there? We're not in a position to say, and the Crown aren't in a position to say either, what *she* was doing... Miss Gunasekera. Fact just appears to be that she was there, on the Sussex coast.'

'Harry, you've lost me. Of course she was there, she was found dead at the bottom of the cliff.'

'But what was she *doing* there? Why did she go down to Sussex in the first place?'

'Well, we don't know. Does it *matter*?'

'I don't know. She was found in a black velvet party

dress...'

Harry was lost in thought again. He was thinking something, and there was quite a pause before he elaborated further.

'Naturally, we've concentrated on what Elton was doing there. Not what the victim was doing there.'

'How does *that* help us, anyway?'

'Well, if – and I know it's a big if, and a pretty remote one – but *if* they are going to consider the possibility that it wasn't Elton, then they're going to ask themselves, well, who was it, then? Sorry, Jim, I'm just thinking aloud. I try not to spout tautologies, but it's either somebody else she knew or a stranger. The loner, the mass murderer, the serial killer yet to be caught, etc. We're drawn to the latter, aren't we?... Drawn there because we know so little about the victim.'

I was concerned about where Harry was going. The last thing I needed was somebody poking their nose deeper into Sarena's affairs. The prosecution didn't have to, because as far as they were concerned they had their man. I really didn't want Harry advising that the defence should start sniffing about retrospectively. I took up the point with him:

'What do we normally know about victims? Just the basics, unless it's particularly relevant to the crime. She was twenty-seven, educated, intelligent, lawyer-to-be... according to her father's statement.'

'I'm wondering if we should ask him to be called?'

The comment sent a shockwave through me.

'You told me to tell the CPS we didn't need him.'

'Mmm, I'm not sure...'

Instinctively I felt that calling Mr Gunasekera, or more likely the fake Mr Gunasekera, would open up a can of worms... a can I'd come crawling out of. I posed to Harry:

'What are the jury going to make of that? There's enough sympathy for the poor girl as it is, without dragging her father halfway across the globe just to have him reminded of his daughter's death.'

Harry thought for a few seconds.

'You could have a point there. Yes, you're probably right, Jim.'

Inwardly I felt a huge *phew* race through my body. Harry suddenly gathered up all the papers in his brief and tied them back together.

'Right... so we'll just have to go for the madman motive. Sarena was killed by a stranger...Not Elton, another stranger. Then for some reason he got involved, which is why there's a smear of blood on his clothes.'

Harry had jolted my brain into top gear. I had to stay sharp. I had to play my role to the full, with a fair degree of skill and flair, and a decent smattering of ball control. I needed to remind Harry of a few cold realities.

'It's hopeless, isn't it?... That bloody interview. Really, what are we doing? The interview alone is enough for a conviction.'

'You know what, Jim: if it was just the interview alone, I think I'd get him off.'

'Really?'

'I'm going to deal with the interview. Elton's psychiatric condition might just be to his advantage on that one. And I was going to say before, about the knife... why wasn't it found?'

'It could have been dumped anywhere. Thrown out to sea, in a bin, could be on the perch of a cliff for all we know.'

Harry paused for thought again, before his next little sermon.

'There was a thorough search of the area. I suppose it could be sitting at the bottom of some distant rubbish tip right now. That's the whole problem with this case. They assumed they had their villain, had their murderer. *Fait accompli*... you know, it's so much easier to defend a murder case when there's a bigger gap in time between the murder and the defendant's arrest.'

'Yes, I know what you mean, Harry.'

'You're sounding like Frank Bruno, Jim.'

I was taken aback by the quip. Though I was well used to Harry's little asides, my nerves were too brittle to cope. Harry ignored my vacant look and carried on musing.

'I'll play on the journey. There's no sightings of him on a train, no evidence that's how he got down to the coast. He doesn't hold a driver's licence, and I'm not sure what all that stuff was about a car. Like I say, one look at him and the jury will doubt he could negotiate his way around a supermarket, let alone drive a car around the roads of Britain. So we'll certainly play on that. Right...'

Harry was getting up a head of steam, and the tempo in his voice was increasing.

'One minute he's tucked up in a bail hostel in Shepherd's Bush, and a couple of days later he's allegedly on a cliff top on the south coast. And we'll play on the blood stains. The lack of spray evidence. I think that's important. What else? Come on, Jim. This is your baby.'

'My baby. My baby...'

Harry looked at me curiously.

'Are you sure you're all right, Jim?'

'Yeah...'

Harry continued, 'The sack... Where did he get that from?'

I couldn't help another swallow.

'In fact why bother to tie her up in two bin-liners, and then cover her in a sack? I've always found that odd. Where did he get them from?'

'I've no idea,' I replied, in a tone which was meant to add to the intrigue. 'Why kill her at all?'I continued.

Harry joined in with the conundrum. 'It's a merry-go-round Jim, isn't it?'

Despite Harry's bouts of enthusiasm, he knew that getting any sort of result for Elton would be a tough nut to crack. Then, quite suddenly, he changed tack.

'I'm surprised the Met dealt with this case. Why did the Scotland Yard murder squad get informed, anyway?'

'I guess her father's phone call went through to them.

Then they liaised with the Sussex Constabulary.'

'I'll see what Lefevre has to say about it. Anyway, maybe someone else had a motive.'

'Such as...?' I regretted asking.

'Well, given that her father held a prominent position in Sri Lankan society... It's not the most stable of countries, Jim.'

'You mean... like a terrorist threat?'

'Could be. Could be business-related, could be blackmail. We really should think a bit more about the victim. I knew there was something in the back of my mind. One minute.'

Harry jumped to his feet, as he always did when he'd just injected himself with a new line of enquiry. As he opened up the door, Lefevre and the woman from the CPS just happened to be passing. I listened in to Harry's conversation with Lefevre.

'Raymond, quick word, please. The victim's father, why did he...?'

Lefevre interrupted, 'Let me just stop you there, old chap. I'd just come looking for you actually. Strange that you should mention Mr Gunasekera. The old boy's dead. Just heard ourselves. Road traffic accident, apparently, some weeks ago, but it's only just filtered through. Doesn't affect things one way or the other as far as we're concerned, but I was going to ask you if you still agree to his statement being read out?'

Harry rubbed his chin.

'Well, I don't suppose we have much choice now.'

Lefevre's look reflected the fact that he failed to see Mr Gunasekera's relevance.

'He wasn't ever a fully bound witness, was he? You weren't going to ask us to call him?'

'No... no. I'll catch up with you later, Raymond.'

Harry scuttled back into our conference room, aware that I'd overheard the news.

'Well, there you are.'

I was lost in thought, and half whispered to Harry,

'...Dead?'

'Sorry?'

'Sarena's dad... dead?'

'Why do you say it like that?'

'No... just, nothing.'

'Go on, if you've got a theory, Jim, I could do with hearing it.'

My mind was racing. Stomach cramps kicked in again, hindering my thoughts. And scary thoughts they were, too. Something stank, absolutely stank. I felt hopelessly out of my depth. I dared not voice any of this with Harry, and finally said, 'I don't think I have a theory, actually.'

'Well, some use you are,' Harry jested, before continuing, 'We'll see what DCI Litton has to say. I'll play it by ear. If you gave me a pound for every time I said that...'

'I'd be even poorer than I am now.'

'Exactly. Right. Work to do. Let's go and see if Elton can remember any more about this phantom car journey... Oh, by the way, his father's in the canteen. Will you just pop in and say hello?'

'Yes, of course.'

'I'll see you downstairs in ten minutes.'

Harry headed for the cells. I didn't want to be away from him for too long. I worried about Elton remembering something, and saying it to Harry when I wasn't there. I had to say hello to Elton's old man, though. It was the done thing.

In the lift on the way downstairs I cursed myself. I'd nearly blown it. I called the victim 'Sarena', for one thing. Shouldn't do that. I couldn't help thinking about Sarena's dad, though. Something mighty odd was going on, but there wasn't time to think. As I walked into the public canteen, the dad I had to focus on was Elton's.

Mr Spears Senior – or Constantine Ignatius Spears, to give him his full title – was sticking out like a sore thumb. Elton really was a chip off the old block. His old man was decked out in almost identical fashion. There must be a second-hand shop in north-west London somewhere that does a hell of a business in old brown pin-stripes. Mr Spears was sitting at a table, alone with his polystyrene cup. He recognised me and stood up to shake my hand.

As I sat down I noticed Loren with Jessica at a nearby table. I guessed they'd probably got underway on Matty's case and broken early for lunch. As I stared across at Loren, I explained as best I could to Mr Spears about what was happening and the reasons for the delay. Mr Spears then said something to me about that weekend. The weekend of Elton's arrest.

He was very difficult to understand, and had lost none of his thick Jamaican accent. Though he was a man of few words, even the ones he did utter were often incomprehensible through drink. He reeked of lager. Making a big effort to make himself understood, he produced a can of Crucial Brew from his inside pocket, as if to explain the aroma. As he poured some into his polystyrene cup he mumbled, 'You look after him, man. I like you.'

'He's a good guy, Elton. I like him too. We'll do our best, Mr Spears, but it doesn't look good.'

'You look after him, man. You always come to see him.'

'I try to, yes.'

I was pulsating with guilt, hating the conversation. Mr Spears looked me in the eye.

'You see him in de police station, man... in de Scrubs... you see him in de hostel too.'

'Sorry?'

I wasn't sure what he meant.

'In de hostel, man. In Shepherd's Bush. Last time he was free. Yeah, on that Sunday, man. I came to visit him at de hostel. He'd gone, man... then I saw him by McDonald's. He was getting in your car.'

I sat there, traumatised and stapled to my chair.

'Yeah, in your car. You give him lift somewhere. You're a good man, Mr Harwood.'

I could feel my knees knocking together. What Mr Spears

had said was well and truly sinking in. It was panic stations again – another brief glimpse of that monster fish that jumps out of the sea at the beginning of *Stingray*; another dose of the credits voice-over saying, '*Anything can happen in the next half hour*'...

I got up from my chair and scurried over towards Loren. She was in the middle of her lunch with Jessica. I spoke a little too anxiously.

'Sorry. Loren, something urgent. Sorry.'

Loren knew instinctively that it was heavy. I could see it in her eyes. She also looked a touch embarrassed, as if she thought I was stupid enough to say something in front of that good egg Jessica Strong. She made her excuses with Jessica and followed me out into the corridor.

We found a quiet corner by the huge stairway window and nestled in among the giant net curtains, all greying at the edges. I tried to slow down, but failed dismally.

'That bloke in there is Elton's dad.'

'I guessed that. So...?'

'He knows I took Elton down to the coast.'

'What?'

'I mean, he knows that I picked him up that Sunday. He was on his way to visit him at the hostel. Reckons he saw me... I mean saw *Elton,* getting into my car.'

'Just calm down, Jim... so he doesn't know you took him to Beachy Head?'

'No, no, but what with Elton rambling on... hell, I'm supposed to be in the cells now.'

'All right. Listen. Take a breath. Calm down.'

Loren put her arms around me and held me. It was most unexpected. She then clasped onto my hand by her side. Someone was passing by, a copper I think, a DS from Paddington Green. We must have looked like two lovers arguing. Perhaps we were. Loren was still trying to placate me.

'Whatever you do, whatever, it will be worthless if you don't keep calm. Who the hell is going to ask Elton's dad after all this time? I mean, if the defence don't ask him, nobody else will.'

'Yeah. You're right.'

'And whose job is it to ask him?'

I knew what Loren was saying.

'Mine, I know. I know.'

'So nobody's going to find out, are they? Pull yourself together. Elton's going to be convicted, Jim. You know it, I know it, Mr Douglas knows it, and pretty soon the jury will know it. All right?'

'All right. You're a brick, girl, you really are. I'm going to the cells. See you later.'

By the time I got to the cells, Harry was already talking to Elton. I opened up the booth door and walked in. Elton was looking at me. So was Harry.

I wanted to know what they were thinking. They both paused for a couple of seconds. My mind was speeding... Oh my God, what's he said? What has the deranged teddy-bear said? Has he remembered something crucial? Has my own client stitched me up? Should I confess now?...

Elton was smiling. His huge white teeth were sparkling. He seemed to be enjoying the hubbub, enjoying being the centre of attention. The whole thing was crazy. Harry addressed me.

'Elton's been trying to recall a little more about his Genevieve.'

'His what?'

'His jaunt down to the south coast.'

I couldn't quite place Harry's reference at first. Then I remembered the old film with Kenneth More, and eventually responded.

'Well, that was Brighton. This is Beachy Head.'

'Is it? Are we saying that? Eastbourne, surely, not Beachy Head? Not on our instructions. Our instructions are that although we were arrested in Eastbourne we've never actually been to Beachy Head.'

'Well, yes, of course. I meant Eastbourne. So what else

have you remembered, then, Elton?'

Elton immediately started to hum.

'La da di da di da da...'

Harry looked at me with a radiant smile – a sort of Eureka. I weakly tried to return the same, but my stomach had just collided with the floor. I just about managed to get the words out.

'You, er... you recognise that song, don't you, Harry?'

'Of course I do. And so do you, Jim. You've got that one, haven't you? It's Led Zeppelin.'

'Yeah, I think it is. Yeah. Bizarre.'

I turned nervously towards Elton.

'Where, erm... where did you hear that, then, Elton?'

Elton repeated the snippet, only this time he was really getting into it, *and* remembering some of the lyrics. I flipped.

'All right, Elton. That will do.'

I was too sharp in my rebuke, which Harry noticed.

'No, Jim, let him finish.'

Elton went quiet. He felt the tone of my voice and it seemed to upset him. Elton never coped well with raised voices, and I'd seen him cry before in situations like that. I didn't want him to cry. He started to rock gently from side to side again. I silently hoped he might be rocking himself to sleep, but no, he piped up again, this time with the sung chorus of *Riders on the Storm.*

If it hadn't been so serious, I would have burst out laughing. If you took one look at Elton and was told he was about to sing, you'd swear it would be some hip-hop, a gangster rap or something. But then Elton always was different.

Somehow Elton's warped brain had recalled the sounds of his journey to the cliff of death. Harry said exactly what I thought he'd say next.

'You've got that one too, Jim, haven't you?'

'*The Doors*?... Yeah'

I had to think of something else to say, and sharpish.

'You know what's happened here... Elton's been in my

car. That's where he's heard this stuff. I don't know why he's associating it with Eastbourne or Beachy Head or whatever, but that's where he's heard it. I've given him lifts home from court before, that sort of thing.'

'I see.'

Did he? Did Harry see? What did he see, exactly? Did he see a murderer sitting next to him? What would he do if he suspected me? What would Harry do if he thought, hang on, is Jim involved in this? Is Jim wrapped up in Sarena's murder? Ken was now trying to reassure me.

-Don't be silly, Jimbo. Don't let that old paranoia resurface.

Harry suddenly got to his feet.

'Right. Elton. I'll leave you here with Jim for a while. I've got some sorting out to do with the prosecution.'

Harry picked his papers up and left me alone with Elton. My brain was ticking over. What sorting out to do? What's he going to say to Lefevre? 'By the way, Raymond, I've got the real murderer instructing me in this case. I think you ought to drop the case against Spears'? Even Ken was momentarily overawed. He was screaming in my ear.

-Harry... don't shop us, Harry. We're going to die.

Harry disappeared down the echoing maze of corridors that run under the Old Bailey. Meanwhile, Elton was still quite buoyant. I wasn't really sure how to play it. I doubted whether aggression would work, and regret that I even tried, but in desperation I did.

'Elton. Will you shut the fuck up with this music shit, do you hear me?'

Elton wore his trademark grin. Then he started to blow out air through his nostrils, as if impersonating a hippopotamus.

'I don't want to listen to it again. Okay?'

But Elton just repeated the same riff as before.

I looked at him and shook my head. I took a deep breath and yawned. Funny how nerves make you yawn sometimes. Ken decided to criticise my tactics.

-Well, you didn't really think that shouting was going to work, did you, Jimbo? You could have put a submachine gun to Elton's head and swore blind that you'd pump him with lead if he uttered another sound, and he still would have done. You created this monster, Jim. You're stuck with him.

Harwood's monster, I reflected... The good townspeople below will be holding meetings and forming committees. They'll be marching onwards with candles in their hands, shouting 'kill, kill, kill the monster'. And they won't stop there, will they? These *Hammer House of Horror* devotees. No, they'll put the creator on trial, and they'll find him guilty. Oh, and it's a certainty, it's a certainty all right that he'll be executed. They'll cut off his head and impale it on the railings.

I'd been sitting there for what must have been thirty seconds, silently staring ahead. Elton was doing that thing with his nose. He can twiddle the end of it and make it look like a rabbit sniffing food. Then he'd blow air out of it. I didn't know what to say to him.

If he remembered anything about the beach hut, or worse still, if he saw me pulling the sack out of the boot on the cliff top, then... then it really was goodnight Vienna. Not for a second had I thought he was drifting in and out of consciousness. Loren had assured me that the drug, with some fancy name or other, would knock him out all night.

I started to speculate over what Harry was talking to Lefevre about. I glanced at my watch. It was ten minutes to two o'clock and the case was about to be called into court.

CHAPTER 26

On Thursday 12th January 2012, at around midday, I had two salient calls in quick succession. The first was from Sarena. She was confirming our date for the following evening, telling me that she was back from Edinburgh and that she'd like to meet first in the bar at the Marlborough Hotel in Holborn. I didn't question her choice of venue; I was just so glad that she was actually going to make it.

Then, no sooner had we finished our call than my office phone rang. Nellie was putting a call through from Acton police station. Elton had been nicked again, this time for alleged theft and indecent assault. By half past one on that Thursday afternoon I was in Acton seeing to Elton.

The officer dealing with the case was DS Hamilton, or Morag, as she was happy to be called. I'd dealt with her before, and we'd always got on well. She was a tough cookie on the outside, but quite a pleasant woman within, with a dry sense of humour. She had severely clipped hair, dark brown eyes, thin pencil-line eyebrows, pale white skin, and an impressive bosom that she struggled to keep locked behind her uniform. She also had a harsh Scottish accent, not at all like the tuning-fork tones of Jean Brodie. As I was led into the custody area, Morag heaved herself towards me.

'Mr Harwood, how are you?'

'Not so bad, thanks. Elton Spears, I understand?'

'Yes. Your client was arrested in Acton High Street this morning.

He'd been causing a disturbance in Playland.'

I wasn't quite sure what Playland was, and my look must have conveyed as much. Morag was happy to oblige.

'It's one of those high-street amusement arcades.'

'Right...'

'Mr Spears was singing or humming something.'

'Is that illegal?'

Morag threw me a look.

'He was doing it in people's ears.'

'Oh, I see.'

'One young girl was very upset. He was singing 'Somewhere Over the Rainbow', or trying to.'

'It's one of his favourites. He must have watched that film twenty times.'

Morag briefly smiled, but she had more to say.

'He followed her out and sang in her ear at the bus stop. Then she says he felt her breasts, and put his hand down his trousers.'

'Oh dear...'

'Exactly.'

I realised that Elton was in a fair bit of trouble.

'Something was mentioned about a theft allegation as well?'

'Yes. Spears was still at the bus stop when we arrived. He was searched. We found a packet of condoms and a copy of 'Deep Throat.''

'Is that a porn mag?'

'Well, it's not a spying magazine, let's put it that way.'

I returned the look, admiring her raillery. She continued:

'They were stolen from the newsagent next door to the amusement arcade. We've got a statement from the proprietor. Elton's on CCTV camera as well. In fact, he smiled at the camera before just walking out with the condoms and the magazine... You'll want a word with him, I'm sure?'

'Yes... Yes, I'd better. Are you aware of his background?'

'I've got Dr Greig coming as a precaution, but he seems fit enough to be interviewed. For what it's worth, he told me that the girl was his girlfriend and that he was going to marry her.'

'The old romantic.'

'Her mother is having seizures. She wants him strung up. There's

no chance of this being dropped. None at all... just so you know.'

Morag was always fair.

'Yeah... thanks.'

'Right. I'll just show you through to the cells.'

The custody sergeant gave her an 'all right, Morag, darling' sort of glance as he handed her some keys. Morag looked suitably bored. The sergeant then gave me a quick look when he'd finally finished ogling her substantial bosom. I ignored him and followed her to the cells. Morag opened up the cell door. We were both confronted by the same vision, and what a vision.

Elton had his trousers and pants around his ankles and was masturbating like a trouper. So engrossed was he that he carried on even when the cell door was opened. There he was, large as life, big brown eyes nearly bulging out of their sockets, a good head of steam going, and the sort of concentrated facial expression you usually see in an exam hall. And to top it all off he still had his pork-pie hat on.

Elton tutted before looking up. He wasn't best pleased about being disturbed. Morag dealt with the whole thing quite admirably.

'Mr Spears, stop that. Your solicitor is here.'

I was still staring, mouth open in disbelief, but I had to say something.

'Elton, please. There's a lady present. At least remove your hat.'

Morag was staring at the cell wall. She knew that if she looked at me, or Elton, she'd totally lose it. Her body was begging her to laugh. Meanwhile, Elton, calm as you like and with his hat still wedged on, bent down and pulled his trousers up, dragging both trousers and Homer Simpson boxers over the offending member. Then he sat down again... and smiled. I caught Morag's eye. She was moving her jaw about, still trying to stop herself from laughing.

Morag closed the big grey cell door and left me to my own devices with Elton. He was staring at the cold concrete floor. I walked over to him and sat on the end of the bench. I went to offer a handshake, but then thought better of it. I wasn't too sure what to say, but took the matter-of-fact approach.

'Finished wanking, have we?'

'Not finished.'

Elton looked genuinely peeved by the disturbance. I blew out a long sigh of disapproval, and he eventually bowed his head sheepishly in response. I needed a few seconds to pass to calm Elton down. I studied him at close range as he bowed his head further into his hands.

He was decked out in a second-hand brown pin-stripe suit, and from somewhere, God knows where, he'd found a security badge and stuck it to his lapel. It was like the badges people wear when they go to conferences or visit factories. It had the words 'Nigel Bates – Horizon Marketing' printed on it, and there was a tacky Horizon logo that looked like it had been designed by a failed art student. Elton also had a red handkerchief sewn into his top pocket, with a small triangle of red cotton sticking out.

When Elton did finally remove his hat, his curly locks reacted to the static, making them stick up in the air. Just for a moment he looked like Don King the boxing promoter – or to be more precise, Don King being electrocuted.

'Right, Elton. Forget about the... erm... you know, the erm, messing about downstairs. Forget about that for a minute. Let's talk about this morning. Do you know why I'm here?'

Elton, for once, had followed my speech. He looked a touch confused as he said, 'To see me.'

'To see you... yes, good answer, that. What I should have said is: do you know why you're here? Do you know why you've been arrested?'

Elton shrugged his shoulders, then fiddled about in his trousers.

'Well? The girl at the bus stop says you touched her. Did you?'

'I never.'

I opened up my bag to get my notebook out.

'Now, I want you to be honest with me, Elton. You remember our conversation about the nurse a few weeks ago?'

Elton pulled a face. He'd all but admitted to me previously that he'd sexually assaulted a nurse outside the Royal Free Hospital.

'This has got to stop, mate, for your own good if nothing else. There's no point lying, all right. Just tell me the truth. Tell me the truth and I'll try and help you. Now, do you remember singing to the girl at the bus stop?'

'Somewhere, over...'

I stopped Elton in his tracks.

'It's all right, I don't need you to sing it. So what happened? Did

you touch her?'

Elton put his hand down into his trousers, grabbed hold of the top of his boxers and pulled them up, so they were visible above the belt line.

'...Wanted to see my pants.' he suggested.

'Really? I don't think she did, did she?'

Elton twitched and blew out some air through his nose.

'My girlfriend.'

'She's not your girlfriend, Elton.'

'Not your girlfriend, Elton.'

I tried not to be irritated by Elton's habit of repeating my last words.

'Well, she's not your girlfriend, is she?'

Elton got up from the bench and paced around. He just walked around in a circle and sat down again. I tried all sorts of tactics but he wouldn't talk about it. He just wouldn't admit touching the girl. He was just as nutty as ever.

I sat in on his interview, but Morag Hamilton didn't elicit any more sense from Elton than I had. The custody officer refused to grant bail, and I could hardly blame him. So Elton was charged with theft of the condoms, the pornographic magazine, and indecently assaulting sixteen-year-old Kelly Fields. He was kept in Acton police station until the following morning, when he was taken to Ealing Magistrates' Court.

I was there to represent him, this being the morning of Friday 13th January 2012. I'm not usually superstitious, but it was the start of a weekend that would haunt me forever. I often wonder what I would have done had I not successfully argued for bail at court.

The prosecution weren't objecting to bail per se. They just wanted appropriate conditions, one of which was a review of his current psychiatric state, and residence at a special bail hostel in Shepherd's Bush. He wasn't exactly under lock and key there, but they were supposed to monitor his behaviour and keep a curfew on him. The only thing in his favour was that he didn't have a history of sexual offences. Well, not officially anyway, though I suspected he probably did.

When I left court that Friday morning, I drove Elton to the hostel in Shepherd's Bush. As I did so I received a text message from Loren. She was out all day on a witness visit in Essex. She said she'd be back late, but wanted me to know that she'd still meet me for last orders in the Swan pub. I'd totally forgotten the arrangement, and despite my planned meeting with Sarena texted her back with an 'OK'. To be honest, I planned to get out of it later.

I met Sarena, as arranged, at six at the Marlborough Hotel. I hated the feelings she stirred but couldn't do a thing about them. For some reason we got chatting about Loren. I'd mentioned her before in passing and Sarena had taken little interest. This time she was a little more curious, asking me things like how long I had known her, and whether I trusted her.

Though she tried to disguise it all as chit-chat, there was a definite edge to her. As ever, I didn't know whether to believe half the things she said.

'I start my course soon... it's going to be really hard work. I'm not going to have much of a social life.'

'So what are you saying? You're going to become a hermit... a slave to your studies?'

Sarena took a sip of her gin and soda.

'Well, yes. I suppose I have to.'

'Have you got all your stuff back in Albany Street?'

'Yes, apart…'

Sarena stopped mid-sentence. She tensed her hands up into balls of knuckles.

'Apart from what?'

'My laptop. It's missing.'

'Really? From the flat?'

'No, from storage. It wasn't there.'

There was something about the way Sarena was talking that I couldn't quite put my finger on. Sure, she seemed concerned that her laptop had been nicked, but there was something else bothering her too.

'And what else went?'

'Nothing.'

I paused and pondered…

'Someone broke into the storage place and only stole the laptop? What about that hi-fi? Must be ten grand's worth, and all the other stuff?'

'...Just the laptop.'

'How odd.'

I felt that she knew a lot more than she was saying, and thought I'd do a bit more digging.

'What did you use it for, anyway? The laptop?'

Sarena lost herself for a few seconds. She briefly smiled into my eyes – a particular smile, and one I'd never seen before.

'Work and... things...'

'So did you report it?'

'What?'

'The theft, the burglary, whatever it was.'

'No point, is there?'

'I don't know, why not? What about the insurance? If you don't report it to the police, get a crime number, then they won't pay out.'

'All right, don't go on.'

The only time I'd questioned her so rigorously was in the car on the way back from Bournemouth all those months ago. I carried on the cross-examination, and thought I'd try and throw her off-key.

'Suppose you've still got the old credit card then... Javita?'

'Of course.'

She'd answered quite matter-of-factly.

'Good, so you can buy us dinner...'

'At the Oasis, I know. I remember.'

She held out her hand and tickled the end of my fingers with hers. A bolt of current shot straight though my spine and down to my legs. I very nearly shed a tear in response. That wicked woman, I loved every inch of her. I worshipped her like a goddess. Right then I could have swallowed her whole.

And there was the ever-present dilemma with the gorgeous Sarena: when she was naughty, and that evening she was very naughty, I fancied her like hell. Despite everything I suspected about her, despite all the mendacity, I just couldn't fight the magic spell.

So we dined at the Oasis, and played and toyed all night. It was like Tom and Jerry: the tease, the chase, and the odd sprint into an oncoming frying pan. We both got high on the adrenaline, on the pulse of lies and deceit and quick-fire repartee. If it wasn't love that was the drug, it was something akin to it.

At around half ten I realised I'd blown it with Loren. I was supposed to see her at about a quarter to eleven. As I couldn't get through to Loren's mobile, the best I could do was leave a message at her flat. The answerphone kicked in, and I lied:

'Hi, Loren. I'm really sorry. I can't make it. I'm ill, must be something I ate. Take care. Don't bother phoning; I'm taking a tablet to knock myself out...'

Two large brandies later – Baileys in Sarena's case – and we were pretty pissed. Although we'd sent him away twice, the waiter came back a third time to ask if we wanted desserts. I had a crème brûlée; Sarena chose a raspberry pavlova.

'Sarena. Tell me. No hang on... let me tell you. No. Sorry, I was right the first time. You tell me... tell me what you think I know about you.'

'You know that I'm a bit of a tease.'

'Yes...'

'And that I... I don't know. What do you want me to say?'

'I want you to tell me the truth.'

And bless her, she couldn't help but form the outline of a smile. I melted into her eyes, and for the umpteenth time gazed at her sheer beauty. I mustered up a speech, and no doubt delivered it with a drunken slur.

'I know you're a scintillating little sham. I know that, but I want you to tell me – and this is a big but – but only if you're still prepared to see me. Understand? I don't care, you see. I did. God, I really did. You know when you went to Australia…?'

I couldn't help it; a wide smile cracked my face. Sarena was about to ask me why the subject of her Australia trip was so amusing when she scowled, grabbed hold of her stomach and said she had to use the bathroom.

She rushed off to the ladies' and seemed to be there forever. When she came back, she was very unsteady on her feet.

'Ugly bitch.'

'Who's an ugly bitch?'

'Some girl staring at me in the toilet.'

There followed a strange period of silence, only broken by Sarena mumbling something. Her eyes wobbled slightly as she stared right through me. Then, totally out of the blue, she piped up with a series of what seemed like random letters and numbers. She carried on mumbling the same, her words getting ever softer before she nodded to herself in satisfaction. I was totally thrown.

'Sarena, what on earth are you doing?'

'I haven't forgotten…'

'Forgotten what?'

Sarena tried to focus on my eyes, but failed.

'Little boxes,' she whispered to herself, before putting her head in her hands, apparently deep in thought.

'What are you going on about? What boxes?'

'Gordon will kill me. I never forget. Never.'

'What? Who's Gordon?'

Sarena raised her eyebrows at me, then let out a moan. I was getting worried.

'Are you okay?'

'Yeah.'

'Talk to me, will you?'

'I am talking to you. You've got lovely eyes, Jim. Sort of sexy.'

'Well, I suppose that's a compliment. Lucky old me.'

Sarena sidetracked the sarcasm and lowered her voice.

'I wish I'd never got into this.'

'Into what? Go on.'

'Maybe I could have been a lawyer, like you. I do actually like you, Jim, whatever happens.'

Sarena leaned back in her chair and yawned. It was one of those false yawns that I'd come to recognise.

'I'm drunk. I'm talking nonsense... C'est la vie, eh? Tu es un espece d'imbicile.'

'What a beautiful accent.'

'I have had practice... believe me, I have. I rogered the George Cinq. You know that?'

'Sarena, what are you on about now?'

'A rather posh hotel in Paris. Don't let me ever go in there again. I'd end up in French prison. No way, monsieur.'

'What did you do?'

'Rogered it, Jim. Dry.'

I was taking it all in. Trying to work out exactly what her admissions amounted to.

'Would I be a million miles away if I said you were some sort of conwoman?'

'Yes, you would. I'm not a conwoman. How awful... how base. I'm beautiful, aren't I, Jim? Kiss me.'

Quite instinctively I leaned forward, knocking over Sarena's already empty wine glass, and kissed her moist pink lips.

'No, you're not a conwoman... you're a beguiler.'

'A big what?'

Sarena smiled, wickedly, before adding, 'I know what it means.'

'My little Aqua Sarena,' I mumbled to myself.

She had no idea as to the mermaid reference. In fact, the very thought of her watching 'Stingray' made me smile. She swayed and hit her head on the padded back of her seat.

'Sarena. Don't nod off. Talk... talk to me, gorgeous, come on...'

'You don't hurt me, you don't hit me. Some of them fucking hit me, Jim. I'm...'

Sarena tailed off into silence.

I realised that it wasn't just the drink, and that she must have taken something else. She was losing her speech and rolling her head backwards and forwards. Then she'd spring into life just for a few seconds and blurt something out, and she was getting louder.

'They all want to fuck me...'

The couple adjacent looked over. Okay, perhaps there was something to be a tad disturbed about, but the woman looked like she was going to cry. I thought that unfair. It was like a footballer exaggerating a dive just to get the defender sent off. The last thing I needed was Sarena being expelled. This was a golden opportunity to find out what she was all about. She needed fleecing, so I ordered coffees.

'It's finished now, Jim. That's what I'm saying... you know, studies and that, it's all crap. I'm not really… I don't know what I'm saying. I didn't really want to hurt you. Fuck it.'

'Sarena... shh. Quieten down. Come on, have some coffee. I've never heard you like this. You lose your accent as well. You sound sort of English... I mean, normal English.'

Sarena let loose a little smile, before morphing into a serious look in a split second.

'You knew, didn't you? Why did you bother, then? Uh?'

Sarena grabbed my wine glass, which was still half full. She swirled some wine about before gulping it back, determined to empty that one too.

'Tell me something, Sarena. What's your real name?'

'Piss off.'

'What sort of a name's that?

The flippancy was purely spontaneous. I guess it was my wont at times, especially when on edge. Sarena then added, quite expressly, 'Everyone knows me as Sarena.'

Other questions were beginning to circle around in my mind.

'All right, what about that football match? Chelsea? I'm intrigued. Who did you go with?'

'You don't want to know.'

'So why did I ask you, then?'

I couldn't believe I'd said that. I'd scowled at her, spat at her, my beguiling beauty.

'I went with Kelvin.'

'Who's Kelvin?'

'The guy I've been with in Edinburgh.'

'Edinburgh?'

Sarena looked at me but couldn't keep her eyes focused on one place for long. She started to shift in her seat. Then she managed to compose herself and held a deep stare, cast many miles into the distance. She spoke in a whisper.

'I was taken there...'

It was the way she said 'taken' that was disturbing. She added, to confirm the point, '...Kidnapped, if you must know.'

'Christ, Sarena! Kidnapped?'

'Yes.'

'Why?'

'To get Gordon's stupid fucking numbers!'

'Clear as mud. Who's Gordon, for God's sake?'

'He'll kill me. Gordon the Goalie, he kills people.'

'Now what are you on about?'

'He forced me to... Kelvin forced me to...'

'To what?'

'Fuck off!'

That really stopped me in my tracks. Sarena swore with an accent born in south London. As I looked into her eyes, she was struggling to hold the expression. Sarena crashed her head into her folded-up arms, and spoke through a mouthful of wrist.

'Don't get involved.'

'In what? How did you really get those marks on your back?'

She looked up at me, flashing her eyelids and wearing a horribly insincere smile.

'A punter. Who do you think?'

'A punter? You mean...?'

'Of course I am, when I want to be. When there's no work on. Three hundred an hour, babe, that's me... fucking three hundred an hour.'

That was the final straw for old starchy-knickers next door. She left in a huff with Quentin following behind her. The waiter looked over knowingly. He didn't have to ask me to keep Sarena quiet. Just a nod of the head sufficed.

'Sarena, keep it down. You'll get us thrown out. I'll have to take you home.'

Sarena didn't respond. She was still wearing that fake smile.

'I don't believe you. I don't believe you're a... in fact, I don't believe anything you say.'

'Good!'

Sarena finally took a sip of coffee. Just for a moment I thought she was playing drunk, to deliberately distract me but then I saw her eyes wobble like the icons sometimes do on my iPhone. There were still things I desperately wanted to know, and sensed she was about to crash out.

'Just tell me this: who's Norton? And the other guy you went to the casino with? Does he look like Jeremy Paxman on the TV?'

Sarena turned pale and her eyeballs disappeared from view.

'Come on, Sarena, who are all these people? And what's this really about?'

'Don't fuck the goalie,' she maundered, before passing out, with her face crashing into the remains of her pavlova.

I had to get some assistance to help her into a cab. When the cab pulled up outside the Albany Street flat, I gave the driver a twenty-

pound tip and a request... and he helped me get her up the stairs.

She was comatose and didn't even stir when I took her shoes off and put her into bed. I discovered some small yellow tablets on her bedside table. I wasn't sure what they were. I looked through her handbag and around the flat but there was nothing to take the mystery any further. It was no good just knowing that Sarena had lied. I wanted to know so much more. I felt somehow that she was in danger.

I decided to have a look around Sarena's flat. I quietly opened drawers and cupboards and looked in a few bags. I guess I found out then what I'd long since suspected: the flat was just a front, somewhere to stay. There were hardly any personal items there at all, just the basics.

In her wardrobe were a couple of dresses, some nightwear, some underwear and two pairs of shoes. In her handbag were a host of credit cards: two in the Sarena Gunasekera's name, one in Javita Srinath's, and many others. Some had sub-continental surnames, others didn't. I wondered then where she really lived, who she really was, how many identities she really had, and how much she was worth.

I left Sarena to sleep it off and walked back to Adelaide Road. I thought about waking Loren up, but what would I say? Why should I be turning up at two in the morning smelling of brandy and cigarettes?

Anyway, I'd already made out that I was ill. No, it wasn't an option. I sat on my sofa and smiled in confusion... 'Who the hell is Gordon the Goalie?' I ran through a few things in my mind. I even tried to remember the names of Chelsea's goalkeepers and wondered for a second whether there might be some link there. I came up with nothing.

I was arguing with myself about how to play things with Sarena. I expected Ken to join in, but he'd gone strangely quiet. As I took off my clothes and cleaned my teeth, I thought about how beautiful Sarena was. Quite ridiculous really: she was a charlatan of epic proportions, and all I could think about was seduction.

I should have been thinking about Loren as well. It was one thing to carry on seeing Sarena behind her back, but I should never have let her down like that. Despite all the duplicity it was the first time I'd cocked things up so blatantly. The last thing I did that night, before crashing out into bed, was listen to my three answerphone messages. I yawned and pressed the magic button.

'Beep... Jim, it's Loren. Pick up the phone. Are you in? Where are you? I'm in the Swan. It's ten to ten. I'll get you a pint in.'

'Beep... Jim? Where are you? Your mobile's off. Are you all right? I'm at the Swan still. I'm going home now. Please phone me... I'm worried.'

'Beep... Oh hello, Jim. Me again. It's ten past midnight. Guess who's just phoned me? Gerry. I got your message. So sorry to hear that you're not feeling well. You shit. You lying little shit. Sorry, let me continue. Gerry's been to the theatre tonight. Guess where he went after... yes, you guessed... the Oasis... because I recommended it to him. He went there with his new girlfriend, who saw this oh-so-beautiful Indian-looking girl swallowing tablets in the toilets. And guess what: she went to sit at your table. I never want to speak to you again.'

CHAPTER 27

The Old Bailey – or 'Central Criminal Court', to give it its proper title – is a grand theatre of illusion, where all still dress in pantomime attire. It's a place where players revel in a daredevil game of truth or dare... and reluctantly, I was a player, in a complex game.

Lefevre had just finished his opening speech, and the first witness, Mrs Rita Brandon, was about to swear the oath. It was then that I suddenly stood up from the defence solicitor's bench where I'd been sitting, immediately behind Harry.

I could hear the words 'fuck off, it's me, I'm guilty' on their way between thought and speech, lost in a Tourettes no-man's-land. I stood there, briefly open-mouthed, causing the usher to cling onto the bible just before Mrs Brandon had a chance to take it. Harry turned around, glaring at me.

'What on earth are you doing...?'

'I'm sorry. Excuse me.' And with that I made my way towards the exit at the back of the court, desperate to escape into the waiting area outside.

Pausing briefly at the door of the court, I made a token gesture of bowing to the judge, in silent apology at my odd behaviour. When I turned to leave, the sight of Sammy's face hit me again. He was looking down from the front row of the public gallery. Sammy briefly shot me a look. One that I couldn't quite make out.

As I walked along the corridor outside court, another vision of the dead Sarena swarmed all over me. A sickly feeling wrenched my stomach and a haze of culpability unsteadied my gait.

I regained my balance again and moved on, taking a few delicate steps into the new part of the building. I paused by an unoccupied bench. I had this awful feeling that something was going to go terribly wrong. I sat on the bench, inwardly chastising myself.

An usher I recognised smiled at me warmly, as if to say *are you okay?,* and I forced a smile in return. Ken felt he had to chip in again, hissing in my ear with a caustic tongue.

-Oh Jim, how could you? You mad fool. You total bastard. What if it all goes wrong?

My chest tightened as I struggled for breath. I needed some fresh air to stop the nauseous feeling that was taking hold. I descended the main stairwell and headed for the swing door.

I stepped outside the Old Bailey to have a cigarette, removing a nearly empty packet from my briefcase. I noticed that my hands were shaking, and it took a good few seconds for me to fish out the little lighter that I'd squashed into the cigarette packet.

I'd found Lefevre's opening unsettling to say the least. I was perturbed by the ease with which these perfidious pictures could be painted. I was well aware, of course, that I'd set the canvas and provided the oils, but nevertheless the smoothness with which Lefevre outlined the facts and rammed home Elton's 'guilt' underlined just how malleable the criminal justice system could be.

I could hear a little voice in my mind. Not Ken, but another more benevolent one, saying 'what if it was someone evil rather than desperate? How many other poor sods are being fitted up with unarguable DNA?' As this was going on I could hear a real voice from behind.

'Jim, over here.'

The voice was calling me from outside the revolving doors.

'They won't let me in,' the voice continued.

I was being beckoned by Sammy Todd, and had no chance of avoiding him. Sammy was wearing a charcoal-grey suit, and could easily have passed for a QC. He must have just legged it down from the public gallery, and was still a touch out of breath.

'Only lawyers and court officials are allowed in there,' I told him, nodding towards the main body of the courthouse.

'I know.'

'What are you actually *doing* here?'

I tried to be as cheery as I could, despite all the turbulent trauma of Elton's case.

'What am I *doing* here?' Sammy mused back, more than a touch cryptically.

He had a locked expression, and was staring straight through me. I thought it odd at first, rather than threatening. I tried to read his face, but he held on to a fixed glare.

'How are you, anyway?' I carried on, while blowing out a plume of smoke in an attempt to calm my nerves.

'Fine, thanks.'

This was even more off-putting. He clearly didn't mean it, with his whole demeanour betraying him.

'I saw you in the public gallery in Court Two,' I said.

'I know you did.'

Sammy had many gifts, one of them being the gift of the gab, but he was deciding not to exercise it.

'What's wrong?'

'*Wrong*?' Sammy let the word resonate around his lips, and then smiled as he added, 'Nothing's *wrong*... is it?'

Sammy manufactured a smile, and then a nasal laugh, as he slapped me on the back with more force than you might expect.

'Why did you want to get into the building?' I asked.

'To see you, *mate*.'

Sammy's emphasis on the word 'mate' took me aback. It was as if he'd thrown it in my face.

'And here you are, having a smoke, so now I've seen you,' he added, with a disingenuous smile.

Sometimes Sammy was difficult to read, but at that precise moment he was indecipherable.

'Look, I know you've been trying to get hold of me.'

'Oh, if I'd wanted to get *hold* of you, Jim, I would.'

I felt my chest tightening as he said it. An unwelcome flush erupted on my face. I knew then that I was the object of his anger, but I didn't know why, or what I'd done wrong.

'What is it?'

Sammy interrupted before I could continue.

'I just need... to confirm a few things.'

I wasn't sure how to continue the conversation. All I could think was, 'please, Sammy, not here... not now'.

'Look, I'll be straight with you, Sammy. I'm up to my eyeballs with this case at the moment.'

'Murder.' Sammy suddenly spewed out, without any particular inflection.

'Yeah.'

'Murder of a Sri Lankan lawyer, by a choice nutter.'

There was something in the way Sammy delivered the line that made me baulk. He was as sharp as many an advocate, and the way he said 'choice nutter' totally threw me. In fact it was the word 'choice' that stood out. I had to take stock, and try and convince myself that I must be paranoid.

'Well, you heard the opening,' I prodded.

'Oh yeah, I heard it all right. Did he do it then, this bloke Spears?'

'Well, that's for the jury to decide. Why are you so interested?'

Sammy looked straight through me again.

'I asked you a question.'

All I could do was release a nervous smile as my mouth dried. Sammy's piercing look was as straight as a laser beam. I could feel it burning my eyes. Then he slowly started to nod his head, but not in a fashion that conveyed agreement.

'She...'

Sammy stopped abruptly. He must have seen Harry Douglas approaching us. I could have done without the interruption.

'She *what?*... *Who* what?' I asked, desperately trying to second-guess what Sammy was about to say.

'Your barrister wants a word with you, Jim.'

Sammy took a couple of steps back, but for a good few seconds didn't take his eyes off me. Harry was now stood where Sammy had been. He was opening up a packet of Dunhill International.

'We've adjourned for ten minutes. Judge probably needs a wee,' Harry announced to the world, in a jovial tone.

I half took in what Harry was saying, but I still had one eye on Sammy, who was now a few paces away, watching my every move. Harry continued.

'Why did you leave court after the opening? You missed Mrs Brandon.'

'Yeah, I didn't think she'd say any more than was in her statement.'

'But why did you suddenly stand up and leave like that? So... dramatically?'

'I don't know. I'm sorry.'

'Well, she did anyway. Have some more to say...'

'But she just found the body at the foot of the cliffs,' I added, as if that was all she was supposed to say.

'She said there was a shoe print on the sack – the sack the victim's body had been in.'

I didn't want to look Harry in the eye as I was trying to manufacture an appropriate response.

'Oh, right...' was all I came up with.

'She pointed it out to the officer after she'd dialled 999. It was sent to forensics, apparently. I haven't been given any statement about it, though.'

I swallowed a touch too obviously. It was a statement I'd kept from Harry. I had to think fast how to play it. A big lie, or a little lie? In fact, I went for playing dumb instead.

'No, sorry Harry, I didn't think it was relevant.'

'Relevant? Forensics say the shoe was a size eight, or forty-two in modern parlance.'

'And Elton's size ten, isn't he?'

'Indeed... or forty-four point five.'

Harry, being as thorough as ever, had obviously done his research.

'What I meant was that forensics have no idea where this sack came from, so there could have been a footprint on it from before.'

'*Could* have been, yes, but equally it could have belonged to whoever kicked her off the edge of the cliff.'

I went to speak but nothing came out. I had to force my thumbnail into the skin of my forefinger to stop myself from thinking of that awful moment.

'At least it was something to have a go at,' Harry continued. 'It certainly wasn't my footprint on the sack, was it?'

Anyone who has experience of the way criminal lawyers converse with each other will know that they often resort to the first person when referring to their clients. 'I'm a burglar with previous', for example, rather than 'my client is a burglar with previous'. Normally I'd take such comments in my stride, but in this instance it caused a shudder to run through me. The words 'it wasn't my footprint on the sack' kept repeating in my mind.

'If you don't mind me commenting, Jim, you seem a little preoccupied.'

That was Harry's way of saying 'get a grip and answer the bloody question.' I had to say something.

'You're right, of course. I should have realised you might have been able to use that. I'm sorry, Harry.'

I looked down at my own size eights and blew out a long

sigh.

'Well, you've had a lot on your plate with this one, Jim. Don't worry, nothing I can't deal with. I'll bring it out when forensics are on the stand. After all, Elton needs every little bit of help he can get.'

'Yeah, I know.'

'I mean, why kick the sack anyway? Why not use hands to shove her?'

'It was freezing cold,' I replied, with far too much feeling.

I looked at Harry. Had he picked up on it? He certainly threw his head back a notch as if to say 'that's a bit left-field...'

'I meant, the evidence suggests it was a cold January night, perhaps it was easier to kick the sack over the frost, if his hands were frozen. Elton's hands... allegedly.'

Harry was used to me talking with a far greater degree of clarity. He nodded a touch emptily and put his cigarette out, grinding it into the gutter with his heel.

'Come on, we ought to get back in.'

I followed Harry through the revolving doors so quickly that we nearly got stuck in the same partition. He must have thought I was behaving very oddly, and couldn't have known that I was keen to escape from Sammy.

Whenever going back into court, you have to go through security again. I was shaking with nerves, trying to open up my briefcase to get my solicitor's ID card out. I briefly glanced back to see Sammy, who was now glaring at me through the window. He gave a little forced wave, and it crucified me... that and the sardonic smile that accompanied it.

Harry and I both showed our ID and made our way back to Court Two. As I pushed past the velvet drapery for the umpteenth time, I felt a pulse of gut-wrenching guilt, as the iniquity hit home.

CHAPTER 28

Saturday 14th January 2012. I woke up with a thumping hangover. I played the messages again, just in case I had dreamed them in some awful nightmare.

I phoned Loren. There was no reply. She usually meant what she said. I hoped not. I didn't want to lose Loren. I wanted to explain things to her. I wanted to tell her the truth and nothing but the truth. Early afternoon, I went round to Loren's flat. Either she wasn't in, or just wouldn't answer the door.

By the time I got to Sarena's it was nearly seven. It was trying to snow and a few flakes had settled on the cars parked in Albany Street. I pressed her entry buzzer. She checked briefly that it was me and let me in.

She looked pretty good, considering the abuse she'd given her body the night before. She was dressed in some sort of house jacket. What do they call them? Not quite a dressing gown, more like an oversized silk jacket. Beautiful, it was. Pure silk, all black with green lizards or kimono dragons or whatever they're called. Come to think of it, it was called a kimono. Or was it? Oh dear... this isn't easy. If only I could pause there and just freeze time. Just talk about Sarena and how beautiful she was.

She beckoned me to follow her into her bedroom. I knew she'd just bathed, and I could smell that caramel perfume again, the one she wore on the pretend flight from Australia... the one that sometimes lingered in the Swedish thing. She stood in front of me by the end of her bed. It was silent in the flat, save for the odd engine that could be heard struggling with the cold outside. Sarena looked at me and stared. She said nothing. I just stood there like a startled baby, locked onto her charismatic chocolate eyes.

Then I noticed she had something in her hand, like a nose spray. She went to put it up my nose. I tried to stop her, but she just made a 'sshh' sound and waved a finger at me. She made me sniff some substance that had a metal-like aftertaste. I have no idea what it was.

Sarena took two sniffs and then threw the little glass bottle onto the armchair. She was choreographing every move. This was the last thing I'd expected. She gently placed her forefinger and thumb on the silk belt of her kimono, then slowly moved her hips from side to side, gently allowing it to fall to the floor. She was naked apart from a pair of silk panties, green silk with a white trim.

She was a perfect specimen. She should have been bottled there and then. Bottled and exhibited, sent into space and fired off to some distant solar system. Some other beings ought to know just how beautiful the human race could be. They would never know what deviousness lies within.

I went to speak. I can't remember now what I was going to say, but Sarena just put a finger to her lips. I didn't utter another word for ages. I stepped up to her. I was still fully dressed: Dr Marten shoes, black jeans, a T-shirt, an over-shirt of thick cotton, a blue overcoat, and a tartan scarf around my neck. I shivered. Sarena didn't.

I put my arms around her waist and she kissed my face. She kissed me so lightly that I could barely feel it. She ran her nails over my jeans and gently placed me onto her bed. She removed every item of my clothing, slowly and seductively, with ease and grace. I was paralysed with pleasure. With gentle thrusts and squeals we were entwined.

There was no call to speak. It was then that I had what I can only describe as an out-of-body experience. You've heard folk talk of seeing themselves from above at the moment of death. Well, I was stuck to the ceiling with a naked Velcro bottom. I was looking down at Sarena from a few feet away. I could see the robot from 'Lost in Space', standing by the dresser, flailing its arms about shouting 'danger, danger, alien life force approaching'.

The next thing I recall is stretching out under the duvet. I felt as if I'd woken from surgery, a touch groggy and unsure of my surroundings. Sarena stroked my hair and spoke, for what I imagined was the first time in ages. If she had a natural accent, then this was it.

'I have to say something.'

'Do you?'

'Last night…?'

Then she went quiet. I caught her eyes They were no longer sparkling, but sorrowed and a little sunken.

'Last night what?'

'I really liked you last night. You were so sweet. You put me into bed, didn't you? You should hate me really.'

I looked at her and tried to – really tried to hate her. I just couldn't. I stroked her face.

'I'm addicted. I can even admit it to you.'

Then Sarena said something that quite threw me.

'I think I was a little bit addicted too.'

'You?'

'I don't have to do this, you know.'

I couldn't get the gist of what she was saying. Sarena realised as much.

'Oh, Jim. You don't understand.'

I felt I was almost there. That any second she might just blurt out what she was going to say. I sensed that half of her wanted to, but the other half was too afraid. I wondered if it might help to expose myself first. I held her hand.

'I've been obsessed with you ever since we met. That's the truth. Oh, I try to pretend I'm not. I've said all sorts of things to myself, and to Loren. But the truth is I'm just not in control when it comes to you. I feel like those idiots who've been hypnotised on TV. I'd eat a lemon now and swear blind it was an apple.'

'A poisoned apple?'

'Maybe.'

'I'm glad you said poisoned,' she added.'

'Instead of rotten?'

'Yes, exactly.'

Sarena stroked me again. Then she took her hand away, as

suddenly as the thought hit her.

'You're not going to report me, are you?'

'Report you?'

Sarena moved away, propping herself up against the headboard.

'To the police?'

'Of course I'm not. What for, anyway?'

Sarena thrust a bare leg out of the duvet.

'Tell me, Sarena. Come on, don't play games.'

Sarena threw back the rest of the duvet and got out of bed. She stood there naked for a few seconds, and stared at me with penetrating eyes. There was something disturbing her, something quite profound. She walked over to the dressing table and pivoted like a ballerina. Then she spoke with a tiniest tinge of cockney accent:

'Jim, tell me to shut up. I'll only get you into trouble. I know you now. You're obsessive about truth, aren't you?'

'What were you going to tell me last night?'

Sarena sat back down on the end of the bed. She shuffled up towards me and clasped her hand around my wrist, looking deeply troubled.

'That burglary... the laptop...'

Sarena's entryphone buzzer pierced the air. The shock of the noise made her bite her lip. She said she wasn't expecting anybody, and said it as if she meant it. She had this hollow-looking face of fear. Her beautifully proportioned body was trembling.

'What's wrong? Who is it?' I said, genuinely concerned.

Sarena seemed frozen with fear. I instinctively got up and peeped out between the blinds. Her fear was suddenly mine. Loren's car was parked outside.

CHAPTER 29

The first day of Elton's murder trial ended at ten past four. Apart from Lefevre's opening to the jury, there had only been time for Mrs Brandon's evidence regarding the discovery of Sarena's body. Although I'd missed the first part of her evidence, I'd returned to court for Harry's cross-examination.

Nothing of any further significance emerged. She seemed proud that her Springer Spaniel 'Banjo' had sniffed the body out amongst the rocks, and from what I saw of her she seemed remarkably phlegmatic about the whole thing. Perhaps her twenty-odd years as a paramedic had accustomed her to such things. It had also heightened her awareness of potential forensic evidence, as on many previous occasions she'd been the first to attend a scene of crime. That probably explained why she'd noticed the shoe print on the sack.

I'd planned to have a coffee with Loren to recap the day's events, and no doubt try and bolster each other's insecurity. I wanted to find somewhere away from the Old Bailey, and escape without Sammy nabbing me again.

As I was about to leave the court building, my mobile echoed to the sound of the Big Ben chimes, alerting me to a message. I assumed it was Loren wondering where we should meet. As I opened the text, I soon discovered it wasn't from her at all. I thought the sender's number looked vaguely familiar, but it wasn't anyone in my phone book database.

I'm not sure I can adequately describe the feeling I experienced as I first read the message. I remember the numbness that pervaded my hand, almost causing me to drop the phone. I also recall shaking the phone in the sunlight, to try and restore a proper grip on it. I looked at the message again. I knew I'd become prone to hallucinations, but to my horror it said exactly the same thing as it had a few seconds before. I hadn't been imagining it at all. The message was in capitals:

'JIM. MEET ME AT THE OASIS BAR. LOVE, SARENA.'

I'd literally stopped in my tracks, blocking the way out of court and causing a commotion behind me. All sorts of lawyers, court officials and jurors were pouring out of the Old Bailey's revolving doors.

-What the fuck...? I heard in my head, but it wasn't me saying it.

Ken was as agitated as I'd ever known him.

-Fucking hell, Jim. You're getting messages from a dead woman.

I needed Ken like a hole in the head. It was bad enough trying to work this out for myself. I leaned back against the concrete wall of the court building, convinced that if I didn't have a secure backing I'd collapse to the ground. I waited for Ken's next interruption, sure that he was about to launch a tirade of swear words at me. He seemed just as shocked as I.

-Text her back.

-What?

-Text her back

-And say what?

-That you'll meet her.

-But she's dead, Ken... she's dead.

I shook Ken away, worrying that I might just have

spoken the last words out loud. I hadn't noticed Harry Douglas approaching with Loren.

'My God, you look white as a sheet, man,' Harry said, in his own inimitable way. I was sure his next line was going to be 'you look like you've seen a ghost', and I was dreading it.

'Are you okay, Jim?' I could hear Loren adding.

'Yeah...' I think I said, but couldn't hear myself saying it.

'What's happened?' probed Loren, staring at me with a 'pull yourself together' look.

'Nothing... nothing'. Repeating the word hardly made it more comfortable.

'Well, I've got a case conference at chambers,' Harry contributed, while checking his watch. Harry seemed more than happy to leave Loren to enquire as to my well-being.

'Sure, yeah.'

'I'd get a good night's sleep if I were you, Jim.'

'I will,' I replied, knowing full well that the prospect was becoming increasingly unlikely.

Harry strode off towards Ludgate Hill, with a parting comment, 'Bright and early in the morning. We need to go through things with Elton.'

'Okay, fine,' I managed, before gripping Loren's suit jacket to steady myself.

Loren waited until she was sure Harry was out of earshot.

'What's wrong, what's wrong?' Loren repeated frantically.

I knew instinctively that it was self-preservation, concern that anything might have implicated *her.* I looked into Loren's bright green eyes. Her new contact lenses made them look like polished emeralds.

'You're shaking,' she said, as much in surprise as concern.

I was so close to telling her, but something stopped me. I had to summon up exactly the same strength as when I was in that police cell with Elton, when he morphed into Basil Brush.

'My... my aunt's died,' I lied, without any idea whether I'd said it convincingly.

'Your aunt?'

'Aunt Marj. She brought me up.'

'Oh Jim, I'm sorry. You poor thing.'

Loren wore one of her smiles, the sympathetic one that was meant to convey warmth and concern. You had to really know her to see through it.

'Why didn't you tell Mr Douglas?' she continued.

'Erm, I didn't want him to worry about me. I'll be okay.'

'What are you going to do? Do you have to go somewhere?'

'Yeah... I have to... go somewhere...'

I think I knew what Loren meant – to liaise with family and all that, but I had no family left. Aunt Marj had actually died years ago. I tried to remember there and then if that was something Loren already knew, but I took from her reaction that I couldn't have told her. I had a vague memory of telling her that we'd lost touch, but that was all.

Loren's reaction seemed genuine, at least to the veracity of the news. She picked up my briefcase, which at some point I must have dropped to the ground in shock.

'Shall we share a cab back to the office first?' she suggested.

'No... no, it's okay. I need a little time.'

'I understand.'

I could sense Loren was finding all this rather awkward. She was trying to sound concerned, but was clearly just mighty relieved that nothing in Elton's trial had gone wrong.

'Is there anything I can do?'

-Fuck off and leave us alone.

I could hear Ken saying it, but fought him for control.

'No... thanks. You get back. I've got to make a couple of calls.'

'Of course, but are you sure there's nothing...?'

'No,' I interrupted, perhaps a tad too brusquely.

A saw a black cab, which had just dropped a couple off further down the road. I walked into the street to wave it down.

'Here you are, Loren. You take this. Camden Town,' I

said, before she could protest.

I watched as Loren's cab disappeared towards High Holborn. I checked my mobile again. As I opened the message I nearly convinced myself that it really had been one of my episodic hallucinations. It must be, I reckoned, as my shaking finger pressed the inbox.

'JIM. MEET ME AT THE OASIS BAR. LOVE, SARENA.'

I checked through the message details. By then I was sure it was Sarena's old number, one I'd long since erased from my phone's memory. I recognised the three fives in a row. Then I checked the further details: *message sent 09.07.2012 at 16.05*. The last remaining hope, that somehow this was an old message that had got stuck in the system, evaporated.

CHAPTER 30

As I strained my neck to look down to street level, I could see Loren. She was standing on the pavement, looking up at all the windows. Then she moved out of sight, back towards the communal front door. I called over to Sarena.

'Jesus, it's Loren.'

'What? What's she doing here?'

I couldn't think straight.

'I don't know, but I'm not here, right... Christ, what am I talking about? She must know I'm here. She must have followed me.'

The entryphone buzzer went again. This time it felt like Loren was resting on it, and she wasn't going to let go until Sarena answered. I grabbed my clothes off the bedroom floor and rushed them on – socks and pants on inside out. Sarena put the first thing on that she could find: her kimono. As we moved through to the living room, Sarena was still tying it up as she picked up the receiver.

'Yes.'

Loren's rasping tone made the intercom speaker vibrate.

'Let me in... I know you're there, Jim.'

Sarena looked at me for inspiration. There was none. All I could do was shrug my shoulders nervously. Sarena pressed the entry button and looked at me again, as if to say 'you deal with her'. Everything now seemed to echo. I could hear the front door slam downstairs. I wondered if Professor Pat Pending could invent me a flying machine so that I could escape. My defence mechanism always seems to revert to childhood celluloid imagery, but there was no escape, and I hadn't a clue what I was going to say next. I could hear Loren's heels clicking their way towards the door.

Sarena swallowed a couple of pills. I didn't know what they were. Then she opened the door and glared at Loren, who simply barged in and stood next to the dining room table.

'Well? Will somebody please say something? I haven't come here to cause a scene. I just want to know where I stand. Well?'

'Loren, I'm sorry. I should have told you.'

'Told me what, exactly?'

'That I was with Sarena last night. That I was coming to see her this evening. I did try and call you earlier.'

'You know what, Jim Harwood? You're a snivelling little turd.'

I accepted the jibe. Loren continued to rant.

'Right. Are you going to be seeing this... whatever she is, or not?'

'Not. That's why I came here.'

'Oh. And what do you say? Sarena, or Javita, or whatever your stupid name is?'

Loren was like a woman possessed, although possessed of what I'm not exactly sure. I would have done anything to avoid this scene. Sarena was eyeing her with suspicion and responded to the bait.

'Does she know, Jim?'

I wasn't exactly sure what Sarena meant.

'Do I know what?' Loren demanded of me.

Loren and Sarena were glued together in a stare. Sarena broke away from it and looked at me.

'Jim? Does she know about me? What have you told her?'

'Nothing.'

Sarena swung around to Loren again.

'Bitch. Are you a policewoman or something?'

'Sarena, calm down. Don't be ridiculous. This is Loren, my work colleague, you know that. Let's all calm down.'

Loren was still locked in a piercing glare, focusing in on Sarena, who snapped at her, 'Don't look at me, bitch. He doesn't want you anyway.'

'He told you that, did he?'

I swallowed for a beat.

'No, I didn't actually.'

Loren took over again, 'Shut up. I'm talking to her. What did he tell you?'

Sarena manufactured an evil-looking smile.

'That you're just a fuck sometimes, but not a very good one.'

'Sarena! You lying sod. I said no such thing, Loren.'

I could feel four eyes fixed on me. Then Sarena made a sort of hissing sound, turned her back and walked into the kitchen. I was mustering up what to say to Loren when a glistening caught my eye. Sarena was in the kitchen doorway, holding a knife. She told us both to stand away from the table. I let out a nervous laugh, my brain telling me that the scene was ludicrous. But not only did Sarena have a knife in her hand, but a menacing look to accompany it.

She didn't speak at first. She just kept prodding the knife towards us, making us back off. I could hear Loren breathing, but she seemed too traumatised to speak. I realised Sarena was trying to get us to move away from the table. She shuffled forwards, jerking the shiny blade out in front of her. Loren and I glanced at each other and then at the knife, as we slowly moved backwards.

'Christ's sake, Sarena, what are you doing?'

Sarena blanked me, choosing instead to fumble around under the table. I could hear a rustling sound. She ripped at some cellophane on the underside of the table. Then she just stood there with an expression that said 'now what are you going to do?' She had a knife in one hand, and a revolver in the other.

The gun was small and neat. My mind tried to tell me that it was a replica. There was a brief war of words with Ken – a replica? No, it's real – but there was no time for debate. It had a black handle and barrel with a tiny white stripe running down its edge. I'd seen countless pictures of guns, and I'd even handled firearm exhibits at court, but I'd never had a gun pointed at me in anger. I looked into Loren's frightened eyes. They said, 'what the hell is happening here?'

Sarena spoke with a broader hint of south London, and aimed her vitriol at Loren.

'You!... Fucking lawyer bitch. Yeah, scary isn't it? Glad you came, are you?'

Sarena held the gun out in front of her, pointing it at Loren. Her hand was swaying from side to side. Loren screwed up her eyes in fear. Then Sarena pointed the gun at herself, slowly lifting it to her temple.

'She's all yours, Jim.'

Sarena was opening up her mouth, forcing the gun towards it. I made a sudden grab for the gun and all hell broke loose. I managed to get a grip on Sarena's wrist. I pulled the gun away from her mouth, catching her eyebrow with a glancing blow. Loren realised what was happening and tried to join in, attempting to grasp the gun with me. I gripped so hard on Sarena's hand that she couldn't squeeze the trigger. She cried out in pain as Loren's hand slid down towards the end of the barrel. I thought she was going to get her hand blown off.

We both yanked away at Sarena's hand with all our might, causing the gun to pop out of it like a bar of soap. It slid across the floor towards a pile of magazines nestled under the curtains. Sarena instinctively went towards it, but I held onto her trailing arm as Loren picked the knife up from the table and blocked her.

'Jim, get the gun.'

I'd expected them to be Loren's words, but they were Sarena's. Loren looked at me in horror, as if she thought Sarena and I were conspiring.

I tried to look for the gun, but I was still clinging onto Sarena's arm, trying to keep her and Loren apart. The two of them were now biting into each other's grip like two pitbulls, each trying to get control of the knife. I had to let go of Sarena's arm to try and force the knife away from the pair of them. I was shouting at Sarena to let go, and at Loren too. I shouted something at Loren, wanting her to look for the gun while I held back Sarena, but neither of them would let go of each other.

Loren managed to force Sarena backwards over a chair. I held on tight to Sarena's wrist, determined that Sarena was never going to hold that knife again. I pulled hard at Sarena's hair with my free hand, hoping the sudden pain would make her let go of the knife. The chair toppled over, with Loren falling into a heap on top of Sarena. I lost my balance as a result and piled on top of them both. Our bodies were both twisted away from Sarena. We'd fallen awkwardly on her. I was expecting Sarena to shout out in pain and swear, but there was silence... then a gut-curdling moan.

I could see Loren's hand clasped over Sarena's hand, which in turn was still clasped onto the knife. Bright red liquid bubbled up over Loren's hand. She withdrew it in shock, leaving Sarena's hand alone on the knife, which was stuck rigidly into her chest.

Blood was soaking her kimono, and a horrible gurgling sound was still emanating from her mouth. Loren's white top was covered in blood. So was my shirt. It was a mess. The whole thing was a bloody mess. I thought Loren was going to scream, and I got ready to cover her mouth. I could visibly see Loren's pupils beginning to grow. A tear dropped from the corner of her left eye, and her mouth began to tremble.

I wanted to flick over the channel and change to another image, but this was real. This was actually happening. There was no television to rescue me from this bloody scene. Sarena made another horrendous noise, like a cry from an animal in the night-time. A final spurt of blood came out of her mouth... then nothing. Not a sound, not a movement... absolutely nothing.

I looked down at Sarena. Her face momentarily morphed into my mother's before changing back. I couldn't move a muscle.

Loren tried to say something, but nothing would come out. The mucus welling up in her throat made her cough and splutter. She eventually spoke.

'She was going to kill me.'

Loren rested her head in my arms, unable to stop the flow of tears. We struggled to take in breaths. I thought I'd feel sick or shake or collapse to the ground, but I was too numb to feel anything. I kept my glare fixed on Sarena. I kept hoping that she might suddenly open up those gorgeous eyes and shout 'joke, got ya!', but I knew she was dead.

It was then I had that flash thought – the one where police officers arrive. I imagined the blue and white tape, the forensic scientists, and all the paraphernalia of murder.

An enormous wave of energy charged my body. If that was an adrenaline rush, then so be it. Whatever it was, I'd never felt the like of it before. I could almost imagine the word 'charging' flashing in a white light on my forehead. I'd been plugged into something, or someone. The purposeful cadence of my voice took me by surprise.

'We're not going to lose our lives over this.'

I was in overdrive.

'This is my fault, Loren. This is down to me.'

Loren was staring at me wildly, unable to take in what I was saying or what had just happened. I held her hand as I spoke, feeling some of Sarena's warm blood on her palm.

'You didn't kill her. I did. Don't ever, ever, say anything different, not even to me. We've got to think, and we've got to think fast.'

Loren's voice shook as she finally managed a few words.

'Think what, Jim? I don't understand. What's happened?'

I looked at Sarena, then looked away again. I forced myself to stay in the same cruise control gear, knowing that if I did things manually I'd crumble.

'I've got a feeling that she hasn't told Gordon about me... at least about me being here tonight.'

Loren looked at me as if I'd just spoken in a foreign tongue.

'I'm going to get us out of this.'

'Who's Gordon?' Loren eventually replied.

'Her boss... I think. Jesus Christ. I've been so fucking stupid I should be dead, not her. Go into the bedroom and take off the sheet.'

'What? What do you mean get us out of this? Jim, it was an accident.'

'Loren, please. Not now. Just do as I say. Do it!'

Loren did exactly what she was told. She must have been volted into action by the same energy that had charged me. Now I was really on autopilot. The force field from 'Lost in Space' was surrounding me. I was invincible and impervious to chemical reaction. I put the sheet over Sarena's body. Then I removed it again and tried to take out the knife. It was stuck. It must have caught in her ribs. I had to really yank it out, and a spray of blood splashed onto my shirt. I wanted to be sick again, but nothing would come.

I went into the bathroom and ran the bath. I took her blood-soaked kimono off and put her in there as the water began to fill. I instinctively tested the water, not wanting it to be too hot for my beautiful girl. I fiddled about with the mixer taps, staring at her with lost eyes.

There's no flow to my memory of this, just flash images of random moments. I can see myself walking out of the bathroom, and sitting at the table, and talking to Loren. It seemed so surreal, so bizarre. I remember saying to Loren, 'Do you want to spend the rest of your life in prison?'

I remember Loren shaking her head, and occasionally peeking through the gap in the bathroom door. Sarena was gently bobbing up and down in the bath. I watched her float as her head banged against the back of the tub. I wasn't sure I was really there at all.

'I don't feel a fucking thing, Loren.'

I didn't get an immediate response. Loren held onto my wet hand.

'You feel everything,' she eventually said. 'Or you wouldn't have sworn.'

I caught Loren's eye, thrown by her perception.

'It's all right. I know you loved her.'

I'm not really sure how long we clung onto each other. It seemed like half an hour, but I guess it was just a minute or so. I remember a voice telling me that we had to get on with it. It may have been Loren's voice. It may even have been Ken's.

Some bits I can still picture, while others have been wiped from the tapes. I can remember draining the bath and drying her off with a navy blue towel. I can even remember that it had a dolphin design on it. I can remember picking out the used condom from her wastepaper bin and stuffing it into my jeans pocket. I also distinctly remember putting Sarena into her black velvet dress, which was on a hanger in the bedroom cupboard.

I can still feel the dead weight of her arms as I dressed her. I'll always remember that horrible feeling, of lifting one dead arm up, then the other.

One particular thing I did, which looking back now was rather odd, was dab Sarena with some of her favourite perfume, or my favourite perfume to be more precise. In doing so I spilt the bottle on her dress, causing a large waft of the stuff to hit my nostrils and make me sneeze.

We cleaned every surface, every possible nook and cranny. I remember putting a new sheet on the bed. It was about then that Ken recovered from the shock, and had his first dig of the evening.

-Good move, that one, Jimbo. Don't want any personal juices discovered, do we? No hairs to analyse.

The old sheet was in a carrier bag and was going back to my flat. Along with our clothes, and Sarena's kimono and towel, it was destined for destruction. All that was left was the blood stain on the rug underneath the table. I folded the rug in two and Loren held open a big grey bin liner as I pushed it in. Then I picked up the small revolver, which had slid over to the window and buried itself in one of many Hello! magazines that were on the floor. I looked at the gun curiously with a look that reminded me of that scene in 'Planet of the Apes', the one where the ape first realises that Charlton Heston can speak.

I had no idea if the gun was real, or a replica. I don't think I wanted to believe that Sarena would have shot herself, or me, or Loren. It was only the not wanting to believe that made me think this at the time. I'm sure the gun was very real indeed, but I wasn't going to try it out. A loud bang might be an inappropriate noise to make in Albany Street at half past eight on a Saturday evening.

I wiped the gun with a tea towel and dropped it into the bin liner along with the rug. Then I dropped the knife and the tea towel in too.

There was nothing left, nothing to say that a struggle had taken place.... nothing to suggest that this had been the scene of a crime. I needed a scenario, one that would provide a different crime scene altogether.

CHAPTER 31

I took the bus along Fleet Street and the Strand, and around Trafalgar Square before getting off at Piccadilly. I'd spent the entire journey flicking the text on and off the little screen. I tried to find answers to the obvious questions... how and who, and why? I couldn't stop the shakes and took two of the little pink tablets I usually save for migraines.

I crossed over the busy junction at the end of Regent Street, pausing outside the Burger King where I'd once sat for hours in turmoil over Sarena. I could feel history pulling to repeat itself. I put my palm against the window pane as my legs turned to jelly. I could feel a bead of sweat finding a channel down the side of my ribs...

...I tried to force myself past the windows, but had to pause as someone caught my eye. It was the same down-and-out guy, arguing with the same Burger King security man. And the same Spanish girls were in the background, the ones with thick dark eyebrows, as excited and giggly as ever. The one in the Barcelona football top pointed at me through the window. She was acting like a child might in a game of war, pretending that her hand was a gun, and firing it.

Then I realised the whole of Burger King was full of people I recognised: Lefevre and Harry were sat at a small table, launching themselves at quarter pounders; Loren was stood behind Harry; And Judge Llewelyn-Davies, in full courtroom regalia, was sat on one of those children's high chairs, his podgy little legs waving about beneath him. He was being fed spoonfuls of baby food by the court clerk. All of the jury were in the queues at the back of the restaurant, waiting patiently for their fast food. Aunt Marj was sat with one of my old teachers from school, Mr Mead. I thought I caught a glimpse of my mum, talking to a younger man who looked like my father. They blended into the background, before slowly evaporating into the throng...

...And there was Elton, in a Burger King security uniform, clearing away the tables. He had huge headphones on and seemed to be singing. Elton opened up a large bin. He put his hand in it as if he was trying to help pull someone out... and he did. He pulled Sarena out of the bin. She was wearing her silk kimono. It was stained with ketchup...

I don't know how long I'd been staring through the window, but the visions were interrupted by a voice.

'Excuse me, sir. Are you all right?'

I paused before answering.

'Yeah... sorry.'

I wasn't sure why I was apologising, or who to at first. Then I recognised him, and it must have been mutual.

'I know you, don't I, sir?'

It was PC Tony Trent, he of dubious club act fame – the officer who had attended the scene after that horrific bullyboy assault in Carnaby Street.

'You do know me, yes. Jim Harwood.'

I wanted to get away from him – nothing personal, but the hallucinations had upset me and I was desperate to follow up Sarena's text message and go to the Oasis. I could tell, though, that he was concerned about my odd behaviour and thought it prudent to engage him in conversation, even if just for a few minutes. So we reacquainted ourselves with the facts of the case, which had turned into Regina versus Derek Clements. After a minute or so, I think I'd at least convinced him that I wasn't a danger to the public, even though I probably had been staring madly through a fast-food restaurant window.

I asked him why I'd never been called as a witness. The officer told me that Clements had been arrested again, on another assault, and that was why the case had been delayed for so long.

'So when's it coming up in court?' I enquired.

'It's been and gone. He put in two guilty pleas. Got five years for the GBH with intent.'

'The Section 18 on the girl?'

'Exactly. As for Melanie, she's doing very well actually, Mr Harwood. A total transformation.'

'Good. So Melanie's her name, is it? I'd forgotten.'

'Yeah... Funny, but she says the incident turned her life around. She's off the smack, and got a full-time job.'

'Good. Well, that's good to hear.'

I was itching to get away. My mobile chimed out the sounds of Big Ben again, but I was too scared to even look at it.

PC Trent kept trying to engage me.

'She asked me to thank you actually, sir. Did the CPS pass that on?'

'Well, no, but it doesn't matter. All's well that ends well, heh?'

'Quite...'

We exchanged a slightly awkward smile.

'Well, I'm sure you've got better things to do, officer. I know I have.'

'Yes, of course. Do you mind me asking, though, what were you actually *doing*? Staring into that window, you seemed lost... I thought you were unwell or something.'

'No, no, I was just... I thought I saw someone I recognised, in Burger King, but I didn't. Mind playing tricks, you know.'

And with that I gave an embarrassing little wave and walked off up Glasshouse Street, without turning around.

It was less than a minute's walk to the Oasis. I passed the

little booth where I'd once enquired about the Chelsea football ticket. The same surly guy in the baseball cap was working there. I stopped outside and dared to look at the text that had arrived a few minutes ago. It was from Loren, asking if I was okay, telling me it was fine to ring her anytime, night or day. No sooner had I read it than another text came through:

'I'M HERE... NOW.' It was Sarena's number again. I was standing right outside the entrance to the Oasis.

I walked down the stairs to reception, where a large black lady offered to take my coat. I declined politely and descended the stairs, passing a man on his way up. There was something about him that made me want to turn around, but I was so fixed on Sarena's message that I couldn't cope with the distraction. Did I recognise him? I briefly pondered.

It had been many months since I'd been there, and the Oasis had undergone a complete makeover, with the 'oasis' theme now far more to the fore. You had to pass under a huge palm tree, which was illuminated by massive floor-mounted lights. The bar was now in the shape of a small lagoon, and lit up by sparkling blue jets of light emanating from somewhere indiscernible. You could see through from one side of the bar to the other, with the shelf of optics forming a partial barrier.

I had an extraordinary mixture of feelings and thoughts. For one thing, I could hardly feel my hands or feet. It felt like I was walking on a carpet of feathers. I circled the lagoon-shaped bar. It was just about five o'clock and the place was fairly empty. Alongside the bar were various booths in cut-out cave style. The first four were empty. But in the fifth, the last, I could see a pair of blue high-heeled shoes resting under one of the benches. I knew instantly that I'd seen those shoes before.

I stopped and tried to peer underneath the row of benches. I could only make out the black leggings and the blue high-heeled shoes. I approached cautiously. Whoever she was talking to was sat diagonally opposite, in the corner and out of my view. I moved like a cheetah stalking its prey, one careful pace at a time, until she came into view.

I recognised her straightaway.

CHAPTER 32

I ferried the bin liners containing the rug and the sheet and the bits and pieces into the car. It was time to put Sarena in there as well. Loren went out to reconnoitre, to check how busy the road was and who could see what from where. While she did that, I tied up the two bin liners. One covered her from head to waist, the other from feet to waist. I folded another up and used it to secure them as a tie. Sarena was nowhere to be seen. She was covered in plastic. Nothing was left to chance.

I had to hold my breath as I lifted Sarena's dead weight over my shoulders. I was about to struggle down the stairs, with Loren holding the lighter end. If somebody had come in through the communal front door, then we'd have been well and truly shafted. 'What's that, mate? Looks like a dead body wrapped up in two bin liners.'

Luckily nobody emerged from the flats, or came in through the communal front door. We made it to the foot of the stairwell, then paused to check outside. Loren surveyed the road, and checked all the windows for twitching curtains. Fortunately the bushes by the side of the block obscured a lot of the view. She gave me the thumbs-up, then opened up the boot. We were as quiet as mice. Six paces later and Sarena was in the boot. The smell of the perfume I'd spilt on her was still overwhelming.

We went back into the flat to make final preparations. I needed to convince myself that the place was as spotless as it could be. Then, as suddenly as it had taken over, my cruise control slipped out of gear, causing me to reel back in pain. My senses were returning, and a colossal colic grabbed my stomach. I had to sit down for a few minutes in the armchair. I wanted to wave a magic wand and make everything disappear. I wanted to be H.G. Wells and twiddle the round spirally bits on the end of the chair arms and go back in time. It was then that the terrible reality of it all hit home. I sat and twiddled the knobs on the end of the armchair, and everything went out of focus...

...I shot back in time. I was seven years old. The air was full of that Robinson Crusoe music that has haunted me before. It was music I was humming in the allotment while taking the cut-through home from school, just moments before I was about to discover the shock of my life. I looked down at myself and could see that I was wearing a pair of grey school shorts and a tank top with pineapples on it. It was stained with my mother's blood. A police officer emerged from the soil around the carrot tops. He sprang out of the ground and approached me. He smiled at me reassuringly. 'We'll catch your mother's killer,' he said, then disappeared into the ground again, burying himself from sight...

...Loren was shaking me in the chair, pulling at my arm. I could hear her voice saying, 'Jim, Jim. Please! Don't pass out. Don't leave me with this.'

'I'm all right. I'm all right.' I was trying to convince the pair of us.

Loren held her hand out and helped me out of the chair. She held me as tight as she'd ever done. I managed to fight the shivers off. We both breathed deeply, several times. I stroked her hair, and for a moment started to groom her, one chimpanzee to another. When I finally calmed again, we carried on cleaning and tidying, as if preparing for a visiting relative. Neither of us spoke as we did so.

Loren followed me back to Swiss Cottage in her new Nissan Micra. As I was driving I pleaded with the mind I've so often cursed, and it began to come up with Elton. God knows where from, but it did. It was just a seed at first, but as the journey went by, and five minutes seemed like five hours, the embryo started to grow. I parked in the little car park behind my flat, and Loren pulled up beside. We went in to my flat and put the kettle on. How very English. What do you do when you've just killed someone? Have a cup of tea.

I thought aloud with Loren as I waited for the kettle to boil. It was time for another dose of adrenaline.

'Loren. What are you thinking?'

'My hand was on that knife.'

'Yeah, I know.'

'Or was it? I can't even think about it.'

I let the comment rest for a beat. I knew Loren must have been seized with shock, but began to wonder if she would try and wriggle out of it. Loren shrugged nervously. I was finding it difficult to read her. As I made the tea I couldn't get a certain thought out of my head.

'Listen, you know I was at Acton police station a couple of days ago?'

'If you say so.'

'Yeah, I was, and it was Elton. He'd been nicked for indecently assaulting a sixteen-year-old schoolgirl. Felt her up at a bus stop on the High Street. I went to court with him Friday, got him bail at a hostel.'

'So?'

'Well, he's not all there. He's a twenty-four-carat head-case. You wouldn't believe what he's like. Anyway, he's suspected of molesting this girl, and stealing a porno mag and some condoms. Well, what if he goes off the rails and kills someone? What if he molests someone else and kills them? I don't know, dumps them in some park or something... or... or over a cliff?'

'A cliff?'

'Maybe. Anyway, let's just say he does. I wouldn't put it past him. Well, the Old Bill certainly wouldn't, that's the main thing. So let's just say that Elton happens to be found in the vicinity of a dead body... and, and there's her blood on his clothes, and fibres from her clothes, and...'

'Stop this, Jim.'

'I'm serious. Look at me, Loren. I'm deadly fucking serious, girl.'

I smiled nervously at Loren. I was hyper. I could hear the Rubettes singing in my head. I was so madly nervous that I could even see them on 'Top of the Pops', with that bloke in a cap: 'I can do it, I can do it, I can really move, from my head right down to my blue suede shoes, I can really make the groove, I can do it I can do it I can really move. Yeah…'

'Sorry, I'm excited. Can you believe that?'

'It must be shock,' whispered Loren, half to herself.

In a way it was, but it felt more like self-preservation. I couldn't stop the words tumbling from my mouth.

'So I need to pin the death – the murder, sorry, I'll have to think of it as a murder now – on someone else. That's stage one. Stage two is this: I'll have to keep control over the situation. I need to know what's going on. I need to have an input. I need to manipulate it. With me?'

'Not really...'

'What if I represent the man accused of the murder?'

'What?'

'I stitch up my own client. I can do it, I can do it.'

'Jim, you're scaring me.'

'I'm terrifying myself... but I can do it. It's do or die, girl.'

I put my mug of tea down and picked up an empty one from the cupboard.

'Jim, where are you going?'

'I'm just popping out for a minute. No, I'm not, actually. Ken is. Yeah. Ken can do the dirty work. I'm staying put and Ken's going out to see Sarena.'

Loren was staring at me as if I'd gone off my rocker, and I had. It was the first time I'd ever said 'Ken' out loud. I picked up my small black kitchen knife. I took the cup and the knife out to the car. At one o'clock in the morning, I opened up the boot. No... Ken opened up the boot. Oh, fuck off, Jim. You opened up the boot. You, James Earl Harwood of 24a Adelaide Road, London NW3. You and only you, Jim. Right? So go on... what did you do?... I ripped off some of the plastic, I ripped off some of the plastic, and I... I stuck the knife back... I stuffed the knife back in... I stuffed... I... I... can't tell you. I just can't say this bit...

I walked back into my flat and put the cup in the fridge. There must have been about a third of a cup of blood covered in clingfilm. I slotted it next to a jar of olives. I sat back down again and carried on thinking aloud with Loren, telling myself, carry on, Jim, carry on. Loren looked at me in sheer disbelief.

'Jim, have you just done what I think you've done?'

'Yes.'

'Jesus, Jim.'

'And I've put her in a sack from the shed.'

'Why?'

'I don't know... I didn't like seeing her in plastic.'

Loren swept her hair back with her right hand. It had a habit of covering her face. She was very unsure as she said:

'You're doing this, aren't you? You're going to do it?'

'Do you want us to spend the rest of our lives in prison?'

Loren never answered my question. She didn't even answer it with a look, choosing instead to bow her head to the floor.

CHAPTER 33

Their name badges had undergone a makeover too: they were now miniature palm trees. It was Claire, the waitress who had once been the bearer of terrible news. Cruella de Vil, I'd called her, when she told me that my Sarena had been lying to me all along.

'Hello,' was all I could get out, and even that one word cracked with trepidation.

'Sorry, I'm on a break. You can get served at the bar.'

Claire shot a look to her colleague opposite, as if to say, 'isn't it obvious'? I had to persevere.

'I'm sorry. Do you remember me?'

'Not really,' she replied, somewhat irritated but unable to hide the fact she really meant 'yes, sort of.'

'Look, I'm really sorry to interrupt, but this is important.'

That seemed to grab her attention, though it didn't diffuse her annoyance.

'It was a long time ago, I know. I once showed you a photo of a friend of mine.'

'How can I forget?'

'What do you mean?'

''Cos you weren't the last.'

'I don't understand.'

'At least three more guys turned up looking for her.'

'Who?'

'I don't know. It was a long time ago, like you said.

All sorts of questions suddenly jostled each other in my mind, trying to get pride of place. One of them won the battle, but I was so nervous my lips got stuck together, causing me to stammer.

'Ha, has she...? Has she been back at all?'

'No, not for ages.'

'Not... today?'

'I said, not for ages.'

I backed away, without any idea where I was going. I eventually found myself perched on a bar stool with half a lager in front of me. I knew I had to call the number; I could think of nothing else. I chose a spot near to the entrance, one that afforded me a panoramic view of the whole bar.

I brought up the number on the display and counted to three. I don't know why, but that's what I did. On the stroke of three I pressed the call button. Nothing. No reply. Then I heard a mobile ringing. I moved closer to the bar and it got louder. A coincidence, I thought, it must be. I stopped the call, waited a couple of seconds and called again. The same phone rang, and this time I could see it light up. It was placed on a small silver tray at the bar. As I looked at it I could see my own mobile number in the caller's display.

Claire shot up from her table and approached me.

'Is this to do with you?' she said.

'Is *what* to do with me?'

I wasn't sure why I said that. It was an automatic response.

'Are you Jim Harwood?'

I knew I'd never given her my name. Not then, not many months previously either.

'Yes...' I told her, tentatively.

'Good. Well, it's yours, then, isn't it?'

'The phone...' I said, without forming it as a question or a statement.

Claire was getting increasingly frustrated.

'You called this afternoon, saying you'd left your phone here at lunchtime... didn't you?'

'I... I...' Nothing of any sense would emerge.

'Why didn't you say when you came over to my table?'

'I don't know... How do you know my name?'

'You gave it to me, on the phone. You said I'll come and collect it after court or something like that.'

'Did I?'

I was trying to think on my feet, but struggling.

'I'm sorry, of course I did.'

Claire finally smiled.

'How long has it been here? I mean, here, on this tray?'

'Since I spoke to you the second time. 'I've just finished work,' you said. 'I'll be half an hour or so'... well, you were nearly an hour, actually.'

My mind reeled in confusion. Who the hell had been impersonating me... and why? I had to stay focused.

'Yeah, yeah, sorry. I got delayed.' Lying had become second nature. I could feel my pants on fire.

'Well, there's the phone. Take it... you *are* Jim Harwood. You obviously know the number because you've just phoned it.'

Claire was trying to convince herself she'd covered all the correct security issues.

'Yes, thanks Claire,' I blurted out.

'Fine... no problem.'

'I haven't paid for this drink yet.'

'You can pay me.'

I handed her the tab, which I hadn't even looked at. I was desperately trying to work out how best to frame the next question. The vital one.

'Three pounds forty,' she said.

Bit steep for half a lager, I thought, before handing over a ten-pound note. But at least it prompted an idea.

'Keep that... the change.'

'What? Are you sure?'

'Yeah.'

'Thanks, Mr Harwood.'

'It's Jim. Just tell me this. At...' I paused to check my watch. 'At about five past four – so just after you said I called to enquire about the phone – somebody else actually used it to send a text.'

Claire looked blank.

'Do you understand what I mean?'

'Yeah, I think so,' she said, shrugging her shoulders.

'And somebody also used it just a few minutes before I came in... so about twenty minutes ago, at the most.'

Claire called over to a colleague at the bar.

'Hang on,' she directed at me, before addressing her colleague.

'Becks, did you see that guy who was in and out this afternoon?'

'What guy?' I spewed out the question before Becks could even answer.

'There was a guy sat here... actually he was here lunchtime too,' Claire added.

'Yeah, he was,' Becks confirmed, throwing back some peroxide locks.

'So he was here literally seconds before I arrived.'

'I guess so. Why?'

'He sent me a text on that phone.'

'I didn't see him using it,' Becks chipped in.

'Nor me,' Claire confirmed.

I took in a breath to pause for thought. I wasn't entirely convinced they were telling the truth. What if he'd given them twenty quid rather than a tenner? I'd become thoroughly incapable of believing the simplest thing.

'Can you describe him, this bloke?'

'Serious,' volunteered Claire, a little to my surprise. Perhaps they were going to be helpful after all.

'Like a librarian,' she added.

'Yeah,' Becks seemed happy to confirm.

'A bit Arsene Wenger,' was another of Claire's suggestions.

'Who's he?' Becks asked.

I let out a little sigh of frustration. 'Get on with it!', I wanted to say, though the comparison to the Arsenal manger reminded me of someone I'd previously met but couldn't quite place. By now Claire had relaxed and was genuinely trying to be helpful.

'He just kept coming in and out, ordering a mineral water, sitting in the same seat.'

'So he actually left the phone there himself...' I mused aloud, and then immediately regretted, realising I'd totally foxed the girls. I picked the phone up and put it in my pocket before they could argue.

'Anyway, thanks. I've got to be off.'

I left in sprightly manner, heading straight upstairs into the bright evening sunshine. I looked left and right in quick succession. I felt certain I was being watched.

CHAPTER 34

The mention of prison seemed to have sharpened Loren's focus. At first she stared blankly at me. In fact, she must have stared for a good ten seconds before replying.

'But it was an accident... I mean, it was, really.'

'I know...'

'So we could tell the truth...'

'The truth!'

Loren was still a novice in the cynical stakes. If she'd been surrounded by the legal system as long as I had, her naivety would have withered away many moons ago.

'It will be a criminal trial, for fuck's sake!' I blazed at her. 'The truth is just a football, Loren. Whoever kicks it in the right direction scores the winning goal.'

Loren battled with the metaphor, mustering another nervous shrug. I made a point of throwing her jacket at her. Anything to jar her from her train of thought.

'Okay. Get your coat on, then. We'll pop down to the police station. Excuse me, sergeant, this young lady and I have killed someone, stabbed her in the heart. It's okay, though, it was an accident. She fell on the knife, honest guv. Oh, I'll just get the body. It's in my boot. By the way, you'll find a cup of her blood next to the green olives in my fridge...'

'Okay, okay. Shut up.'

'We get this wrong now and you may as well forget about your life. I'm trying to keep you out of it... don't you understand?

'Of course I do, but...'

'Triangles, Bloody maths again.'

'What?'

'Love bloody triangles. That's what it's going to look like. We've got no chance, Loren. Do you really think either of us would stand a chance on an accident defence?'

'Jim, I'm just trying to help you think. Don't be angry with me.'

'I'm not angry with you. I'm explaining how the Prosecution will put it: boy kills girl to get girl, or girl kills girl to get boy. Either way, Loren, we're shafted.'

I could feel my heart thumping rapidly against my chest. I realised there and then that I would have to take responsibility. I needed to protect Loren as much for my own sake as for hers.

'But why do we have to blame it on someone else? Why not just dump the body and forget about it?'

'Try and think straight, Lol... Young woman murdered.... They'll want to know where she's been, who she's been with, get me?'

'Yeah.'

'Yeah, exactly. And eventually they'll find out about her... find out about dodgy credit cards, find out where they've been used and God knows what else... and they'll make enquiries and ask people, and there'll be a little trail leading to me. And they'll search my car, and they'll find blood stains and...'

'Okay... okay. I know.'

I tried to take in a deep breath to relax, but it was hopeless. I was still suffering from hyperactivity and my mouth just wouldn't stop chattering. I was zooming about the kitchen like a pinball, collecting points for bouncing off the dishwasher and the oven. I don't think I've ever talked so fast in my life.

'Now if this doesn't work out, they'll do that anyway, and you can rest assured that I'll do what I can to clean the car and everything else. But they've got a habit of finding things. The point is, Loren, that if they've nothing else they'll search and search and search until they find something. Anything. But... but if they've got their man... if they've got their little mitts on a prime suspect, and latch on to him, well, it's a

whole different ball game then. The whole thing's done differently...'

Loren tried to interrupt, but I was still steaming.

'...Last thing they want to do then is follow other trails and make more work for themselves. I mean, don't get me wrong, it's a murder. It's big time. They'll go for it; they'll want a conviction. But believe me, if I can set them up with someone like Elton, they'll take the easy route. One-track mind. Go for it. That's what they're like.'

'Jim. Calm down.'

'Calm down, she says.'

I tried to, but failed. Loren was taking in what I was saying. At least, I thought she was. You could almost hear the little warning bell ringing in her head, just as she began to argue with herself.

'But you can't do it...'

I ignored her and carried on in the same vein.

'I need to give them enough to convince them they've got a suspect. Once they're convinced, it will steamroller. Don't you see? If you did more criminal law, you would, Loren. That's the beauty of it. They'll actually do the rest for me. They'll make up bits and add bits and build on what they've got. Might even get the cell confession if we're lucky.'

'The what?'

'It will land on your lap just before the trial starts... the old cell confession. Some poor bastard will be pressurised into saying that Mr X confessed all while sharing a cell on remand. And then you find out Mr X has had three years knocked off his sentence. Always view it with suspicion, Loren. Sneaky trick, that one.'

'You're serious about all this, aren't you?'

'It's a devious game, this criminal justice thing, but we've got to play it. It's our only chance. What I have to do is keep in touch and keep on top, and the only way of doing that is representing the guy accused of doing it.'

Loren took a sip of lukewarm tea as she mulled it over. I made one short sharp attempt to ram the point home.

'It's either that or we spend the rest of our lives in prison... for something we didn't actually do: murder!'

I almost shouted the word, and then chastised myself. After all, it was two o'clock in the morning and hardly the cleverest of things to shout at the wall of my nearest neighbour. It seemed to have done the trick, though. Loren stroked back her hair as she spoke, in idiosyncratic style.

'...it might just work.'

It was just a spark at first, a whisper to herself, but it was as if I'd made her tick over with a starting handle, and she was about to rev up. She continued slowly, deliberately, as if she was trying to convince herself as much as me.

'So, somehow you've got to get Sarena's blood on Elton's clothes... and fibres or whatever... but what about a motive? You're saying that he's just molested a young woman, schoolgirl, but why should the police think that Sarena was molested?'

'Well, they won't at first, but they're bound to consider a sexual motive. And given that Elton's just done it to someone else...'

'Yes, but where's the evidence? It's not as if he raped her.'

'Well...'

What I wanted to say was 'they might find evidence of recent sexual intercourse.' I very nearly did, but something in the back of my mind told me that it might just tip Loren over the edge... and she might fall down on the prosecution side. I disguised the thought with a look.

'Well, the point is, Elton's prone to this sort of behaviour. It's only one further step along the line.'

'Well, you know him better than anyone.'

'Yeah, I do. Poor bastard. I really like the guy.'

'Uh?'

'I know. You wouldn't think so, would you? But if things did work out, I might actually get a manslaughter verdict. It's crazy, I know, but he'd end up in the very place he needs to be.'

'What do you mean?'

'Because of lawyer privilege I can't say. Well, I can tell you... I know for a fact that Elton has already committed a serious sexual assault on a nurse. Not only did he tell me, but I know that the nurse told the police the suspect asked if she wanted to see his pants. It was the first thing he said when he approached her. I knew straightaway that it was Elton, but I can't tell the police that. All I can do is advise Elton that he ought to speak to them himself, but of course he won't do that. See?... He ought to be inside, anyway. In fact, he ought to be getting proper mental health treatment, but nobody cares... Nobody gives

a shit!'

Loren slowly nodded her head in understanding.

'I actually like Elton... Oh, maybe I'm being ridiculous. Maybe we should just go to the police?'

I collapsed onto my sofa. I was drained, but still managed to keep an eye on Loren, to take in her reaction. I couldn't detect one.

'I'm exhausted, Lol. What do you think?'

Loren blew out some air. Some of the tissues on the coffee table dropped onto the floor.

'Yeah... No... Oh, I don't know. Oh God, I really don't know.'

She started to cry. She cried for ages. I put my arms around her and hugged her firmly.

'We've got to try and stay focused.'

Loren pulled away from my hug.

'I could go the police...?'

I panicked then, immediately regretting what I'd said earlier. I had to shake her out of it.

'And say what?'

'That it wasn't my fault...'

I let the comment float around awkwardly in the air. I knew where her mind might be going.

'You had hold of the knife too.'

The silence of the night was disturbed by a gritting lorry sweeping past my front window. I needed to remind Loren of a few home truths.

'Well, I didn't actually... have hold of the knife. Not when... not when it stabbed her.'

Loren was now breathing in and out as if she'd just finished a marathon. I think it might have been shock kicking in.

'It was your fault, though... your fault you were cheating on me!'

'You wouldn't, would you?'

'Would you? Eh? Would you, Jim, if it was the other way around?'

CHAPTER 35

The following morning, the second day of Elton's trial, I arrived at court early, at about half past eight. I knew that Harry wanted to see Elton, to find out if he could remember anything more about his Eastbourne experience. As I was about to approach the revolving doors, I found myself being tugged backwards. Someone had got hold of my suit jacket and was yanking at it.

'*You're* coming with me.'

Sammy was with somebody else who was lurking a few yards behind. I looked at the guy a couple of times because I knew I'd met him before. Then I realised that not only was it the same guy who I'd passed on the stairs at the Oasis, but the very same guy who'd once given me a key to a money bag in the Cotswolds.

I was still frozen to the spot as Sammy pulled me again.

'I said *come on*.'

'Sammy, what are you doing?'

His associate then stepped right up next to me. He took the briefcase from my hand, wrenching it out of my grip. I could see people I knew going into the court building - other lawyers, court staff, police officers, etc. I thought it best not to cause a scene. I addressed Sammy with trepidation.

'What's going on?'

'It's time to talk. Properly.'

Sammy's steely look still penetrated.

'But I'm in the middle of a trial. I've got to see my client.'

'Later.'

Then I heard his associate say, 'Gordon. See you over the road.'

He walked off with my briefcase in his hand. I looked inquisitively at Sammy.

'What's he doing? And why's he calling you Gordon?'

'I want the fucking truth, Jim... and I mean it.'

There was a purposeful resonance to his voice, with more than a touch of hostility. I was taken aback. Though Sammy had been obstreperous when I'd met him outside court the previous afternoon, he'd never spoken to me in those tones before.

'About what?'

Sammy didn't answer; he just looked at me with menace. I wasn't sure what else to say, so referred back to my opening shot.

'Why Gordon, anyway?'

'I thought you were a football man.'

'I am, sort of.'

'Gordon Banks, mate. Our World Cup-winning goalie?'

Sammy glared at me.

'What? You haven't heard of him?'

'Of course I have.'

'When I used the name Banks back at Harrow Road nick, Bamber came up with Gordon as a nickname. Better than the Robin you came up with.'

I remembered the awful joke name and smiled, hoping that it had broken the ice.

'He's Bamber's hero, ain't he? He was actually born in Wembley, 30th July 1966, the day we won it. His dad told him he could hear the roar of the crowd through the hospital window.'

I instantly remembered that 'Mr Bamber' was the name Sammy had given to me. 'He'll sort you out', I seemed to recall Sammy saying, and he did too, giving me a huge wad of cash for my deeds.

I glanced over at Bamber with half a smile. He was now loitering over the road, outside the pub, and still holding my bloody briefcase. He nodded at Sammy and walked into the pub.

'We're having breakfast. They do a decent fry-up in there.'

I could see the chalkboard sign outside: 'Full English – special offer – 7 'till 10.' There was something quite disturbing about the subtext.

'Sammy, for the last time, what are you actually *doing* here?'

'You really don't know?' he asked, as if I must have done.

'No.'

Sammy looked at me again. Just for a moment he looked quite foxed, as if he couldn't work out whether to believe me.

'You remember Bamber?'

'Yeah, sort of.'

Sammy didn't pick up on my puzzlement. He just grabbed my arm.

'Come on. Let's go.'

'What, now? You've got to be joking.'

'Do I look like I'm joking?'

Sammy was in a dangerous mood. I knew he could be as hard as nails when he wanted to be.

'Look, just let me go into the building and explain to my barrister.'

'No.'

Sammy knew I couldn't argue the point, but rammed it home nonetheless.

'You can't get in without ID. Nobody can. I had to make my own.'

Sammy smiled, the same sardonic smile he'd used the day before.

'And mine's in my briefcase,' I slowly revealed, realising

why Bamber had taken it.

Sammy took hold of my arm. I could feel him pinching through to the bone.

'So come on. Now!'

'Okay, let go, will you.'

Sammy pinched me even harder and pulled me towards him. Then he pulled me into a little recess further up the street, away from public gaze.

'Got your phone back then?'

My face was no more than six inches from Sammy's. I could see the little pink growth on the outside of his eyelid. I was totally lost for a response.

'We used to visit the Oasis a fair bit... back then.'

'Sammy, please tell me what this is all about!'

'Why would anyone respond to a message from someone who died six months ago... eh?'

'I don't know...' I said, quite pathetically.

'I mean, you weren't expecting a fucking miracle, were you?'

'Please just tell me.'

'How do I know you didn't fuck the silly bitch up yourself to get some of the action?'

Sammy was causing a pain to shoot up my arm as he increased his grip some more.

'I promise you I haven't got a clue what you're talking about. What action?'

Sammy whispered, from only three inches away, with that distinctive wheeze piercing in my ears.

'If you're fucking with me... you cunt. I will tear your fucking balls off.'

CHAPTER 36

Sleep was ineffectual and episodic. I lay next to Loren for the rest of the night, still dressed, and occasionally drifting in and out of consciousness. I kept thinking about how to get Elton and Sarena in the same place.

I took myself back to the day when Sarena had broken my heart. When that waitress had told me she was still in London, cavorting with other men. That was the day I'd called Loren in a panic, and I remembered her little speech:

'Loren Granger, twenty-nine next March. I've got a mum and a dad and a brother called Simon. Dad's a consultant anaesthetist; Mum's a care assistant. Oh, and Simon's a bum. I'm a solicitor at Johnson Gower. Been there just over a year. Before that worked for London Transport as part of their legal team. Got bored with it. Wanted to go into private practice. I'm ambitious; I want to be a partner at Johnson Gower. I want to run my own firm eventually. I want to have children, anytime will do. I want to have a nice home and a husband who loves me. There you are, simple. Actually, I'm not sure about the husband bit. It seems to go with the children, that's all…'

Through the open bedroom door I could see the lights on the graphic equaliser still gently bouncing up and down to quiet but endless repeats of Morcheeba: 'Left my soul there, down by the sea'. It was another of my scratched CDs. Suddenly I shouted out at Loren.

'Your father!'

'Uh.. what? Jim, I was trying to rest, like you said!'

'Your dad's an anaesthetist.'

'So?'

'So he's on call sometimes, for emergencies. He carries the stuff around... It's what I need for Elton.'

I waited for the penny to drop.

'No. I can't.'

'Of course you can.'

After convincing her that it was the only way I could see of getting Elton where I wanted him, she reluctantly caved in. She eventually agreed to steal one of her father's anaesthetic syringes. She really was very reluctant to do so, but she was as desperate as I was to see this through.

We talked for ages that Sunday morning, planning and scheming. At half ten she left for the hospital. She would join her dad at work for a while and then take him to lunch. He would be delighted. She'd lost count of the number of times he had invited her to do exactly that on his Sunday shifts. I had a list of jobs to do and we would meet later that evening.

When Loren had gone, I popped out to the boot to shove some of those plastic freezer-block things into Sarena's sack. I don't know why... I thought perhaps it was the right thing to do. I guess I was worried that she might start to smell, and I didn't want my final sense stimulation of Sarena to be that of rotting flesh. I was hardly thinking straight, anyway. It was bad enough having to actually deal with a dead body, but dealing with a body you'd come to worship, a body you'd adored, a body that had been so appealingly alive, was unbearable. I needed every sinew of energy to shield the trauma from my senses.

I tried to set about my plan. I drove to the tip and disposed of the bits and pieces from Sarena's flat. I decided not to get rid of the gun or the knife, at least not there. I worried that the gun might clog up the grinder – stupid, maybe, but that's what I thought. I counted away the minutes of the day wandering around Camden Market, completing my little tasks.

Later that Sunday evening, at a quarter to nine as planned, I went out to use a public call box. I had driven to Baker Street to do so. I picked up the phone and called the bail hostel in Shepherd's Bush. I did one of my lyrical chameleon jobbies. General brain-dead scally:

'Yeah... er, Elton there, mate?'

'Elton? Elton Spears?'

'Yeah.'

'Who shall I say is calling?'

'Just get him mate, will ya?'

I could hear the TV on in the background. Elton was watching a Roadrunner cartoon. I could distinctly hear a trademark 'beep beep.' As I waited for Elton to get to the phone, I wondered if my own hare-brained scheme was no better than one of Wile E. Coyote's elaborate plans. A few seconds later I could hear fumbling on the line, then Elton's voice.

'Yeah?'

'Elton. Got some money for ya... can't wait... Be outside McDonald's on the Green, in fifteen minutes.'

There was no need to say anything else. I'd known Elton long enough to learn how to plant the bait.

Fifteen minutes later and there he was, gormless as ever, standing at one of the bus shelters on Shepherd's Bush Green. I don't know what he thought he was doing, or who he thought he was going to meet, but I just knew that he'd be there. I suppose the sad truth was that if you told Elton to go and stand in the middle of a crocodile-infested lake, he'd do it without a second thought... especially if there was the lure of money, or a 'go large' burger, or a giant Snickers bar.

I kept Elton in shot, drove up a side road, and pulled over in the Swedish thing. Sarena was already in the boot, quiet as a dead person. Loren was in the passenger seat, equally quiet. We'd gone over it enough times. Loren knew exactly what to do. All we had to do was get Elton into the car.

I started up the engine again and pulled away, soon turning left onto Shepherd's Bush Green. I slowed down alongside Elton before coming to a halt. I got out of the door and walked over to the bus shelter. He was looking at the entrance to McDonald's.

'Hiya, Elton.'

'Yeah.'

Elton didn't even look confused, and had no concept of the incongruity of the situation. He smiled at me.

'Some money.'

'What money?'

'Dunno.'

'Someone's got some money for you?'

'Yeah.'

'I'll give you some money, Elton. Come on, in you get.'

By this time Loren had positioned herself in the back seat on the passenger side. I opened up the front passenger door. I didn't say anything else. Neither did Loren, or Elton, come to think of it. He just sat in the car and stared out of the window as we drove off.

I drove just a few hundred yards to the roundabout where the Kensington Hilton is. I pulled up opposite there on a dark side street, away from any street lighting. As I did so, Loren had been focusing on Elton's huge, thick neck. Without warning she stabbed him with a syringe. Elton jerked forward and I picked up the Evening Standard and started wafting it about, shouting something about wasps. Ridiculous, I know, particularly in early January, but there you are, that's what I did. Elton was trying to slap the back of his own neck with his hand, and soon got the message that he'd been stung.

'Wasps.'

That's all he said, and I wanted to laugh and cry at the same time.

I smashed the Evening Standard against the windscreen, said 'got it', and it was all over. I kept glancing across at Elton, hoping I'd see him suddenly collapse in a heap on the seat. It took about ten seconds or so before he started to lose consciousness. He rocked gently forwards, and started muttering nonsense.

'Money burger. Don't want money with cheese. Don't eat cheese. Eat sardines. Sardine burger, no cheese...'

Then, plonk. His head would have hit the dashboard if his seatbelt hadn't stopped it. I gently pulled him back and rested him properly in his seat. Elton was sleeping like a baby.

Loren shuffled from the passenger-side rear seat to the driver's side. Once she'd moved, I turned the plastic knob by the side of Elton's seat, slowly lowering him to a semi horizontal position. The top half of his body was out of view, making it look like I was alone in the front of the car.

When we approached Loren's flat in Camden, she started to argue.

She wanted to come too, but it wasn't the plan. It wasn't an argument I could afford to lose, either. I had to do things on my own. I eventually dropped her off on the Camden Road.

I took a deep breath to compose myself, before setting off on my journey. A drugged six-foot-four mentally unstable giant and a gorgeous dead young charlatan were about to be taken on a trip to the seaside.

CHAPTER 37

As Sammy marched me over the road to the pub, I was trying to work it all out. I knew then that it must have been Bamber who texted, pretending to be Sarena. I knew they were trying to spook me. I had absolutely no idea why, or even how either Elton or Sarena were connected.

Even though Sammy had loosened his grip, it still felt as if I was being frog-marched. He plonked me down on a seat next to Bamber, who was already at a table.

Sammy then pulled a stool right up next to me. If he was trying to intimidate me, then he was doing a pretty good job. All sorts of information was racing around in my head. My little computer was trying to put it all together. Sammy smiled... a disingenuous Bob Monkhouse-type smile. Then he spoke again.

'That day in Harrow Road nick. Cheers, Jim. Top bloke.'

Sammy was suddenly sounding all cheery. I tried to respond in kind.

'Well, that was ages ago, Sammy. And you... erm, you thanked me before.'

'Paid off your debts, so my bookie tells me.'

'Yeah.'

Then I saw him, coffee mug in hand, at the bar. I can't say my heart sank, because it all tock a few moments to register. The man was looking over at Sammy, who briefly nodded in response. Then the man limped over to the far side of the bar. I could feel the fear in my own voice, 'Jesus. I know that guy. He's called Norton, isn't he?'

'He tells me you were asking questions?'

'Uh?'

'About Sarena. Ooh, let's see, summer last year?'

Sammy peered at me with those raging eyes. It was all beginning to come into focus, horribly into focus. I blurted out, 'Fuck. You're Gordon, aren't you? You're *that* fucking Gordon. You're Sarena's Gordon?... Aren't you?'

Sammy wasn't buying it.

'You do surprise me, Jim. Man of your calibre.'

But my shock was totally real.

'Sammy. Oh my God… can we speak in private?'

'No, mate, we can't. Bamber's me ears; Bamber's me eyes.'

I slowly slid my head down into my folded arms, as a certain vision hit me... I was at the casino with Loren. We'd spotted Norton limping into the entrance hall. The doorman had given titbits of info... I was so open-mouthed I could have swallowed a goat. Bamber, I thought. Shit, bloody Bamber Gascoigne, isn't it? The bloke's a dead ringer. Absolute spitting image. Old quizmaster. They used to sit on top of each other. It *was* University Challenge. You idiot, Harwood. Before Jeremy Paxman it was Bamber Gascoigne. All that time spent watching telly as a kid and it still hadn't hit me. I finally said out loud, 'Bamber-bloody-Gascoigne!'

'Jim, you wanna tell me what the fuck you're on about now?'

'The doorman at the Victoria casino. It doesn't matter. Sammy, I had no idea, I honestly didn't... please, tell me what this is all about.'

For the first time Sammy could see I was genuinely frightened.

'You're shaking, Jim. Calm down...'

All I could do was smile in trepidation. Sammy added,

with a facetious tone, 'So, you reckon he did it, then? Your guy... Elton Spears.'

I had to try to keep my mind in focus as I answered.

'Um, yeah. Looks like it. I mean, that's why I was making enquiries about Sarena.'

Sammy didn't like that. He screwed up his face and placed it six inches in front of mine. I could see that small pink growth on the outside of his eyelid again. This time it was twitching in irritation. As he snarled at me I could feel a spray of spit hit my eye.

'Don't *fucking* lie to me.'

'Okay, Sammy, okay.'

'You didn't have a case until 16th January this year, when the body was found, so why the fuck should you be making enquiries about Sarena six months previously?'

'Erm...'

I had no answer. No answer at all. I was sinking. I struggled to put a few words together, not really sure what they were going to be.

'Yeah. Right. Sorry... All right, let's be straight with each other.'

'Just tell me,' snarled Sammy.

I asked, tentatively, 'Did Sarena work for you?'

'Just tell me how you met her.'

'I just bumped into her. In a pub, not far from here, actually. It was early summer last year.'

'After you'd seen me at Harrow Road nick?'

'I don't know. I suppose so, yeah. *Why?*'

'What did she tell you?'

'About what?'

'You better not be fucking with me.'

'I'm not. She didn't tell me anything. She only mentioned the name Gordon a short while before she... before she was found dead.'

'What did she say?'

'Just... I can't remember. I honestly can't remember. All I can remember is that she said Gordon would kill her if she said anything.'

'About what?'

'Well, I don't know, do I?'

Sammy ran his fingers over his stubble. I started to shake again, and I think he sensed that my unease was genuine. He grabbed my arm, this time almost pinning it to the table.

'She died with certain information in that little brain of hers. Ha, little brain... fucking huge brain, mate. Information we couldn't risk writing down anywhere. You know, the sort of thing the donkeys produce in court when they find the right discs. I lost a lot of revenue, Jim. A fortune.'

'Please...'

It was all I could say in response. Sammy must have filled in the 'I really didn't know' for himself. He finally released his grip.

'Look. Sammy. I don't know anything about that. I risked my career for you. I...'

'Fuck off! You couldn't resist forty grand any more than the next man.'

I had to take that on the chin. I was more concerned about Sammy thinking I'd put one over on him.

'Sammy, I haven't said anything to anyone, I swear. I didn't know about this. And I wouldn't stitch up my own client.'

Sammy laughed like a demented *Family Fortunes* contestant.

'Do you want to say that again? That bit about fucking over your own client? What the fuck are you doing to that pudding in there, then?'

I realised Sammy was referring to Elton, and the trial.

'Jesus, Sammy. What do you know?'

'No, mate, it's what *you* know that matters.'

My head was spinning, still trying to piece it all together. I looked over at Norton again. He was now sat at the bar, eating a bacon roll.

'Who *is* Norton, anyway?'

'Norton's safe. He's a trader. That's all you need to know.

He's my man in the City.'

Then some of things Sarena had said came back to me.

'She mentioned some bloke called Kelvin, I think?'

'What do you know about Kelvin?'

'They'd been to things together. Football matches. And they went to Edinburgh.'

'Now you're talking. Tell me about Edinburgh?'

'It was ages ago, last Christmas time. Sammy, hold on a minute. I'm being honest with you. Tell me, was my meeting with Sarena a coincidence or what?'

Bamber shuffled nervously. I wanted to say out loud 'here's your starter for ten', but fought against it. My mind always plays these games in times of panic. Sammy seemed intent on talking to me from about six inches away. He was very alert, in criminal mode I'd say. He spoke powerfully but with that menacing wheeze.

''Course it wasn't a fucking coincidence! Sarena had worked for me since she was sixteen. The girl was a prodigy, a fucking beauty. She'd built up identities all over Europe. She was perfect. She'd set things up. Run cards, laundering chains, all sorts. She was dead clever. She could store numbers like a computer. You wouldn't believe it. PIN numbers, card numbers, safety deposit box numbers...'

Safety deposit box numbers? I silently repeated it in my mind, getting a flashback to Sarena mumbling something similar.

'Little boxes,' I let out involuntarily.

'That's it,' said Sammy. 'What do you *know*?'

'She said something about little boxes, but I honestly hadn't a clue. She passed out a few minutes later.'

Sammy was glaring again, trying to work out if I was lying or concealing. For some reason he picked up a plastic bottle of HP sauce and started ripping off the Houses of Parliament label.

'But what's all this got to do with me?' I asked in desperation.

It prompted quite a tirade from Sammy.

'Christ's sake, Jim, she was my number-one kiter... my flying fucking ensign. When I got busted on that art gallery shit, she was pissed off. It took me a while to find my feet and she lost out on her income. Couldn't pay her for a while, could I? So she set out to get the forty grand back. Greedy twat.'

'The forty grand Bamber...?'

'Exactly.' Sammy interrupted.

My brain couldn't think fast enough.

'Did you send her after me, Sammy? Am I being thick here or what? You did, didn't you?'

''Course I didn't. She *came* after you. She wanted a piece of the action. Saw you as easy pickings, mate. I told her that you'd earned it, that you were safe, but she must have set out to track you down.'

I knew that Sammy was spot-on, and it hurt.

'Pretended to meet you by chance, yeah?' Sammy guessed.

I briefly mulled it over, before accepting the inevitable.

'Yeah,' I replied, weakly.

'Had a little story for you, and a decent cover?'

'...Yeah, I guess she did. She'd bluffed her way into doing work experience at a barristers' chambers.'

'Yeah. She's good at that. She didn't tell me, though. No... see, by the time I find out there's something's wrong, listen to this.... by the time I find out, she told me she'd fallen in love. Twat.'

'She told you *that*?'

'Why? Didn't she tell you?'

'You mean with *me*? Erm... No. She didn't.'

I jerked my head back in disbelief. Sammy added, 'She even forced herself to keep away from you for months.'

'The Australia trip?' I thought out loud.

'If that's what she told you. Is this Kelvin guy black?'

I was still reflecting over what Sammy had just said about Sarena, but knew I had to answer.

'I never saw him... I remember now. She said something

about him being a rival.'

'He's the fuck who was drugging her up, trying to break through.'

'She said she'd been kidnapped.'

'The cunt,' Sammy whispered to himself.

A few more pennies dropped into place, and my slot-machine of a brain rolled around. It came up with three £-signs in a row. Sammy felt the need to explain.

'He wanted her brain, not her body. Numbers, that's what he wanted. Numbers we'd had to kill for. Worth a fortune.'

Sammy got right up close again. He was going nowhere without the answers.

'Think... did she write down any numbers? Did she ever say that she'd written them down anywhere?'

'I thought she kept them in her head.'

'Fuck's sake, get up to speed. She knew her time was up a couple of months before she died. She knew. Must have done.'

'Are you telling me that someone was trying to kill her? That she was going to die anyway?'

'If she was forced to reveal the info, yeah. There'd be no use for her then. She'd be a liability. Kelvin would have dumped her. We thought he had, but she must have escaped. Then this Spears guy gets nicked and the trail leads to you.'

Sammy wasn't bothered about my liaisons with Sarena, or the fact that poor innocent Elton had been framed. He wanted Sarena's code numbers, and the money they unlocked. With information coming at me like a train, it was tough to clear a thought. I reckoned one wrong step and maybe Sammy would do away with me.

'There was something... a laptop. She had it when I first met her. She said it was stolen from storage. Sammy, you better explain this to me because I'm out of my depth here.'

'No, you're not... Think!'

I was thinking as hard as I could, but I had to be careful about what I revealed – or in what order I revealed it, to be more precise. There was one question I had to ask, though the fear of asking made me stutter in hesitation.

'Do... do you actually *know*... how Sarena died?'

'I know that great oaf didn't kill her. And I know that you know he didn't either...'

Sammy was anything but hesitant. He waited for me to respond. I slowly nodded my head. Sammy continued.

'Norton's got a contact in the Serious Crime Squad. He's a goldmine. Come the end of last year, we're really concerned about Sarena. She's behaving oddly; she's under pressure.'

'Yeah, I noticed the change.'

'So Norton's mate on alert. Her body's found on some beach in January. She's been tooled up and dumped. We put the emergency plan into action. Make out like it might be a political killing. We play on the father, the fantasy student, all that crap the prosecution barrister said in court.'

'I knew someone was behind that. I knew there was something dodgy about this father business.'

'They haven't got a clue about her.'

'So, what *is* her real name, then?'

Sammy gave me a look that suggested I'd just asked the world's most stupid question.

'You don't need to know,' he delivered, with a growl. Then carried on.

'We thought someone must have got to her, tortured her, God knows what. So we reckoned they'd got the numbers. But nothing happens. There's no activity, no blackmail, no offer of any deals, nothing. It's just a dead end... We're waiting for this Kelvin bloke to approach us for a cut, but he never shows. Then guess what? Months later I find that me old mate Jim Harwood is acting for the man accused of killing her. Now, there's a coincidence, thought I. A mighty odd little coincidence. Sarena goes off after you and a few months later you're representing the bloke accused of killing her.'

Sammy stared at me as if I ought to say something of

import. Confess, maybe? I knew I should have put more of it together, but I'd been dealing with a degree of criminal sophistication I hadn't bargained for. I really did feel out of my depth. In fact, I didn't want to be swimming there at all. As I was thinking all this, Sammy got even closer. He breathed coffee all over me as he said, 'You killed Sarena.'

'It was an accident, Sammy.'

'Jesus fucking Christ...'

Sammy squeezed the HP bottle so tightly that a blast of brown sauce shot up from the top and splattered onto the table. I could almost hear his blood on the boil. I had to try and simmer it down.

'Look, firstly I knew nothing about this. Sarena was loyal until her death, I swear. I've got a colleague called Loren. Sarena flipped. She got this knife. And she had a gun.'

Sammy briefly swapped a look with the mute Bamber. I wasn't quite sure what they were conveying to each other, but the gun revelation clearly wasn't a surprise. If anything, I think the look meant 'so that's what happened to it.' I knew I had to explain some more.

'There was a struggle. All three of us fell to the floor. She fell on the knife. That's the truth... I loved her too, you know.'

Sammy was slowly shaking his head. I had to convince him.

'I know it sounds crazy. I was hooked, Sammy. So I panicked. I wanted to keep Loren out of it. In truth it was her hand on the knife, but it doesn't matter. Fact is, I didn't fancy her chances or mine on an accident defence.'

Sammy was pulling at his bottom lip in thought.

'It's true, I swear. I didn't know what they'd find out about Sarena, did I? With no suspect they would have dug up her background. So I had to give them one... and sharpish. You've seen what it's like in there. It's a sham. The whole justice system is a sham.'

I sensed Sammy might finally be taking it in.

'It's a game, Sammy. A dangerous one sometimes... but

I'm not a bad player, you know that. So I framed Elton. Then, well, I knew he'd want me to act for him. He doesn't trust anyone else.'

I'm not exactly sure what Sammy was thinking, but he came out with, 'So, where's this laptop?'

'I don't know. She said it had been stolen.'

I felt a further beat of relief as Sammy exhaled for the first time in ages. I wasn't sure if he believed me, but something had changed within him. Then he took another deep breath, as if he was going to stay underwater for some time.

'After I got nicked, we decided to store all the info with Sarena. Get me? We couldn't risk storing the box numbers on disc, so we tested her and tested her. I tell you, you wouldn't believe it. She could just reel them off on demand. So, we planned to strike in December.'

'You were still banged up.'

'Well done, Jim. So I was. So fucking what? I could still pull a few strings.'

'Yeah, I guess.'

'I was running the show from Ford Open. Bamber had it all geared up. Norton was gonna do the wash and spin-drying, and we'd be laughing.

'What went wrong?'

'It went knob-shaped. Sarena starts going all funny, acting weird, taking drugs... She's under pressure. Her moods keep changing. We reckon somebody's onto her, but she keeps it all under wraps. I don't know if it's the donkey's serious crime mob or some bastard trying to cut into our scam. Then a few weeks later she's snuffed it. Fuckin' washed up on some poxy beach. Now I reckon she knew she was about to snuff it, only the last person she thought was going to blow her out was you.'

I felt sick at the thought.

'Jesus, Sammy, I'm sorry.'

Sammy swapped another look with Bamber just as Norton joined us at the table. I think he was piecing it together himself. He thought out loud.

'Sarena put the stuff on this laptop. That's what she's done. Now where the hell is it?'

'I'm telling you, I don't know.'

I could sense a slap around the face in the offing, but it didn't arrive. I visualised being taken off to a remote warehouse, being tied up, being tortured until I revealed its whereabouts. I remembered Sammy once telling me how his mate had sawn off a rival gang member's fingers with a breadknife, before stuffing them in the guy's mouth. I recall Sammy laughing about it, telling me his sick joke: 'How's that for handy work?'

I struggled to piece together as much as I could. I needed to understand exactly what it was that Sammy needed. It was do or die.

'You can't get the numbers again, then?' I asked in desperation.

'That contact's dead as arseholes.'

I smiled nervously, and knowingly. Then said, half to myself, 'Like Mr. Gunasekera?'

'Spot-on, boy. Sad, eh?'

Though I'd always suspected Sammy was ruthless, to have it confirmed like this really brought it home. He'd use people to fabricate stories, then dispose of them so they could never spill the beans. I could feel all six eyes glued on me: Sammy's, Bamber's, Norton's...

Sammy waited for the little Irish fella to put his breakfast in front of him. I hadn't even heard him order it. I could still feel myself shaking.

'I don't want anything to do with this...'

Sammy picked up his knife and held it.

'Jim. You're a blind beggar. You're entitled to a shout. That's what she wanted. Don't you see that? She only tapped the stuff in because she feared she was going to be kidnapped, tortured, God knows what...'

I was trying to take in what he was saying. Sammy then picked up his fork and stabbed at a sausage. I don't think he had any intention of eating it.

'She told you about the theft in case anything happened. Probably thought sooner or later you'd make the link with me. But she didn't expect to go so suddenly in January, without the chance to say anything else.'

Sammy pushed his face up to mine again, as he said, 'How many Swedish geezers do you know?'

'None, why?'

'Think!'

'I know a clerk who's Swedish. Billen the Swede. Billen Ben we call him. It's possible Sarena might have met him through a guy called Giles. A barrister she ripped off.'

'No, I know about that.'

I was a touch thrown at the give-away line, but ignored it to concentrate on the point.

'She never said anything to me, Sammy, honest. I really don't know anyone from Sweden.'

'She was stoned senseless. Said if anything happens, find the Swedish person, or something like that...'

A bolt of lightning shot through me. I felt like the monster when Dr Frankenstein flicks the switch on. Sammy looked on as my eyes lit up like spotlights. I slapped Sammy on the back, quite spontaneously.

'Give me one minute. Stay put. I promise. Trust me. Stay put.'

I rushed out of the pub, literally pushing chairs out of the way as if I was Harrison Ford in *Raiders of the Lost Ark*. I didn't know if Sammy was following me. I didn't really care. My mind was telling me to run.

Into the main entrance, past the kiosk, past the big yellow notice that tells you that you better hand over your life savings if you want to park the car there overnight. Don't take the lift, run down the slope, to level two, level three, level four. There it is. My Swedish thing. There it is, winking at me as I press the magic button.

I checked under the seats. Nothing. Then the boot... the boot where Sarena had lay dead. Nothing. But underneath the spare tyre, the edge of a carrier bag was sticking out. A PC World carrier bag. I tugged at it, but it was stuck. I peeled back a little more of the boot cover and had to yank away the jack that was jutting out. I pulled the bag towards me. It was heavyish... about the weight of a Toshiba laptop, I thought. You cunning little devil. If only you'd have told me, you might still be here. If only Loren hadn't had such abysmal timing. If only her stupid little gleaming white Nissan Micra hadn't followed me. If only... if only...

I tucked the charger lead back into the carrier bag and instinctively decided to call Loren. I'm not really sure why. I pressed her stored mobile number.

'Loren, where are you?'

'On my way to court. Just left St Paul's Tube.'

'Something's happened, Lol. I'm by that pub opposite the Old Bailey.'

'What?'

'In that pub by the car park.'

'It's quarter to nine in the morning, Jim!... What's happening?'

'Just get here now! Please...'

'What's *wrong*?'

'Everything. Nothing. I don't know. Just get here.'

I walked back towards the pub, trying out a couple of breathing exercises, slowing it all down. I could see Sammy standing outside the pub with Bamber. I smiled and held the bag up in the air like I'd just caught the world's biggest fish. Sammy gesticulated madly, as if I was holding some sort of unexploded bomb. I realised I shouldn't exactly be attracting attention. After all, we were right outside the Old Bailey, and a cross-section of the legal hinterland was walking past.

Sammy and Bamber were joined by Norton. I briefly thought about testing out my old rugby skills by doing a nifty dummy and sprinting off down Ludgate Hill, then thought better of it. I always used to get flattened by the opposing flank forwards. Anyway, there was nowhere to run.

Back in the pub, I put the carrier bag in front of Sammy.

He peered in. He pulled out the laptop, then, bold as brass, plugged it into one of the pub's sockets. Norton and Bamber were leaning over us as Sammy waited impatiently for Sarena's 'documents' icon to appear. I studied his face as he waited. Then his mouth began to fill with teeth.... and his mouth slowly opened in a wide smile of elation.

'Cock-a-doodle-fucking-doo!'

I could see question marks, pound signs, something like '£/?"8^.' I said the daftest of things: 'It's all in code.'

Sammy looked at me.

'Which I gave her! If the worst came to the worst... It's beautiful, that's what it is.'

I could sense the excitement in Sammy's voice. Then, quite out of the blue, he put his arm around my shoulder.

'Jim, about earlier, about getting heavy and that. It's just, I couldn't work out what the fuck was going on. I doubted you. I did.'

'You're not the only one.'

'Numbers. Lovely little numbers. I'll get you a piece of the action.'

'I don't want it.'

Sammy could feel me trying to move away. That's when I realised that Norton and Bamber had been joined by two other well-built guys who were still pinning me to my seat. Sammy nodded at them and they moved away.

'Well, that's up to you, Jim. But you'll have to turn it down yourself. Because I'm a man of my word, and you'll be offered it.'

'I know you are, Sammy. I know you're a man of your word. I only wish I was.'

Before long they were on their way. Sammy, the mute Bamber, the limping Norton, and the two heavies. Off they went to plan their little escapade. I would imagine that we're talking several million, knowing Sammy.

All sorts of emotions were coming and going. It struck me that Sammy didn't give a toss about Sarena's death. Not once he'd got his box of magic tricks.

I dared think. So, Sarena loved me after all, in her own sort of way. Those little bits and pieces made a little more sense. I guessed Loren didn't need to know everything, but she'd find out the truth sooner or later, lingering along the track, sneaking along those parallel lines.

CHAPTER 38

I drove off with my two remaining passengers, Sussex-bound. A hip flask containing Sarena's blood was now in my jacket pocket. I'd used a tiny funnel to pour it in from the cup.

From Camden I chose the shortest distance to the M25: straight up the A1 to the South Mimms junction. Then I went east towards the Dartford bridge. It might have been quicker to drive through central London on a Sunday evening, but I had to cut down on the chances of being stopped by the police. I thought of all the traffic lights and roundabouts – potentials for innocuous disaster. Somehow the M25 seemed safer.

I set the CD on remote, or tried to. I must have been halfway down the M23 on the way to Brighton when the Doors came on, and about fifty minutes later it was 'Led Zep Four'. The CD was playing up again and I'd be stuck with Led Zep for the rest of the journey. If I hear 'Stairway to Heaven' one more time, I'll stab someone. Bad choice of words.

I drove around the outskirts of Brighton and picked up the coast road to Eastbourne. There were remnants of the weekend snow on the roads. I constantly had visions of crashing on the ice. We'd all be found at the foot of the cliff in a mangled wreck. What would the donkeys make of that?, as Sammy might say. a wrecked and squashed car, a wrecked and squashed and already dead Sarena... a wrecked and squashed Elton and a wrecked and squashed Jim. I let out a nervous chuckle. How preposterous.

I drove on past Newhaven and briefly followed the river inland. At a gate next to a small bridge I stopped the car. I'd put the gun and the knife into a carrier bag. I'd put a large stone brick in there too. I'd tied the bag with brown tape, around and around until it looked like an old-fashioned leather football. I threw the 'ball' into the river and it sank straight down. I started up the Swedish thing again and drove back towards the coast road.

My tear ducts were itching to water. I drove on and turned up a small track. I parked there and got out. I could feel the cold claw at my hands as I opened up the boot. I peeled back the top of the sack and turned Sarena over, not wanting to see her face.

I took out the clothes brush I'd bought that day in Camden Market. I brushed it over her black velvety dress. I stroked it one last time. I removed the cooler bags and forced the sack back over Sarena. Then I picked up the brush and closed the boot.

The cold was unbearable. It must have been minus ten with that wind chill, and my thin latex gloves were beginning to freeze over. The moonlight was enough to see, so I turned off the Swedish thing's interior light. Elton seemed as dead as Sarena. It was only when I unzipped his anorak that I also noticed he was wearing a QPR football top. I took the sponge from the glove compartment and smeared some of Sarena's blood onto it.

I screwed the top back onto the hip flask. I smudged the blood on Elton's top, then wiped his shirt and jacket with the brush. I tried to do up his anorak again, but it was too cold, and I couldn't get my fingers nimble enough to fit the zip into its socket.

I put the blood-soaked sponge and the brush into the carrier bag. I added another brick, which I'd put on the back seat. I did the same as I had done before, making a solid football by wrapping it with heavy tape. That one was bound for the river at Newhaven on the journey back. But first there was another job to be done – one that I was dreading.

I shut the passenger door, walked back round to the driver's side and started up the car again. I drove to the brow of the hill. From there

I could see the coast road from both directions, coming up the hill from Eastbourne and winding away west in the direction of Seaford. The car clock flicked over to 01.42. I sat there in the moonlight for a while.

It was twenty minutes before a car had passed in both directions. Now I knew how much time I had, should some headlights be spotted in the distance while dumping Sarena. I checked and double-checked. All was clear.

With headlights still off, I carefully negotiated the track to the main road. I turned right and within a minute I was at my chosen spot: a small lay-by. A sign was telling me that this was an area of outstanding natural beauty. It was then that my mind first cast pictures of Sarena on the windscreen, flicking through them like a slide-show. I closed my eyes to block them out, but they continued in the darkness. I wound down the window to take some cold, clear breaths.

Though it was still frozen underfoot, the heavy frost helped me slide the sack over the ground, leaving a snail-like trail. I looked out to the sea and focused on the cliff edge. I imagined taking a run at the cliff top, and a jump. I heard the sound of the sea echoing along the cliffs, telling me to carry on, to stick to plan A. I remember thinking I had to give it my best shot, but that if it did all go wrong I'd end it all later. I stared out into the void.

Even in the darkness you can still see the white salt breaks of the waves. I started to take exaggerated deep breaths. The sack was at my feet. I pulled it until we were both just a foot or so from the edge of the cliff. I had this vision: I'd take Sarena from the sack. I'd cling on to her and jump with her. We'd live together, forever, in No Man's Land... I wondered whether tears freeze. I could stand it no more.

In a sudden surge I kick-pushed the sack over the cliff, then closed my eyes. There was an almost immediate thud onto a rock that jutted out ten feet below. I could hear the sack bounce off, and then... nothing. Sarena was in full flight on her way to crashing two-hundred feet below. I wasn't sure if it was the salt-water spray or the tears I could taste, but I couldn't lick my lips because of the cold.

I edged my way back to the car, though by that time my eyes had become more accustomed to the light. I got back in and drove back to the same spot on the country track, then turned off the engine and tried to catch my breath.

I'd already planned what to do with Elton. I'd worked it out countless times on the motorway, but this was the final 'mental' dress rehearsal. I knew that one mistake would blow the whole thing sky-high. I did what I could to calm down. I needed a time-out, needed to recharge the batteries. I turned the radio on and flicked through the frequencies.

The radio locked on to a local phone-in. It was twenty-five minutes to three on a Monday morning, and 'Clive from Lewes' was talking about censorship, and television, and how disgusting Emmerdale was. I had a private bet with the comatose Elton that he was probably a magistrates' court clerk. He was droning on and on. I sat there and listened to the discourse between presenter and callers.

'It used to be a nice little programme about a rural Yorkshire farming community. Well... it's just filth now. Filth and nonsense, what with all these affairs and abortions and drugs. I don't know.'

'Okay, Clive, thank you. Now on to Maggie from Eastbourne. Hello, Maggie, and what would you like to say?'

'Rowan Atkinson makes me sick.'

'Does he?'

'Is that programme supposed to be funny?'

'Which programme, Maggie?'

'It was on UK Gold. The policeman one. Can't people be funny without being rude?'

'I remember that series, Maggie. 'The Thin Blue Line', wasn't it? I thought it was rather funny, actually.'

'Oh, did you. Well, you're sick too, then. Goodnight.'

'After the break Clara Bewley will be here to discuss your personal and emotional problems. Next, it's the news headlines with Barry Carter...'

I wished Elton hadn't been anaesthetised. I needed someone to talk to, just like those callers did. I spoke to him anyway, as my hyper-shock momentarily returned.

'Did you hear that, Elton? Eh? Who are these people? They're out there somewhere, mate. Insomniacs, probably. Poor old Maggie, she'd be better off getting her vibrator out and having a good old J. Arthur. What do you reckon, Elton? Know what, Elton? J. Arthur Rank was actually a devout Methodist. Wonder what he'd make of those cockneys

nicking his name for their slang, eh?'

Elton didn't answer.

'Well, Elton, may the Lord forgive me for what I have done... and what I am about to do. I just hope Loren's singing 'Stand By Your Man'... and not 'Backstabbers'. Remember that one, Elton? Temptations, was it? Four Tops, O'Jays...?'

Of course this was all too much for Ken. But as it was company I sought, I couldn't really complain. He forced his way in.

-You pick up the phone then, Jimmy. Go on. Tell Clara all about it. Clara Bewley... Listen, love, someone here's got some personal and emotional problems. Why don't you? You renegade. You slimy snake in the grass.

-Piss off.

-Ooh. We are vicious today, aren't we? Jimmy's a murderer, aren't you, boy?

With a mighty kick I dismissed Ken onto the gravel path and drove off. I turned back onto the coast road as 'Black Dog' was blasting out over the CD again. As I drove into Eastbourne I turned the sound down a little. A sign on the roadside urged me to drive safely, and 'keep death off our roads.' I looked over at Elton, who was still sprawled out on the reclined passenger seat. I shot him a look, and couldn't help a little comment.

'Keep death off our roads, Elton. I've failed on that one, mate.'

Elton let out a little snore in response.

Along the front there was a row of small wooden huts, just like I remembered them. Aunt Marj had taken me to Eastbourne for a holiday... to 'escape from it all' after Mum's murder. We stayed in a guest house for four weeks, and it had its own beach hut on the front.

I parked up along the sea road. I got out and walked over to the beach huts. I'd got as close as I could with the car. I walked up the little wooden ramp and kicked one of the doors in.

I knew this was going to be the tricky part. This was the moment of optimum risk, my take-off and landing time. I was constantly looking about in every conceivable direction. The front was deserted, but I kept thinking I could see someone clambering out of the cold sea. It was Sarena. She'd really done a Harriet Houdini this time, and had escaped from the sack. I strained my eyes. I was witnessing the greatest escapologist trick of all time. I tried to take in another deep breath, but all I could get was a wheezing sound and a pain in my chest. The vision disappeared. I quietly whispered to myself.

'See, Loren, she was only a mirage.'

I couldn't afford to let my mind slip. It kept trying to show me visions of my dead mum again... and me running through the allotment, screaming, getting home, letting myself in with the spare key, seeing that my pet rabbit 'Pringle' was okay, and turning the telly on… and watching it, with my grazed knees stuck to the wooden floor, glued by my mother's blood…

With an inner thrust of propulsion, I blasted the thoughts away. I walked back to the car, opened up the passenger door and dragged the giant out. I got one of those surges of energy that people talk about in moments of panic, like when you have to escape from a burning building. Elton flopped over each step. I had to get him up the little wooden platform that ran along the front of the huts.

I lifted his top half, then walked around him to lift up his feet. I stepped into the hut and dragged him in. I picked up his feet again and rested them on a stack of deckchairs. I glanced at my watch. It was a quarter past three. I wondered when Elton's drugs might wear off. I was concerned that he might freeze to death. There was a stack of towels on a shelf. I opened up several and placed them over Elton. I tucked him up for the night, satisfied that he'd be warm enough to keep ticking over.

I pulled the door to, but the beach hut wouldn't close properly because there was a dent where I'd kicked the door in. I pulled it to, as close as I could. I stared out onto the front. It was deathly quiet.

There was a light on in one of the flats over the road. I wondered if Maggie was peering out of her curtains. Maggie the Rowan Atkinson hater. I got back into the Swedish thing to begin my nightmare journey back to Swiss Cottage. I'm sure there was a quicker route back to London, but I chose the old Newhaven road and skipped the outskirts of Brighton. Apart from anything else, I had this odd desire to pass the point on Beachy Head where I'd kicked the gorgeous Sarena off the cliff.

Once on the M23, I found myself following the Norbert Dentressangle juggernaut. That was when the hauntings returned, as

Sarena's face appeared on the windscreen.

CHAPTER 39

I stood alone outside the Old Bailey, waiting anxiously for Loren to turn the corner from Newgate Street. Then I recognised some of jurors from Elton's case. They were on their way to court for day two of the trial. One of them gently broke away from the others. She waited for them to enter by the juror's side entrance, holding back. Then, to my surprise, she came up to me.

She was the pretty young woman who I'd noticed during Lefevre's opening – the one in the white cotton smock, with the African beads. She came up close and spoke softly.

'Excuse me. Can I talk to you?'

'Erm, not really. Certainly not if it's about the case. You're a juror.'

I had to smile to myself. There I was, in the middle of the most astonishing breach of confidence the Old Bailey had ever known, and I was politely fretting about chatting to a juror. In any event, she was insistent on talking.

'I was looking at you when the prosecution barrister was doing his opening speech.'

'Were you?'

I stopped and puzzled. What was going on here? Was she chatting me up? Wishful thinking, as she added, 'I know you, don't I?'

'I don't think so...'

'I do. I recognise you.'

'Do you?'

'My name's Melanie.'

Nothing happened at first. Then it clicked... but it couldn't be. Melanie? Wasn't that the name of the girl who...? I smiled into her eyes.

'You?... The girl who was attacked in Carnaby Street?'

She nodded.

'You look so... different. You look great.'

'Thank you.'

'Sorry, I didn't mean to be rude.'

I was quite taken aback, and worried that I might have offended her. I needn't have worried at all. She smiled back, and a radiant smile it was, too.

'That day changed my life. The policeman said it was your statement that forced him to plead guilty, otherwise I would have had to give evidence at court and face him again... and... If you hadn't called that ambulance, I might have lost my sight.'

I could sense a tear forming in her eye. Then I reminded myself that we shouldn't really be talking at all.

'Melanie. I'm not actually allowed to talk to you. In fact, you shouldn't...'

'I know, but I wasn't sure at first. It was only yesterday, when I left court, and saw you close up when you were talking to Mr Douglas outside. You didn't notice me, but I had a good look... and I knew it was you.'

At which point I could see Loren turning the corner, about thirty yards away.

'I really *can't* talk to you now, Melanie. I'm sorry. But I'm so glad you've recovered.'

Melanie was still nodding in thanks as I made my way up towards Loren. She was clicking those heels again, and didn't appear to be in the best of moods.

'What the fuck's going on?'

'Loren! It's not like you to swear.'

'Just tell me!'

'It's a long story. I'll tell you over breakfast if you want.'

'I don't want breakfast.'

Loren had a prickly tone. In fact, spiky would have been more apt.

'Just tell me what you want to say. And what were you doing in a pub so early in the morning?'

Loren was snapping out words like a terrier. I tried to throw the girl a bone.

'Well, let me buy you a coffee and I'll tell you.'

Loren huffed in response. I ignored it.

'The pub will do. They do a good fry-up, apparently... and it's got sockets.'

'What?'

'For plugs. Never think about pubs having sockets for plugs, do you? Of course, there's the gaming machines... and they've got to do the hoovering.'

Loren scrunched her nose up, lowering her eyebrows as she said, 'Jim, are you losing it again?'

'No... I'm not, actually. I'm just trying to calm down, like you always tell me to.'

I escorted Loren into the pub, where the aroma of bacon and sausages hit you long before the vision of the hotplates did. I smiled at Loren, and deliberately kept it cryptic. The seed of plan B was taking root. Melanie, I thought, you beauty. You might just have saved my bacon.

CHAPTER 40

It must have been Loren who secretly texted Harry to say that I was in the pub having breakfast. At least, looking back now, I'm sure it was.

We'd only been there five minutes when Harry marched up, sat down opposite me, opened his briefcase, and immediately said, 'Jim. Look at this.'

'What?'

Before Harry answered, Loren made her excuses and left, saying she had to meet Jessica to discuss Matty Campbell's trial. Harry waited for her to leave, then he spoke in rather a serious tone.

'I asked Lefevre if there was any 'unused material' we hadn't seen. He said no. Only what had been sent to you.'

A bleep registered on my guilty Geiger counter, but Harry sprang to my defence.

'Of course I told him that you hadn't received it. Otherwise you would have sent it to me.'

'Yes, of course.'

'Anyway, he handed me this after court yesterday.'

I studied the statements that Harry thrust in front of me. I pretended to read them, hoping I wouldn't betray the fact that I'd read them many times before. Harry began a commentary, helpfully explaining their contents.

'First one's a statement from another forensic guy. They examined the victim's home address: Albany Street. There were traces of blood in the floorboard crevices. The victim's blood. There's also a statement from a neighbour who heard raised voices on that Saturday night. Like two or more people arguing. Two of them women.'

I swallowed a hot gulp of the cappuccino that had been placed in front of me, and collected as many deceitful thoughts as I could muster. I briefly glanced into Harry's eyes. I had that awful feeling I always get when I can't quite read someone. I had to stick to type, though, and painted on the most earnest look I could as I listened further to Harry.

'Lefevre will just say that a few spots of blood in the crevices are neither here nor there, and he's right. She could have cut herself at home. There's certainly nothing to suggest any impropriety.'

'No...'

'The Crown might not want it, but we might be able to make use.'

'Yeah...?' I questioned, a little too naively.

Actually, I wasn't sure *exactly* what Harry was getting at, and listened on.

'That's not all, Jim. I've been examining the black dress, exhibit five, whatever it is. She obviously wasn't wearing it when stabbed. So on the Crown's case, Elton must have stabbed her when naked. That might suggest that he took her clothes off by force, or threat of force. Why stab her then? If she'd refused him, if she'd felt threatened, she's more likely to be stabbed with the dress on.'

'Possibly.'

'But more importantly, what if she was wearing something else? What if she was attacked in her own home and then taken down to Beachy Head?'

'Why would anyone want to do that?'

As I asked the question I dribbled some saliva in pure terror. It was as if my mouth had been anaesthetised by an over-zealous dentist. Harry added, 'To divert from the scene of crime, maybe? Say it was someone she knew. Considering what this neighbour says?... Raised voices, two of them women. A domestic? What if she was having an affair, say with a married man, the wife follows her husband to his love nest, there's a confrontation. It gets out of hand. Someone grabs a knife. There's a panic. They clear up the blood.'

I was nodding along, trying not to make myself look stupid.

'Makes sense,' I somehow managed to say, with an air of intrigue.

Harry wasn't really listening. He was in one of his motormouth moods.

'If we can convince this jury that the woman was killed in her own flat, on that Saturday night, when Elton was tucked up in the bail hostel... and I'll come on to that in a minute.'

'You're right, Harry. But what about the forensics on Elton?'

'Okay. We have to accept Elton was in Eastbourne. Obviously. What if he caught them in the act? What if he saw someone trying to dump the body? You know how curious he is. What if whoever it was got involved in an altercation with Elton? That's how he might have got her blood on him, and those fibres. If I can get Stefanovic to accept that she would have expected the knifeman to have been sprayed with blood – not simply smeared, but sprayed... We're building a few bricks here, Jim...'

'Yeah, sounds like you are.'

I was in turmoil, not quite able to work out if Harry could get Elton off without dumping me in it. Harry was steaming ahead.

'There was another statement as well. Arthur Collins, bail hostel receptionist...'

Now that was a genuine surprise. Even the CPS had kept that one up their sleeve. I listened on as Harry read some of it out loud:

'I have been asked to confirm the whereabouts of resident Elton Spears during the weekend of Friday 13th through to Sunday 15th January this year. Spears came to us via the probation service on Friday 13th January, having been granted conditional bail at Ealing Magistrates' Court. He had been remanded to us pending psychiatric assessment. I can confirm that at about nine o'clock on the Sunday evening, 15th January, Spears received a telephone call. I do not know who it was from. I later became aware that Spears had left the hostel and was in breach of his curfew. His father had come to visit him and I had to inform him that his son was missing. Elton Spears never returned to the hostel. On Monday 16th January I was informed he had been arrested and detained by police.'

I tried to force another intrigued look at Harry, who carried on talking.

'Interesting. Right, Jim. Get Elton's dad back here. Take a statement from him.'

'Sure. Yeah.'

'I thought you told me that the hostel couldn't help?'

'I did, yeah. They said they couldn't.'

I wondered there and then whether to stop lying, give up and confess all to Harry. I very nearly did, but I had formed a different escape route, at least a potential one, and I had to clear it with the Colditz committee. For once Ken was in subservient agreement.

-Plan B, Jim. I like it.

-So do I.

-Will it work?

-I don't see why not.

-It's either that or let Harry balls it up.

-That's a bit unfair, Ken.

-Fuck unfair. Why risk it?

I regained concentration and listened to everything else Harry had to say. I thanked him for trying so hard for Elton. Harry was a touch thrown, no doubt thinking that it was the sort of thing you said when a trial had ended, not when it was about to enter its second day. Then we both made our way over to the Old Bailey.

I spent ten minutes or so alone in the canteen, thinking through my strategy. At about a quarter to ten I made my way up to the barristers' robing room on the fifth floor. As the lift doors opened, I unexpectedly caught Harry and Loren in a compromising position.

They tried to make it look like they had just greeted each other with a 'good morning', but there was something about their body language and the look on their faces. And I was sure I had seen the tail end of a kiss. Instead of asking to speak to Harry, I addressed Loren.

'I need a word. It's important.'

'Okay...'

Loren then turned to Harry.

'Thanks, Mr Douglas. I better go.'

I escorted Loren down the steps, suspecting that she had thrown in the 'thanks, Mr Douglas' as a cover. What I had gone up to the fifth floor to say was soon replaced by a growing suspicion.

'Got something to tell me?' I snapped at Loren.

'I thought it was *you* who wanted to speak to me?'

'What's going on with you and Harry Douglas?'

Loren stopped in her tracks.

'Nothing.'

'Really?'

Loren was thinking on her feet as she descended the stairs again.

'He just... I just bumped into him. I was looking for Jessica Strong.'

'Oh, yeah?'

'Mr Douglas was helping me with something, that's all.'

'Mr Douglas was kissing you.'

Loren let out a nervous laugh, a dreadfully guilty one. It was then that I noticed she had something in her hand. I immediately recognised it.

'Weren't you about to talk to him about something?'

'No.'

I snatched the report from her hand. It was the original

forensic report from JD Sound and Vision. I headed into the canteen, knowing that Loren would have to follow. She sat down next to me and lied, 'Nellie said she found it in your desk. That she was worried about Elton.'

'No, she didn't.'

Whatever Nellie might do, I always knew that my secretary would speak to me first. Loren looked as blank as a liar, so I filled in the blanks for her.

'You found the original that day... didn't you? And copied it.'

Loren tried to keep herself together. I roared at her, inches from her face.

'Didn't you?'

Loren's bottom lip began to tremble.

'I needed to know.'

'Insurance, was it?'

Loren tried her blank look again.

'About to show it to Mr Douglas, were you?'

Loren tried to remain cool for a few seconds, but soon her whole body was trembling.

'I panicked, Jim.'

'You panicked? Ms Cool. You're the one who said Elton was going to be convicted.'

'I didn't want that. The poor guy.'

'Oh, fuck off, Loren. You were saving your own skin.'

Loren swallowed the comment, and continued to wriggle.

'I had dinner with Mr Douglas last night. He told me about those other statements. I thought, it's all going to come out, what happened in Sarena's flat. I couldn't stand it. I couldn't face prison.'

'You idiot. It wasn't 'all going to come out.' It's just muddied the waters, that's all. You were going to shop me, weren't you?'

'Well, it wasn't my fault, was it! It was you... *you* and *her*.'

I looked at Loren in disgust.

'So you were going to show him the original report! What? To get him to believe that I'd framed Elton? And then tell him your version of the truth, which no doubt involved only my hand on the knife? And what then? Tell him I forced you into silence, or some crap like that. Close, am I?'

Loren tried hard to rebuff the argument, but just couldn't muster it.

'How long have you two been bothering, if you'll pardon the phrase?'

Again Loren attempted an escape, but it was only with a brief look, before admitting to it.

'Few weeks... He... he went to Tunisia with me.'

'Bloody hell. He told me he had flu. We had to cancel Elton's last conference.'

Loren looked sheepish.

'And did you tell him in Tunisia that you were sowing the seeds of blackmail?'

Loren didn't bother with a reply.

'It was only yesterday morning you pretended that you'd never met. I knew, you know. You don't act the way you did with him if it was the first time you'd ever met.'

'I'm sorry, Jim.'

'I don't give a shit about that. Really, I don't. I *do* give a shit about you shopping me, though.'

'I wouldn't have done it. I wouldn't have shown him the report, or said anything.'

'I see. It just happened to have moulded itself to your hand this morning, did it?'

'Oh, fuck you.'

Loren went to descend the final step of the stairs. I pulled her back.

'Fuck you, Granger. Just stand there a minute and listen. All you've got to do is sit in court in fifteen minutes' time and stay schtum.'

Loren looked puzzled.

'That's all you've got to do. Okay?... Something's going to happen. Something quite out of the blue, really.'

Loren quickly had to pull herself together, as Jessica

Strong was now approaching.

'Morning, Loren. Jim.'

I replied; Loren didn't.

'Morning.'

'Well. Your man's jumped out of the soup and into the fire.'

Already thrown by the Loren episode, I failed to get Jessica's joke. She bristled with frustration as a result.

'Out of the soup... Campbell. He's pleading.'

'He's what?'

'Pleading guilty. Hasn't Loren told you?'

Loren whimpered.

'I was just about to. Sorry.'

I felt the need to explain to Jessica.

'We've been... erm, preoccupied with something else.'

Jessica accepted it.

'Oh, well anyway, the Flying Squad came up trumps with an enhanced security photo. Matty's thrown the towel in and copped a plea. He's being sentenced this morning.'

'I didn't really fancy Matty's chances anyway.'

Jessica shot me a knowing look.

'He wants to see you.'

'Yeah, okay. I'll pop down and quickly see him. Thanks.'

Jessica strode off to prepare her mitigation for Matty. I caught Loren's eye again.

'So just stay schtum. Got that?'

Loren nodded obediently. I could tell she was itching to ask me why, but she was still chastised by the discovery of her betrayal.

'See you in court in fifteen minutes.'

Loren tried her best at a smile. I headed towards the lifts, glancing back at Loren as I did so. I put my finger over my lips, and after a seconds thought, Loren nodded again.

I had to see Matty, and make it snappy. When I met him in the cells he was remarkably phlegmatic.

'Fuck all point, Jim.'

'In fighting it?'

'Yeah... I mean, you could see the cunt's face. Clear as fuckin' day. Even this fuckin' tooth.'

Matty pointed to his one black tooth.

'What yous reckon? Double figures?'

'I doubt it. You'll still get some credit for a plea, even at this late stage. No shots fired, so maybe eight?'

'Bastards.'

As it transpired, I was spot-on. Matty Campbell was to get eight years. Before I left him in the cells that morning, he said, 'You okay, Jim?'

'Me? I'm fine.'

'Tell Jessica thanks, yeah. Aye, she was all reet.'

'Yeah, I'll tell her.'

'Posh fuck, that one, Jim?'

'If you say so, mate.'

I left Matty with a forced smile and went upstairs to find Harry. He was outside Court Two. Everything was happening at a pace.

'Jim. Have you seen Mr Spears Senior yet?'

'No. It doesn't matter now, Harry.'

'What do you mean?'

'There's something I need to tell you.'

CHAPTER 41

The usher called everyone into court at ten fifteen precisely... everyone except the jury. Judge Llewelyn-Davies addressed Harry with an air of intrigue.

'You've asked for the jury to be kept out, Mr Douglas?'

'Yes, my Lord. Indeed, I'm going to have to ask that they be discharged.'

Harry proceeded to explain how his instructing solicitor had only just informed him that he was now sure that he actually knew one of the jurors.

He told the judge how Mr Harwood had left court prematurely the previous afternoon to check the names of the jurors against the name of a young woman he had previously come into contact with. He explained to the judge that this was why Mr Harwood suddenly stood up so unexpectedly when Mrs Brandon came into court to give her evidence. He also told the judge how, many months earlier, Mr Harwood had 'performed heroically' and rescued the juror from a thug who was sentenced to five years' imprisonment.

The ultimate irony was that 'Mr Harwood' was then actually praised by the judge... for his sense of public duty and his integrity. I wanted to curl up and die in embarrassment.

Loren was as shocked as anyone to hear the news. The trial was abandoned and Elton was remanded into custody pending a retrial. I went downstairs to see him with Harry. I let Harry explain it all to Elton, who barely understood. Then I had five minutes with him alone, during which time I just held onto him in a big bear hug, and promised him everything would be all right.

I left the little booth with tears streaming from my eyes. I crossed the road, got into the Swedish thing and headed back towards the office.

CHAPTER 42

I checked into this place. A little B&B called The Limes. It's perched up on the hills, a mile or so from Beachy Head.

This is where you've caught up with me, lying on my bed, staring up at the ceiling. This is my self-imposed exile, and I can almost feel part of me dissolving.

Having resigned from Johnson Gower & Co., there were a few loose ends to tie up, and important loose ends at that. I made sure that Elton's new lawyers had all the information they needed, at least all the information they needed to do Elton proud. I knew full well that Loren would protect her precious career and never utter a word. I'm pretty sure she never will. That girl knows how to look after number one.

As it transpired, Elton's retrial never took place. The Crown's pathologist, Helda Stefanovic, reconsidered her view on time of death, and it dovetailed in with a further statement from Arthur Collins, the bail hostel receptionist. Elton had a rock-solid alibi.

I reckoned the officer in the case, DCI Litton, must have known all along that something was awry with Elton's case, but never bothered to see it through. Why should he, I guess? He had what looked like a watertight case, so why weaken it?

It really is such a lottery, and somewhere lurking beneath

the surface of the criminal justice system lies this thing called truth. The players know how to manipulate it; they cut it and spin it and bend it every which way. Prosecution and defence, just the same.

The CPS had no option but to discontinue the proceedings. Elton was eventually released from Wormwood Scrubs on 16th July 2012. Guess who picked him up and took him to his dad's? Well, I had to really.

Sarena's 'murder' remains unsolved. I'm sure there must have been all sorts of spotty little CPS clerks scratching their heads, trying to work out who framed Elton, and why for God's sake. How did his clothing come into contact with her blood? How did those fibres get there? Why had he falsely admitted to killing her? I'm sure the first part of the enigma is a conundrum of some magnitude to unravel, but nobody even bothered to analyse Elton when he was released, or find out what sort of condition leads him to behave the way he does.

It isn't the first time someone like Elton has confessed to crimes they haven't committed. This one will be seen as more trouble than it's worth. After all, the whole of the system would come under the spotlight, and we can't be having that. Maybe that's the greatest irony of all: that the system remains unscathed. Despite all the extraordinary comings and goings, despite all the contrivance and deceit, if I wasn't telling you all this, nobody would ever know.

The official court note will tell you that Regina versus Spears was abandoned after lawyers for the accused had to withdraw for 'professional reasons.' It will then tell you that the CPS discontinued the proceedings against Elton Spears, on the basis that 'on the balance of probability a jury would be unlikely to convict'. It won't tell you any more than that, though. Only I can.

Had something quite extraordinary not hit me, then Elton would be facing that old stark reality: that there is no 'care', and very little 'community' either. However, there is capital. There is the ubiquitous authority of money, and it sprouted a gem of an idea.

I had to wait for a few little money transfers to be processed before putting it into action, but now it's all done and dusted. I didn't tell Elton. He wouldn't understand. So instead of informing him about Sammy's loot, and how he really did stick to his word after all, I told Elton that his luck had changed. That scratch-card I bought for him, the one with the teddy bears on, had come up with three little teddy bears all in a row.

There was no point handing over the cash to my favourite delinquent giant, as he wouldn't have had a clue what to do with it. So I made sure that the Cranbourne Institute have had a year's rent in advance. As far as they are concerned, Elton had an unexpected windfall, and solicitor James Harwood, his licensed Power of Attorney, invested the windfall wisely. Who would have thought it? Elton's scratch-card coming up with the teddy bears... Bless him. If only they knew.

All this means, of course, that somewhere in West London a wealthy old chap woke up one day to find his security box empty. As the old joke goes, the police are still looking into it. In fact, a number of terribly wealthy folk have made an unwitting donation to the Elton Spears Trust Fund. Sammy had emptied their little boxes. I wonder how much they would have put into the tin outside their local Knightsbridge store?

The Cranbourne Institute is one of the world's leading centres for mental health studies. Dr Healy will be helping Elton with his pioneering techniques. It's just up the road from St Vincent's in Epsom, so he's near his less fortunate mates. I'm sure Elton would be delighted to see you if you're passing that way. He finally has all the help and care he could ever need, and Scooby Doo on demand.

Meanwhile, I'm contemplating whether I want to return to a world of lords and your-honours and worships and pomposity and deceit and mumbo-jumbo. If I do lose touch, then at least I've gained from my loss. I think I've lost Ken.

I'm sure he was just hiding behind my father's mask.

My instinct tells me to make a clean break. My chemistry tells me that one day there might even be another reaction, though nothing could compare to Sarena. It's a thought that might just tip me over the edge.

Should the likes of Stingray and the beastly Basil Brush resurface again, I feel that they will do so without inherent malice. Alone they cannot torture me. Whatever venomous substance it was, it has now begun to dissolve and disperse. I hope that it is buried because it is finally dead, and not merely hidden... but sometimes latent reactions are always the most difficult to second-guess.

It's time to take a walk now, along the cliff tops of the stunning Beachy Head. I think my soul is probably waiting for me, down by the sea...

....

....

18451687R00147

Made in the USA
Charleston, SC
04 April 2013